DIDO

In this hauntingly beautiful book which begins with the fall of
Troy, David MacNaughton traces the wanderings of the Trojan
hero Aeneas and his companions from shore to shore of the
Ancient Mediterranean in search of a new home, until at length
after many adventures they arrive at Carthage, the city recently
founded by Dido on the North African coast. She too is a
refugee from her native land, as is her sister Anna, and her
past is no less tragic than that of Aeneas.

These events are recalled by Aeneas's son Ascanius, then a
young boy, as he looks back on it all in old age long after
Aeneas and his Trojans, predestined to be the founders of the
Roman nation, have left Carthage and settled in Italy. From
the outset the story is full of atmosphere and the characters
have the dimensions of real people. The reader finds himself
sharing not only their adventures and their trials and tribulations
but also their fears, their doubts, their hopes and their despair.
Far from being a mere retelling of the opening part of the
Aeneid, this novel is a work of imagination inspired by it.

DIDO

A love story
by

DAVID
MACNAUGHTON

COLLINS
St James's Place, London
1977

William Collins Sons & Co Ltd
London · Glasgow · Sydney · Auckland
Toronto · Johannesburg

First published 1977
© David MacNaughton 1977

ISBN 0 00 222158-6

Set in Garamond
Made and Printed in Great Britain by
William Collins Sons & Co Ltd Glasgow

GODS AND GODDESSES MENTIONED

Names used in this novel are given in block capitals.
Names within brackets have been inserted purely for
identification purposes.

Greek name	Roman name	Phoenician name if used
ZEUS	(Jupiter)	—
(Hera)	JUNO ('Queen of Heaven')	ASHERAT
HERMES	(Mercury)	—
APHRODITE	(Venus)	ASTARTE
POSEIDON	(Neptune)	—
DEMETER	(Ceres)	—
APOLLO	(Phoebus)	—
DIONYSUS	(Bacchus)	—
HECATE	—	—
(Athene)	MINERVA	—
(Heracles)	HERCULES ('The Pillars of Hercules')	MELKART

PRINCIPAL CHARACTERS OR PERSONS MENTIONED

The prologue is set in Italy to the south of Rome. Lavinium is now called Pratica di Mare. The site of Alba Longa is close to Castel Gandolfo beside Lake Albano. The narrator is ASCANIUS, *the son of* AENEAS, *the Trojan hero whom the Romans regarded as the founder and originator of the Roman nation.*

AENEAS   The hero of Virgil's Aeneid. Father of Ascanius.

ANNA   Sister of Dido, Queen of Carthage.

DIDO   Queen and founder of Carthage.

CREUSA   Trojan wife of Aeneas. Mother of Ascanius. Daughter of Priam, King of Troy.

HECTOR   Greatest of all Trojan heroes. Brother of Creusa and husband of Andromache. Killed by Achilles.

ASTYANAX   Hector's son.

ANDROMACHE   Hector's widow, and mother of Astyanax. Later wife of Helenus.

CAIETA   Aeneas's old nurse and nurse of Ascanius.

ANCHISES   Aeneas's father. Grandfather of Ascanius.

PANTHUS   Priest of Apollo in Troy.

ILIONEUS   Trojan officer who accompanies Aeneas on his wanderings.

ACHATES   Another Trojan follower of Aeneas and his favourite companion.

PALINURUS   Helmsman of Aeneas's ship.

ANIUS   King of Delos, and priest of the oracle of Apollo there.

PYRRHUS   Son of Achilles. Murderer of Priam and Astyanax. Later King of Epirus.

HELENUS   Priest of Apollo and King of Epirus after death of Pyrrhus. Andromache's second husband.

ACESTES   King of the Elymians in West Sicily.

SYCHAEUS   Dido's husband.

PYGMALION   Dido's brother.

IARBAS   King of the Numidians in North Africa.

IMILCE   Anna's handmaid.

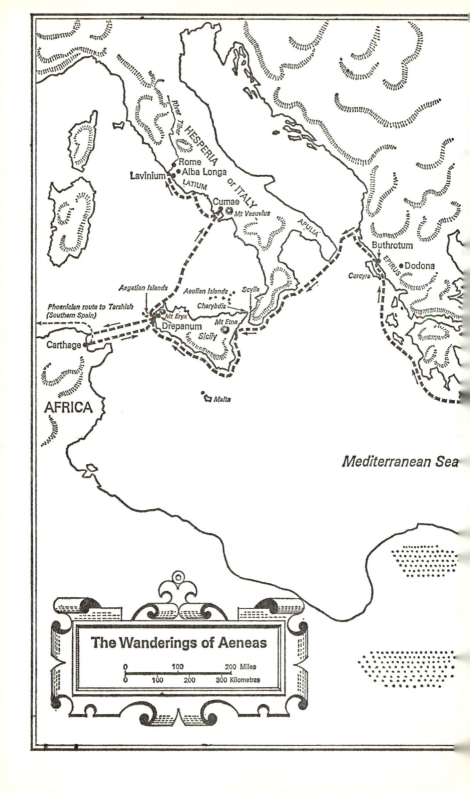

The Wanderings of Aeneas

0   100   200 Miles
0   100   200   300 Kilometres

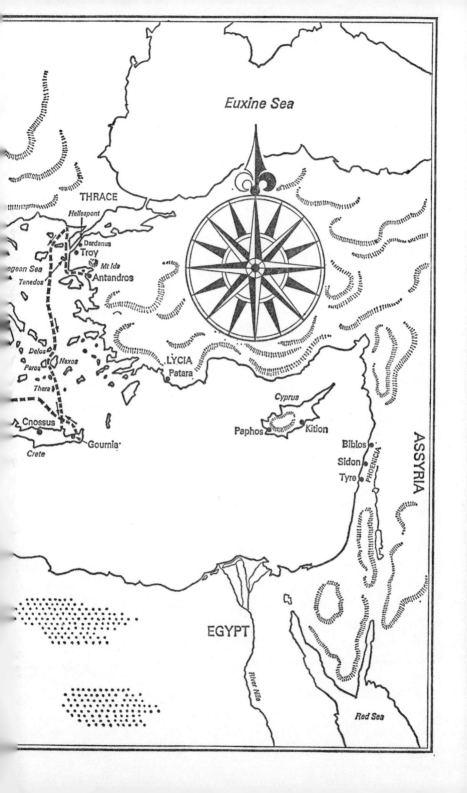

'L'amour tel que le concevaient les anciens
n'était-il pas une folie, une malédiction,
une maladie envoyée par les dieux?'

Gustave Flaubert.

'Did not the Ancients think of Love as a kind of madness, as a
curse or malady inflicted upon mortals by the Gods?'

AUTHOR'S NOTE

The hymn to Asherat-of-the-Sea taught by Anna to Ascanius in
Chapter IX is based upon the hymn to Ishtar Queen of Heaven
quoted by N. K. Sandars in the introduction to her translation of
The Epic of Gilgamesh (Penguin Books 1972).

I
PROLOGUE

Three days ago I rode inland from Lavinium to Alba Longa, the new capital which I have founded for my people among the Alban Hills, in obedience to Almighty Zeus. High upon a cliff it stands, and beneath there lies a still and radiant lake of unfathomable depth. In winter no doubt the site will be cold and windswept – but no more windswept, surely, than Troy, my birthplace, now a heap of ruins but once the glory of the Hellespont. Besides, who am I, the son of pious Aeneas, to challenge the inscrutable wisdom of the gods?

The omen was clear – or so my father told me when he founded Lavinium, mastering his misgivings for he thought the site ill-chosen. But it was there that he saw the white sow with her thirty offspring which the prophecy had foretold; it must be there, and not beside the Tiber, that we refugees from Troy were intended to build our settlement, naming it after the Latin princess whom my father was foreordained to marry. Thirty years were to pass; and then I, Iulus, was to found a new capital inland among the hills.

Three years later my father died. But no one could find his body after the battle, and for me his death has been without significance. His heroic image has not ceased to haunt my dreams, now checking, now encouraging me, and wherever I go his invisible presence seems to loom over me like a shadow. To be the son of a hero is to be his prisoner even when he is dead.

There is no glory in having waited thirty years to found

Alba Longa. For too long I have had to bide my time in patience, no more than a nominal king of a dwindling band of Trojans and an uncouth tribe of herdsmen. The Latins respected my father; he was a hero and Lavinia's predestined husband; but for as long as she was alive they had little respect for his son. Now that she is dead at last my hour has come. But I am growing old. I know that my descendants will build a city called Rome: I know that Rome will grow into the mightiest empire the world has ever seen: I know that an age of justice and peace will dawn upon the earth. But I am only a mortal, an instrument of the gods. My eyes are too dim to see the shining lustre of this distant golden age. I have seen too many visions, I have dreamt too many dreams. I have been dutiful, pious, obedient, frustrated and disappointed. Such as it is, my new-found independence has no savour; it has come too late.

Such were my thoughts three days ago when, leaving the plain beside the sea, I turned my horse's head inland and began to follow the forest track that ran beside the sacred river Numicus, where my father fought his last battle. Usually I travel with an escort; this time I rode alone. Suddenly I heard, borne by an autumn breeze, the distant cooing of pigeons. It came from a grove of ilexes perched upon a rounded grassy hill, and instantly I thought of Anna, Dido's sister, and the doves that had fluttered around the temple of Asherat in Carthage. When her sister died, Anna had fled from Carthage and after many adventures had landed in Italy. My father had welcomed her but she had tried to avoid him although I sensed that she still loved him. Many years had passed since I had seen her. I had heard that she had become a priestess of Juno at a sanctuary upon a promontory far to the south of Lavinium. Sometimes I had wondered if she was dead. Now, in a flash of vision, I knew that she was still alive, that the cooing which I had heard came from her doves, that she herself was there in the grove waiting for me. I was seized with an overwhelming desire to see her. Driving my heels violently into my horse's sides, I lashed him into a gallop up the steep smooth hill. At the edge of the grove I dismounted, tethered my horse, and listened. No sound came now from within; the breeze had fallen, the sun had disappeared. I had never been told that the grove was sacred, but as I moved forward beneath the trees I seemed to feel an invisible presence watching me, and remembered with a thrill of fear that Asherat had long been our enemy. In the half-darkness I saw the faint gleam of mistletoe; muttering the propitiatory words my father had taught me, I seized a branch and broke it off. I felt its magic course through my veins, and my instinctive fear left me. Before me lay a glade. With each step that I took I had the strange impression that I was returning to a place that was infinitely familiar and was awaiting my return. 'Anna must be there,' I said to myself, and quickened my pace, tingling with a childlike excitement I could not explain.

The glade was deserted; but at the further end, partly concealed by overhanging foliage, I saw a grotto such as a nymph or satyr might dwell in, and beside it a spring which trickled down the rocks into a little pool. And might not that flat stone before the grotto's entrance serve as a primitive altar? I made my way towards it, and as I did so a woman came out of the cave. I saw that she limped, and knew that it was Anna. I called her name. She turned her head, and I realized that she was blind. 'Anna,' I repeated, and moved towards her. She stood quite still, with a grave smile on her face.

'I knew that you would come, Ascanius,' she said.

I stopped: 'That is my old Trojan name. Now I am called Iulus.'

'To me you will always be Ascanius,' she said quietly.

Yes, I had been called Ascanius then, but now that I was close to her I hesitated. Could this indeed be Anna, this emaciated old woman with dishevelled grey hair? I looked at her skinny arms. She guessed my thought.

'Here is the mark where you jabbed me with an arrow because Dido would not take you hunting with her.'

She held up her forearm and showed me the mottled scar; then she put out her hand and touched me.

'Kiss me, Ascanius, for Dido's sake.'

I hesitated no longer, and embraced her like a sister.

'But Anna,' I said, 'what are you doing here? How did you know I would come? How did you recognize me? My voice...'

'Yes, your voice has changed, Ascanius,' she said smiling, 'and I am blind now, as you can see. But the goddess I serve, whom we call Asherat and you call Juno, has not forsaken me. She showed me this grove in a dream, and told me that here I would meet you, and you would build a shrine in her honour. It has been a long journey for an old woman, but Imilce has guided me. Now she has gone.'

'Imilce,' I said, 'I remember her.'

'Yes,' said Anna, 'Imilce was my handmaid in Carthage; but that was long ago.'

'Then you are alone,' I cried, 'alone and blind! You must come with me to...'

'To your new capital, Alba Longa,' said Anna.

Suddenly her frail body was shaken by sobs, and tears began to stream down her face. I took her in my arms and tried to comfort her.

'What is the matter, Anna? Let me take you with me. You shall travel in a cart, and I will ride beside you.'

'No, Ascanius, no. I will not come.' She felt for the skirt of her robe and began to dry her eyes: then she said unsteadily, 'Carthage was Dido's new capital. In our language it is Karthadasht. Don't you remember?'

I was silent, and she continued: 'Your father never learnt Punic, and you will have forgotten it. Dido sometimes spoke to you in Punic... but with your father she always spoke Greek. Once, I remember, he tried to say "I love you" in Punic, but the words would not come. It was a bad omen, they both knew it; but Dido was so happy that she only laughed and kissed him.'

'Dido was afraid of nothing,' I said. I waited for a moment, and then added gently, 'Anna, is it because of her that you have come?'

She raised her face to mine:

'Yes, Ascanius. We must lay her ghost before we die.'

Suddenly I was afraid:

'You are her sister, not I, and you are a priestess. You need no help from me with your magic arts,' I said roughly.

'I need your help, Ascanius,' said Anna steadily.

'Why should I help you? Your sister was a sorceress, a demon queen; she bewitched my father, she bewitched us all. And then when Almighty Zeus broke the spell, and set my father free to fulfil his destiny, she called down curses upon him and me and all our royal line. It was the gods alone who protected us from her fury.'

I was trembling with anger.

'Who told you that she said this?' asked Anna slowly.

'You were with her,' I answered, 'is it not true?'

'Yes, it is true,' said Anna. 'Those whom the gods wish to destroy they first drive mad.'

She turned away so that I should not see her tears. I felt my resolution weakening:

'She cannot hurt my father now,' I said, 'but what of me and my sons?'

'She cannot injure anyone, even if she would. Did you not hear the doves calling you, Ascanius?'

'The doves?' I repeated in astonishment. 'It was the sound of their cooing that brought me here. Where are they?'

'They have gone. It was Asherat who sent them to bring us together; but they came from Dido, I know it. They spoke to me.' Suddenly she stiffened and put her finger to her lips; 'One of them is returning,' she whispered. 'Listen.'

Through a gap in the trees I saw a flutter of white wings as the bird flew towards us and alighted on Anna's outstretched finger. She spoke to it in soft liquid sounds, then brought it close to her cheek so that she could hear its reply, nodding her head as she listened. The bird looked at me, as it seemed, inquiringly. 'He is not used to men,' whispered Anna. For a moment she held the bird close to her breast, and suddenly as I watched, she was transformed into Dido in the courtyard of Asherat's temple at Carthage – Dido in a flowing white dress

[15]

with a golden girdle about her slender waist. She was stroking a dove that had tried to nestle in her breast, while my father watched her with eyes of adoration. The next moment the vision had gone. There was Anna once more before me; but the bird had disappeared.

'You saw her?' asked Anna quietly.

'Yes,' I said, my voice shaking.

'You will help her, Ascanius?'

I could scarcely speak:

'I would do anything for her.'

'Anything, Ascanius? And what of Aeneas's royal line? You must not endanger its glorious future or the new capital you have founded.'

She must have sensed the fear in my eyes for she went on:

'But Dido does not need so great a sacrifice to bring peace to her restless ghost.'

'What then does she need?' I asked.

'Someone who will tell her story for her with passion but with truth. A wicked sorceress, a demon queen you called her. Is this what you truly believe?'

'No,' I answered, 'she is the only woman whom I have ever loved.'

You who listen, you who may catch the echoes of my story across the ages, remember this, remember this. I was a child then, but these are not only an old man's memories. Hermes the winged messenger of Zeus has taken me back with him into the past. I have stood upon the threshold of my life once more, seen what I saw then. I did not see what my father saw, nor feel what he felt. My story is no less true, but it is very different. You must follow me into this vanished world which I have revisited, a world that is sometimes innocent or dream-like; you must listen to the voices that I heard; you must see Dido as I saw her in all her beauty.

II

I was born during the siege of Troy. My father, Aeneas, was not himself a Trojan. He came from Dardanus, a neighbouring city, which he ruled in the name of his aged father, Anchises. At first my father tried to stay aloof from the war; but the ruffianly Greeks showed no respect for his neutrality for they were always short of food. Without warning, Achilles raided his territory, drove off his cattle, killed his herdsmen and sacked the city in which he had taken refuge. My father, deeply angered, threw in his lot with the Trojans who welcomed him and Anchises within their walls. King Priam gave him his daughter, Creusa, in marriage. One year later I was born. I was their only child.

I have little recollection of my early childhood before Troy fell. I remember my father's daily departure from the palace in armour to lead his men into battle – a noble figure with herculean shoulders. Once I remember him being carried back on a stretcher after Diomed, the only Greek of whom he could speak without loathing, had hurled a huge rock at him and broken his thigh-bone. I remember my mother running with tears to greet him, and how he took her hand and kissed it, saying that with her to nurse him he would soon be fit for battle once more. It was not the answer she had looked for.

We Trojans are nothing if not horsemen. My first toy was a wooden horse on wheels with a bridle – a present from my father. To the horse was later added a chariot, and on the same day a nurse brought my cousin, Astyanax, to play with me. Although I was a little older than he, I felt embarrassed and tongue-tied for I knew he was the son of the great Hector, our leader, who had met his death at the hands of Achilles. I felt almost ashamed because my father was still alive.

Astyanax and I looked at each other without speaking. Then I showed him my horse and chariot.

'My father gave them to me. He commands the army now, and he is the bravest man in all Troy,' I said proudly.

'I know,' said Astyanax.

He stared at the horse and chariot for a moment with a kind of horror in his eyes. Then he lay down on the ground with his sandalled feet pointing towards them.

'I have thought of a game,' he said. 'Fasten the thongs of my sandals to the back of the chariot.'

Wondering, I did as he asked.

'Now fasten the chariot shafts to the horse.'

I obeyed him.

'Now stand by the horse's head and take hold of the bridle. Whatever happens, promise me you will not let go. Do you promise, Ascanius?'

'I promise,' I answered.

'And will you promise to do what I say? If not, it will spoil the game.'

'Yes,' I replied, feeling more and more perplexed but determined not to disappoint him.

Astyanax lay motionless for a moment with a strange smile on his face. Then he raised himself on his elbow and looked at me with a kind of fury.

'Run, Ascanius, run,' he shouted at the top of his voice, 'and pull, pull, pull.'

I broke into a run, dragging the horse and chariot behind me. The wheels shrieked and squealed as they sped across the tiled courtyard.

'Go round and round the courtyard,' shouted the voice behind me; 'make the chariot swing out round the corners.'

I looked back; Astyanax was slithering along the paving behind the chariot, face downwards, his long hair trailing out behind him. He raised his head.

'Faster, faster. The Greeks will catch us.'

[18]

At the word 'Greeks' I broke into a panic and ran like one possessed. As I rounded each corner, I felt Astyanax's body swing out behind the chariot and strike a pillar or a wall. I dared not look back, I dared not stop. I ran until I felt that my lungs would burst and my legs stiffen into bronze. Suddenly I heard a woman's voice give a great cry:

'Stop, Ascanius, stop!' Gasping and shuddering with exhaustion I came to a halt, wiped the sweat from my eyes and looked up. It was Andromache, Hector's widow, with my mother beside her. She was deathly pale.

'What have you been doing? Do you call this a game?' she asked, her voice trembling. She ran to Astyanax, who lay sprawled upon the tiles, his arms and face bruised and covered with blood. 'Who thought of this . . . game?' she whispered, 'you or Ascanius?'

'I did,' said Astyanax faintly.

'Why?' asked Andromache. He looked at her dully without answering.

'Why?' she repeated with a note of urgency in her voice.

'Because Achilles did it to my father,' said Astyanax slowly, 'and I wanted . . . to share it with him.' His eyes closed. Andromache hugged him close to her, weeping. My mother took me by the hand and led me away. I never saw Astyanax again. When the Greeks took Troy they hurled him from the walls because he was Hector's son and they dared not let him live.

Except for the last day that I ever saw her, my memory of my mother is curiously indistinct. She was affectionate but remote. Only once can I remember seeing her smile. Her face was thin and pale. It was not until later, when my father told me of the acute shortage of food, that I realized why she ate so little. She loved my father deeply, and every time he left the palace to return to the battle raging outside the walls, she would accompany him silently to the porch and then stand watching him with an anguished expression of foreboding in her eyes as he strode away along the narrow street. She would answer my childish questions gravely, and sometimes I would see

[19]

her looking at me with great tenderness; but even when she caressed me she seldom spoke. Several times I asked her innocently if she would take me to the walls so that I could watch the fighting; she only shook her head. My mother's silence added to my sense of solitude: it was like living with a mournful ghost. No doubt it was from Caieta, my father's old nurse, that I first learned to speak.

Caieta is the only servant whose name I can remember. The remainder are only faces, women's faces, for by this time all the men in the household had been killed.

Except when he was recovering from his wounds, my father came home only to eat and sleep. Apart from him I can remember only one other man, once afire with vigour and beloved of Aphrodite for his youthful beauty, now an aged cripple, hobbling about the palace chafing at his uselessness – my grandfather, Anchises. Who could have foreseen then that he, infirm and feeble as he was, would play so vital a part in charting our destiny?

Our palace stood at some distance from the city walls from which it was partly screened by trees; but not so far off as to escape the din of battle. The clash of arms, the rumble of siege engines, the battle-cries, the screams and groans of the wounded or dying, the bray of trumpets, the furious neighing of horses – all these were sounds that we who took no part in the fighting regarded as the normal accompaniment of our daily lives. And then one morning I awoke at dawn to total silence.

I had been forbidden to go on to the roof and went to find my father. He had gone. I found my mother in the courtyard.

'Why is there no fighting? Is there a truce?' I asked.

She shook her head. 'No, there is no truce. I do not understand it; we must wait for your father to tell us.' She looked anxious as always but tried to smile at me.

'Do not worry,' I said, dutifully repeating what Caieta had told me, 'I am sure the gods will look after us.'

'Sometimes the gods are powerless,' said my mother slowly, 'and sometimes they are . . .' She stopped.

'Sometimes they are what, mother?'

'Sometimes,' said my mother gravely, 'they are merciless.'

'But if there is no fighting,' I persisted, 'perhaps the gods are being kind to us, and you ought to be happy not sad.'

'Perhaps you are right, Ascanius,' she answered, stroking my head, 'but happiness is something I have learnt to mistrust. Your father is too trusting. He trusts the gods, he trusts his mother, he would even trust the Greeks.' She shivered. I was puzzled.

'But who is his mother? I have never seen her.'

'Your father believes it is the goddess Aphrodite. Sometimes she appears to him, and twice she has saved him from certain death.'

I digested this information.

'Has she ever appeared to you?' I asked.

'No,' said my mother sadly, 'I am only an ordinary mortal – I have never seen her. Nor has your grandfather since . . . long ago.' She paused: 'I do not know what to believe, or what to hope for except that the war will end, no matter how.'

The entrance gate leading from the street to the porch was wrenched violently open, there was a sound of rushing steps and my father burst in upon us. He was in a state of intense excitement. My mother caught my eye and put a warning finger to her lips.

My father flung his arms round her and kissed her passionately. Then he swung me off my feet into his mighty arms and hugged me like a bear.

'The Greeks have gone,' he cried. My mother put her hand to her throat.

'Aeneas – it is impossible. It simply cannot be true after all these years.'

'It is true enough, sweet love. Their camp is deserted. I have been there myself. Not a man is left.'

'But why did they leave so suddenly?' asked my mother incredulously. 'When did they go? Why have they gone?'

My father shrugged his shoulders.

'They must have given up all hope of taking Troy now that Achilles is dead, and sailed away during the night. No doubt they are on their way back to Greece. There is not a single Greek ship left on the beaches, not a sail in sight. Come on to the roof with me and see for yourself. Ascanius must come too.'

'No,' said my mother. 'He is too young. He might fall.'

'The Greeks have gone,' repeated my father. 'I want him to see for himself. Don't you understand, Creusa? The war is over. It is a day he must never forget.'

Grasping their protecting hands, my father's massive and horny, my mother's slim and white, I climbed out on to the roof and up the steep ladder that led to the watchtower. My father held me up so that my feet rested on his shoulders. Far below me lay the rectangular courtyard of the palace flanked on one side by its wall and row of cypresses. Beside the central fountain stood Caieta shading her eyes as she looked up at us. I tried to wave, but my mother checked me for fear I should lose my balance. My father shouted the joyful news to her and she rushed off to tell the other servants.

'Don't look down, Ascanius,' said my father. 'Look beyond the city walls and tell me what you see.'

It was the first time that I had ever seen beyond the walls of Troy. For a moment I was spell-bound and completely bewildered.

'I can see the plain below, and the river Scamander and Mount Ida, and the sea and an island and a camp,' I said at length in a breathless rush, repeating such names as I had heard and could remember.

My father laughed. 'Good. Is the camp empty?'

'No, there are people walking about in it, and there are many more walking towards it. Some of them are women I think. Are they Trojans?'

'Yes,' said my father. 'They have gone to look at the Greek camp now that it is empty. Look, all the gates of Troy are open.'

'Then we are safe now?' I cried, wildly excited, 'and I can go outside the house with Caieta; outside the walls even, and play and swim in the sea?'

My father gave a happy laugh.

'Yes, you are safe now. Safe and free. Tomorrow I will take you riding with me, and soon I will teach you how to fight with a sword and spear.' He lifted me off his shoulders and turned to my mother.

'Why, what is the matter, Creusa?'

'The Greeks have gone,' she said bitterly, 'but all you can think of is fighting.'

My father flushed. 'Ascanius is not a babe in arms. It is time for him to start behaving like a man.'

'And I want to sail to that island,' I interrupted. 'I want to sail far beyond the horizon.'

'So you shall, so you shall,' said my father gaily. 'It is not far to Tenedos as you can see, and one island leads to another.' He smiled at my mother but she did not seem to be listening.

'Aeneas,' she said suddenly, 'suppose the Greeks have only sailed to Tenedos and are hiding there out of sight?'

My father looked at her in surprise: 'Why should they want to do that?' he asked. 'We would find out soon enough that they were there. Besides, most of Tenedos is rocky and inhospitable. They could not stay there for long. Where would they moor their ships?'

'They might be planning to sail back and take us by surprise.'

My father shook his head. 'They will not be able to do that. Remember, it was Poseidon the sea-god who built these walls; they are impregnable.'

'But are the gods on our side?' asked my mother quickly.

'Yes,' said my father deliberately, 'and the Greeks have at last realized as much. They have failed – failed miserably – and they know it. That is why they sailed away secretly during the night. They will not come back; they have gone for ever. I think it means peace in our time.' He spoke with a quiet authority that carried complete conviction.

'Oh,' said my mother fervently, 'I am glad. I feel happy at last.' She put her arms round my father's neck and kissed him with a kind of maternal tenderness.

'Let us go to our room,' she whispered.

'I ought to go to the citadel. There is much to be done,'

said my father doubtfully.

'Not now. Later,' said my mother softly.

He looked at her without speaking, and I realized that he was suddenly hungry for her body.

'Yes, later,' he said. 'Come, Ascanius, you can go back to the courtyard and play.'

We made our way back along the roof and down the staircase, my father impatiently leading the way. He halted for a moment outside my grandfather's room.

'I ought to have told him at once,' he said uncertainly.

My mother took his hand and pressed it to her breast.

'It will only confuse him if you wake him now, poor old man,' she whispered. 'You know that he always sleeps late.'

It was on the same afternoon that I saw the gigantic wooden horse which the Greeks had inexplicably left behind them. My mother had gone with Andromache to perform the Rites of the Dead before the funeral mound where Hector's bones lay buried – Hector the guardian of Troy, whom they treasured the more in their hearts now that others had forgotten him amid the general rejoicing. All the servants had left the palace to join in the festivities. My mother had agreed to let Caieta take me with her; only my grandfather remained at home.

I was hopping from one foot to the other in my excitement at the prospect of going outside the palace.

'Why, Ascanius, you will grow into a stork if you go on like that,' said Caieta laughing.

'Let's go, let's go,' I chanted, impatient with her slowness, and dragging at her arm as we made our way to the porch. Once in the street I realized that I had forgotten something.

'Perhaps I ought to bring my horse. He will be lonely.'

'I think it would be best to leave him behind,' said Caieta. 'He might be frightened by the crowds. Besides we are going to see another horse – a much bigger one that the Greeks have left behind.'

'Do you mean a real one or a toy one?' I asked quickly.

'Well,' said Caieta, 'I suppose you might call it a toy one, but they say it is very big – much bigger than a real horse.'

I clapped my hands in excitement.

'My father never mentioned it. I wonder why the Greeks did not take it with them? Perhaps it was too big. Or do you think they left it behind as a present for us or for one of the gods?'

'They might have left it for Poseidon to ensure a calm journey home,' said Caieta thoughtfully, 'but if it is a gift for us, I hope that King Priam will have nothing to do with it, for it can only bring us bad luck. Never trust the Greeks, Ascanius. They are treacherous and cruel.'

'I am sure my father will know what to do with the horse,' I said firmly, seeing that she was suddenly looking troubled, 'and it can do no harm for us to look at it. Where is it now?'

'I think the soldiers have dragged it up to the walls,' said Caieta, 'but we will soon see. May the gods preserve us! What was that?'

A confused deafening roar suddenly filled the air, the ground shook beneath our feet and a cloud of dust rose high into the sky behind the tall buildings on our left. Caieta clutched at me and looked frantically about her.

'Keep still, Ascanius. It may be an earthquake.'

From the distance came the sound of wild cheering.

'I cannot understand it,' muttered Caieta. She looked up and down the deserted alley. 'Perhaps we had better go home,' she added doubtfully.

'No, no,' I cried, 'I want to see the horse. Look, there is a man coming towards us. Ask him what is happening.'

'What was that noise? Where is everyone?' asked Caieta peremptorily; but the man lurched past without reply, talking confusedly to himself, his face flushed and his hair tousled.

'Why doesn't he answer? Is he mad?' I asked, for I had heard that my mother had a mad sister called Cassandra to whose incoherent ravings no one paid attention. Caieta took a firm hold of my hand.

'No, he is not mad,' she said slowly, 'he is drunk.' She seemed to find his drunkenness reassuring, and began to walk quickly in the direction of the cloud of dust. As we drew closer we heard more intermittent shouting followed by a tremendous burst of applause from thousands of throats. I wrenched myself free from Caieta and broke into a run. Then suddenly as I rounded a corner I saw all Troy before my eyes.

The great square was crowded with a multitude of people singing, shouting and dancing. Many of them wore garlands in their hair. The women were dressed in their richest robes and flaunted their costliest jewellery. Of the men most were bareheaded and few if any bore arms. Some were eating, others gulping down wine from leather wineskins. Everyone whether drunk or sober was filled with the same unbridled excitement. Men and women, young and old, embraced each other joyfully and indiscriminately. Some made love openly, rolling on the ground in an ecstasy of passionate abandon, the women tearing open their robes to reveal their naked breasts. From the flight of steps leading to Aphrodite's temple, where a group of musicians had assembled, came the furious rattle of tambourines, the feverish twanging of psalteries and the continuous screaming of flutes. The dancers below were working themselves into a frenzy; sweat poured from their faces, their eyes glittered, their lips were frothing with excitement as they vibrated their bodies to the insistent remorseless rhythm of the music. And there in the middle of the square, surrounded by a crowd of admirers but towering over them all, stood the monstrous wooden horse the Greeks had left behind, with its long and flowing tail, its brazen hooves, its mane of purple and gold and its fixed unwinking eyes as red as blood.

I was terrified and looked round wildly for Caieta. To my relief I found her close beside me, but she was staring in another direction and scarcely seemed to notice me.

'Merciful heavens!' she gasped. 'Has all Troy gone mad? They have pulled the Scaean gate off its hinges and broken down the wall.'

She pointed, and I noticed for the first time that a great jagged gap had been torn in the walls at the further end of the square. A huge gate, studded with spikes and nails, sprawled on the ground like a crippled monster surrounded by mounds of rubble.

'They must be mad,' repeated Caieta loudly.

'No, mistress, not mad,' said a soldier standing beside us, in a thick voice; 'it was the king himself who ordered us to bring the horse into the city even if we had to break down the gate and knock a hole in the walls to do so. It is a sacred horse it seems – sacred to Poseidon who built these walls. By bringing it into Troy we are showing him honour, King Priam says, and doing the Greeks a bad turn as well.' He chuckled. 'As for the gate, we will have it back in its place again by sundown – if any of us are still sober that is.' He took a swig of wine from the leather bottle attached to his belt.

'What does Prince Aeneas have to say about the horse?' asked Caieta.

'It does not matter what Prince Aeneas has to say,' said the soldier abruptly. 'Now the war is over it is what the king says that matters.' He caught sight of a pretty woman ogling him, shouldered his way through the densely packed crowd and disappeared.

Caieta looked up at the great horse, which stood motionless in the midst of the seething mass of people, and shivered.

'It is evil, whatever the king may say,' she muttered. She glanced once more at the ruined gate and the shattered walls, and shook her head. Then she took me by the arm. 'Come, Ascanius, this is no place for you,' she said firmly. I felt sick and frightened, and allowed her to lead me away without protest.

As we left the great square with its shouting screaming multitude, I seemed to feel the horse's blood-red eyes watching me.

As soon as we returned home Caieta decided that I was feverish and put me to bed. On such occasions I slept in my parents' room according to my mother's wishes. Although it was still daylight I fell asleep instantly.

[27]

I was awakened by a voice, as it seemed, close beside me. A thick curtain had been drawn across the window and the room was very dark. After a moment I recognized that it was my father's voice, and that it came from the near-by bed. My mother's regular breathing told me that she was fast asleep. I realized that my father was talking to someone whom I could not see and did not know. With racing heart I sat up in the darkness.

'It is you at last,' said my father distinctly. 'How glad I am to see you.'

There was a pause. 'But where have you come from,' he added with a kind of agonized entreaty, 'and why is your body covered with wounds and filthy with dusty blood?'

There was a moment of silence, then my father gave a terrible groan. 'No, no,' he shouted, 'it cannot be true.'

He sat up convulsively, leapt out of bed and lit the lamp with trembling fingers. My mother awoke at once.

'What is it, my darling?' she asked anxiously.

'It was Hector,' he cried. 'I saw his ghost. I saw his wounds. He told me . . . Oh God! It cannot be true.' He ran out of the room and raced up the stairs making for the roof.

'Please do not go, mother,' I said quickly. She came across to my bed without speaking, sat down beside me and held me in her arms. Suddenly her body stiffened. From afar off came a burst of wild shouting, and for the first time I became aware of a dull but insistent roar in the background. I began to ask my mother what it was, but she cut me short.

'You are to dress at once while I awaken the household,' she said. 'When you are ready go down to the courtyard.' Before I could question her further she had gone.

I began to pull on my clothes, trembling with excitement.

Presently Caieta burst into the room with my cloak and a miscellaneous collection of toy soldiers.

'Come at once, Ascanius. We are in great danger,' she said. She had scarcely begun to shepherd me below when my father was upon us, buckling on his sword and leaping down the

[28]

stairs with great strides. His eyes were ablaze with a desperate fury.

'The Greeks are in the city,' he snarled, and vanished into the night.

By the time we reached the courtyard the terrible truth could no longer be concealed even from an ignorant child. The western sky was bright with flames. From the direction of the Scaean gate came shouts and cries and the clash of arms. A small group of servants was cowering, whimpering, in the shadow of the courtyard wall where the moonlight could not reach them. Caieta stood beside me weeping as though her heart would break. I looked round for my mother.

Then I saw her. She was coming slowly down the stairs holding a lamp in her left hand; with the other she supported my grandfather as he hobbled jerkily down the steps. Crooked over her left arm she carried his stick.

As she reached the bottom step there was a violent knock on the entrance gate, and a man's voice called my father's name.

'Who is there?' said my mother sharply.

'Panthus, priest of Apollo,' answered the voice. 'Where is Prince Aeneas?'

'He has gone,' answered my mother. 'What do you want with him?' Her voice trembled a little. There was a moment's silence, then the gate rattled again.

'Then I must see King Anchises,' shouted the voice. 'Let me in. Hurry, hurry.'

My mother hesitated, fearing a trap, but my grandfather intervened.

'Aeneas is not the only man in the household, Creusa. There is myself and there is Ascanius. Open the gate, Ascanius.'

I became aware that I was clutching my toy soldiers in my hand. Once I had treasured them; now they were meaningless. I dropped them on the ground and went to open the gate.

I saw before me a bearded old man wearing the headband of a priest and carrying a hastily-wrapped bundle in his arms.

He brushed past me without a word, went up to my grandfather standing in the moonlight, and flung himself at his feet.

'Your Majesty,' he gasped. 'I came to tell your son that Troy is lost. The Greeks are in the city. The gods have deserted us.'

'Not so fast, not so fast,' cried my grandfather. 'How did the Greeks break in? Were no sentries posted? Who holds the citadel?' He motioned to the man to rise.

'The citadel is surrounded, Majesty,' answered Panthus more calmly. 'I alone escaped.'

'Escaped?' repeated my grandfather angrily. 'What sort of talk is this? Priest though you are, have you no sword to fight with? Is this how the Trojans defend their city?'

The priest made a gesture of despair.

'You do not understand,' he shouted. 'It was the horse, the wooden horse.'

There was an incredulous silence, and he went on:

'The gods blinded us all save for a few whose warnings went unheeded. We thought the horse was sacred to Poseidon. It was not; it was an engine of war devised for Troy's destruction. The Greeks sailed away so that we should think they had lost heart and gone for ever, but they went no further than Tenedos. There they waited out of sight, watching to see what we would do with the horse they had left behind them. We thought that they had abandoned it reluctantly because it was too large for their ships. We thought that they had tried ineffectively to hide it from us. We thought that we would bring them ill luck if we took their offering to Poseidon into Troy. Like the fools we were, we fell into the trap that the Greeks had laid for us. They always intended us to take it into Troy; they made it so huge that we could not bring it through even the largest of our gates without destroying the adjoining wall. Hidden in the cavernous belly of the horse, out of sight, out of reach, crouched nine armed men, waiting silently till night had fallen and the city slept. Yes, even the sentries at their posts were in a drunken stupor although the wall was only half-repaired. I alone was wakeful after an ominous dream. Suddenly, as I looked down from Apollo's shrine in the citadel, I saw to my stupefaction hundreds of Greeks silently disembarking on the beaches. Full of misgivings, I glanced instinctively at the wooden horse standing in the deserted moonlit square, and as I looked, its monstrous belly seemed to open, a rope issued from it and one Greek after another slid silently to the ground . . . Nine men – no more,' he gave a sob, 'but it was enough to massacre the sentries on the walls and open the Scaean gate. At once I gave the alarm. It was too late. The Greeks were surging through the gate before I could rouse a single man. Drunken sluggards – such are the guardians of Troy, my lord. Troy is lost I tell you; Troy is lost as Cassandra foretold. Alas, poor girl, doomed by Apollo to prophesy in vain.'

He stopped. Behind me the servants broke into a chorus of wailing and lamentation. My mother stood motionless, clasping and unclasping her hands. My grandfather held up his hand for silence, then turned to Panthus.

'I believe you,' he said simply, 'but if Troy is lost why do you need my son?'

Panthus bent to pick up the bundle he had been carrying. 'I have brought him the gods of the city, the tutelary gods of Troy. The Troy we know is dying, dying before our eyes; but another mightier Troy will arise to the west beyond the seas. Your son will be its founder. I know not how nor when. I only know that these things shall be.' He unwrapped the bundle and gave it to my grandfather. 'You shall take charge of them, my lord, until your son returns. He will take them with him to the new Troy.'

'Until Aeneas returns?' echoed my grandfather. 'And who told you he would ever return? He has gone to die fighting, sword in hand, as a hero should.'

'It was Hector who told me,' said Panthus. 'It was his ghost that I saw in my dream.' His despair had vanished, his voice was calm and solemn. He bowed to my mother and grandfather, and raised his hands in blessing on us all. Then he turned on his heel and was gone.

I had been listening so intently to Panthus that I had forgotten the distant shouts and screams, and the roar of the advancing fire. A thunderous crash close at hand brought me brutally back to earth. I began to cry. My mother shook me by the arm.

'Stop it, Ascanius. Remember your father.'

'When is he coming?' I sobbed.

'Soon, soon,' she said mechanically, stroking my hair. 'Oh God! What was that?'

A terrible clamour had broken out to the south near the city wall. There was a fierce sound of crackling timber, and suddenly a great sheet of flame soared into the sky.

'The king's palace is on fire,' shrieked one of the women.

My mother covered her face with her hands.

'Do not weep, dearest Creusa,' said my grandfather, 'at least your father is not a cripple. Old though he is he will have died a hero's death.'

There was a pause, and he added sadly and gravely: 'This is the end of Troy.'

My mother looked up.

'Yes, this is the end, I know it; and the servants must go while there is still time. Fetch them, Caieta.'

She was speaking calmly once more, and I can still see her standing there as she addressed the group of women – a slight but erect figure in the moonlight.

'You must leave Troy before it is too late. Take all the food that you can carry and make for the northern postern gate – the Greeks should not have reached it yet. Then follow the path to the grove where the ancient temple of Demeter stands. Caieta knows the spot. There we will meet if the gods allow. Go now at once without farewells and weeping, and may the gods protect you all.'

Caieta flung her arms round me without speaking. Then she picked up her pitiful bundle of belongings and beckoned to the other women. One by one, sobbing quietly and with bowed heads, they filed past us out of the gate.

My mother, my crippled grandfather and I were left alone. Suddenly I was afraid.

'When will father come?' I asked plaintively.

'Soon, soon,' said my mother, taking hold of my hand.

'You should tell the child the truth now, Creusa,' said my grandfather. 'In your heart of hearts you know he is in the thick of the fighting and will never come at all. Even if he is still alive, how will he get through that inferno?' He pointed with his stick.

The western and southern quarters of the city were engulfed in a raging sea of fire. We could still hear intermittently the clash of arms, the triumphant shouts of the Greeks, the screams of their victims, but the sounds of battle were increasingly submerged by the sullen roar of advancing flames. As my grandfather spoke, a series of tremendous reverberations shook the ground, cracks appeared in the tiled courtyard and a shower of rubble poured down from the surrounding walls. My mother hastily led us to the shelter of the porch. My grandfather continued with a wry smile:

'The very walls of Troy are collapsing as you can hear. Poseidon must be pulling them down with his own hands. What have Aphrodite or any of the gods done to help us? Aeneas is surely dead or trapped by the fire. How can we believe the mouthings of Panthus about a new Troy beyond the seas?'

'Yet here is Aeneas as Panthus foretold,' cried my mother, and the next moment my father burst into the porch, helmetless, his face and arms scorched and splashed with blood. He sank down against the wall gasping for breath. My mother ran to fetch him wine, and he drank it staring fixedly before him.

'Are you wounded?' she whispered. He shook his head.

'It is Greek blood,' he muttered. 'Such horrors . . . I have seen such horrors,' he went on, brushing his hand across his face. 'The Greeks massacring and raping in the streets. I saw them dragging Cassandra away by her hair. I saw Priam . . .

[33]

Oh God! Forgive me, Creusa.' He buried his face in his hands.

'Tell me,' said my mother quickly.

'I saw your father butchered in cold blood before the palace altar,' cried my father. 'And I stood there powerless to save him, powerless, do you understand?' He struggled to his feet. 'I must go back,' he shouted. 'It would have been better to die than to see such sights and live.' He began to strap his shield on to his left arm.

'Then we will go with you,' said my mother quickly. My father stared at her.

'That is impossible. You would be killed. I came to tell you to escape while you can – you and the servants. How can I leave Troy while there is fighting to be done?'

'Better die by your side than live without you,' said my mother quickly. 'Have you thought what the Greeks will do if they take us?'

My father groaned and covered his face with his hands. Then I heard my grandfather's voice:

'You do not know what to do, my son. I will tell you. Panthus has been here. He brought you the gods of the city. He said that Hector had told him to do so and that you were to found a new Troy beyond the seas.'

'He brought me the gods of the city!' repeated my father. 'Show them to me.'

He took the bundle from my grandfather and unwrapped it carefully.

'Then it is true,' he said at length in a shaking voice, 'these are the gods that Hector took from their inner shrine and gave me as I awoke from my dream.' He paused: 'He meant that I should leave Troy, taking them with me. Now I understand.' He turned to us peremptorily.

'Where are the servants, Creusa?'

'They have gone. I bade them go to Demeter's temple.'

'Then we will follow them there. The northern quarter of the city should still be safe. Father, I will bear you upon my shoulders. You will carry the gods and their sacred vessels. Ascanius will hold my left hand to leave my sword arm free.

Creusa will follow close behind us. If we are separated, we will meet at the solitary cypress tree near the temple walls. Come, let us go.'

My grandfather shook his head. 'Not I,' he said.

'Do you think I would go without you?' cried my father. 'I would rather disobey Hector than leave you.'

'I am too old to leave Troy,' said my grandfather slowly. 'Go, Aeneas, with your wife and son, and be sure that my blessing goes with you. You are young and strong, but I have neither strength nor faith enough to face the hazards of an uncertain future. My world is in ruins and I have nothing to hope for. Why should the gods or you care for a useless cripple whose life is well-nigh spent? This is my home; here I will stay; and here I will die.'

My father stretched his hands to the sky in supplication.

'Oh, almighty god of Heaven,' he prayed, 'if it be thy will that thy servant Anchises leave this city, send us a sign.'

We waited breathlessly. Suddenly my mother gave a cry.

'Look! A shooting star.'

High above the city we saw a star blaze across the sky towards Mount Ida. Then it had gone.

I looked at my grandfather, leaning on his stick; his face shone with a serenity and hope such as I had never seen.

'Give me the gods, Aeneas,' he said quietly. My father handed the bundle to him without speaking. I could see that he was deeply moved.

'Now, my son,' said my grandfather cheerfully. 'I am ready for you.'

My father bent down, lifted him on to his broad shoulders and took hold of my hand. He glanced at my mother:

'What is that large bundle you are carrying, my darling?'

'Food,' she answered quietly. 'You and Ascanius will be hungry.'

'Is it not too heavy for you?'

My mother shook her head. He gave her a smile of love and gratitude. 'How could I live without you?' he said.

We went down the steps to the gate, and out into the street

without a backward glance. A moment later the palace was out of sight, and we were threading our way rapidly through narrow passage-ways hugging the shadows. I had to run to keep up with my father's long stride. I could feel that he was on the alert and tense with anxiety. We changed direction with bewildering speed; every now and then he would halt and listen.

'Is your mother following?' he would whisper.

Once we had to wait several minutes before she came in sight behind us at the corner of a moonlit alley. I could feel my father becoming increasingly nervous and realized that, anxious though he was about my mother, his main fear was for my grandfather and myself.

I could see that we were gradually leaving the fire behind us, and hitherto there had been no sign of the Greeks. By avoiding the main streets we had also avoided the stream of panic-stricken refugees fleeing from the city. But as we approached the postern gate it became impossible to circumvent them any longer. We found ourselves caught up in a dense mob all trying to force their way through the narrow gate. My father protected me as best he could with his left arm.

Suddenly there arose a wild cry to our left: 'The Greeks are coming,' and in an instant the scene before us had changed into one of terror-stricken pandemonium.

My father broke into a run, dragging me bodily along beside him, forcing his way through groups of hysterical people until we reached a secluded passage-way far from the gate. I heard him gasping for breath in the darkness as we listened intently.

'It was a false alarm, father,' he said at length, wiping the sweat from his face, 'and I have lost my way. But Creusa never panics as I do. By now she should have reached the temple. Let us go.'

He took hold of my hand once more, and we made our way forward stumbling with exhaustion. After what seemed an interminable length of time we emerged once more near the gate. The crowd had disappeared and the moon had set. We seemed to be alone.

At last we reached the grove where the derelict temple lay. Scattered about on the grass lay hundreds of people, some of them moaning or weeping, others inert or asleep in the last stages of exhaustion. Here and there torches flickered in the darkness. My father seized one of them, and picked his way through the bodies lying on the ground until he reached the solitary cypress tree. No one was there.

'Creusa,' he called, and looked about him. There was no answer.

'Creusa,' he cried in a loud voice, and listened intently. From nearby came the sound of sobbing. 'Surely that cannot be Creusa,' he muttered to himself.

He hesitated, then set my grandfather down upon the ground and let go of my hand.

'Stay here while I look for your mother,' he said. He disappeared into the grove in the direction of the temple, calling her name repeatedly.

There was a crackle of twigs behind me. I turned quickly and saw a woman's figure approaching. I ran towards it.

'Mother, is that you? Oh, I am glad we have found you.'

'No, Ascanius, it is not your mother. It is Caieta. I heard your father calling.'

'Have you seen her?' I asked quickly, trying to disguise my disappointment.

'No, I have not seen her, but no one else is missing. Your father will find her soon enough. Lie down and try to sleep,' she added soothingly. 'You are safe now.'

She took off her cloak and wrapped me in it. I must have fallen asleep almost instantly for when I awoke daylight had come and the birds were singing in the nearby grove.

I sat up and looked about me. My grandfather and Caieta were fast asleep. My father was nowhere to be seen. Then I saw him coming slowly towards us along the path with bowed head, and ran towards him.

[37]

'Where is mother?' I cried.

He looked at me without speaking, then took me in his arms.

'She will not be coming with us, Ascanius,' he said gently. 'We have lost her for ever. She is . . . she is dead.'

His self-control suddenly crumbled. With a hoarse cry of grief he flung himself upon the ground and wept with great searing sobs that racked his whole frame, while I stood watching him, appalled by such sorrow which I was powerless to assuage.

III

We never discovered how my mother met her end – whether she had been crushed to death in the mob, or collapsed and died under the weight of her heavy load. For long my father could not bring himself to speak of her without giving way to agonies of self-reproach. It was not until later that he told me how, after leaving us at the derelict temple, he had returned to Troy to look for her. In a frenzy of anxiety he had retraced the route we had followed, calling her name. Careless of danger he had even returned to the palace although the Greeks were looting it and the building was ablaze. More than once he was set upon by the Greeks, but each time he cut down his enemy or made his escape, for the gods did not mean him to die and he bore a charmed life. At last, worn out with grief and all his exertions, he came once more to the postern gate by which we had left the city. It still stood open and un-guarded, but at the further end of the square he saw, guarded by soldiers, a band of captive women and children whom the Greeks had rounded up like cattle. Dawn was breaking, and although he knew that he was courting death, my father began slowly to advance towards them. He felt that if he found my mother in their midst his reckless folly would not have been in vain and he would die happy.

Suddenly he saw her shape, tall and strangely luminous, before him. With a cry of joy he stretched out his arms towards her, but she evaded his grasp and he realized that what he saw was not his wife but a lovely wraith.

'Speak to me, sweet love,' he implored her.

The figure pointed to the postern gate, and he seemed to

hear a faint sigh like a dying breath, 'Farewell, Aeneas.' Then it vanished. Her last gesture had been to save her husband's life; as if she knew that she belonged only to his past, she was never to visit him again.

Left to himself, my father might have succumbed completely to the terrible despair that descended upon him during the first few days after my mother's death. He railed against the gods for their treachery and injustice in delivering innocent Troy into the bloodstained hands of the Greeks. He cursed them for their cruelty in snatching his beloved wife from him. He defied them to do their worst, calling upon them to send the Greeks to massacre us all. He poured scorn on the prophecy of Panthus that he would found a second Troy to replace the flattened smoking ruin we had left. And yet I realize now that his faith in the gods never entirely deserted him. However much he longed for death he no longer tried to court it. His words were sacrilegious but not his actions. He reviled his divine mother but continued to pray to her. He spoke contemptuously of the tutelary gods of Troy – the vanquished gods which had failed to protect the city – but he treasured them none the less. The truth is that it was not so much his faith in the gods which had been shattered as his faith in himself. Over and over again he cursed himself for having weakly agreed to the wooden horse being dragged into Troy, for having slept while the Greeks were pouring into the city, for having failed to rescue Priam and, ultimate disgrace, for having abandoned his wife in a moment of blind panic.

'I am not fit to live,' he would groan, and then his eye would fall upon his crippled father and myself, he would sigh deeply and relapse into silence. Little by little my grandfather coaxed him from his despair. Yet it was above all the pressure of circumstances, the hand of fate if you will, which roused him to action. A whole concourse of refugees, men, women and children, had assembled at the temple, for the news that he was there had spread like a forest fire. One and all looked to him to be their leader. They would follow him, they said, to the ends of the earth. My father could not abdicate from the position they thrust upon him; there was no one else to act as shepherd to these hungry frightened sheep. Yet, so unsure of himself had he become that he would do nothing without consulting my grandfather whose calm confidence in the gods had remained unshaken.

To remain for long so close to Troy was out of the question. Trojan resistance had collapsed completely. The sacrilegious Greeks might attack the temple at any moment, and we were desperately short of food. Late the following afternoon after a pitiful meal, we set off for the mountains where we would be beyond the enemy's reach and there were friendly herdsmen. My father led the way carrying the gods of Troy – a limping dishevelled figure with unkempt hair; and behind him trailed a dejected, straggling, exhausted band of refugees carrying their scanty belongings. My grandfather being a king travelled in the only cart with the pregnant women and the youngest of the children. A Trojan officer named Ilioneus brought up the rear bearing his aged mother in his arms. Next morning as we were nearing our destination he found that she was dead. We buried her beside the steep, stony path with weeping and lamentation.

'Was it for this that we were born, my lord?' Ilioneus asked my father bitterly, pointing to the wizened body. My father made a gesture of despair. It was my grandfather who answered.

'She had done all that the gods wished her to do in this life,' he said gently. 'Your destiny is not hers – that is all.' He looked at my father as he spoke, and added slowly:

'All that matters is that we should try to obey their will. Whoever does so can die happy.'

'But how can we do so?' cried my father wildly. 'Where is it, this western land beyond the seas of which Panthus told you? Whither should we sail? Where are the ships to carry so great a company of people? Where are our sailors, our gold, our victuals?'

'We will ask Apollo's guidance since it is he who reveals the future to mortals and Panthus was his priest,' answered my

[41]

grandfather. 'You are tormented and bewildered, my son, but our plight is not so desperate as it seems. Patience in adversity comes more easily to the old than to the young, yet it is this rather than heroism in battle that the gods will require of you in the years ahead.'

My father looked at him and silently bowed his head.

Throughout the rest of spring we stayed in the foothills of Mount Ida near Antandros where the simple people befriended us and gave us shelter from howling winds and heavy rain. My father set the men of our company to work on building ships that were to take us on our journey; but he himself, on my grandfather's advice, departed with a companion to consult the oracle of Apollo at Patara, far to the south in Lycia. There he would be told our ultimate destination – or so they believed.

He was gone for so long that many decided he was dead, and deserted us. Others lost heart and refused to work any longer, saying that it was foolish to build ships which might never put to sea. Even Ilioneus began to waver; only my grandfather seemed unperturbed as summer declined into autumn, and still my father did not come.

At last, one rainy wind-swept morning, he and his companion Achates rode into our forest camp. He dismounted without a word and went into my grandfather's hut. An eager crowd gathered round Achates, embracing him and plying him with questions. At length my father appeared at the door of the hut.

'My friends, I will not waste time in greeting you,' he said formally. 'You have waited long enough to hear the oracle's pronouncement.

'Whither should we sail? What is our destination? These were my questions. And here is the answer the god vouchsafed me after many months of waiting:

"You are to sail towards the setting sun till you come to a land where you will eat your own platters." '

There were cries of bewilderment and dismay. My father held up his hand for silence.

'What does this answer mean? you ask. Does it mean that we are to sail to the very edge of the world? I cannot tell. Does it mean that we will suffer hardship? Surely it must. Does it mean that we are destined to die of hunger in a barren wilderness? I cannot think so. If such is to be our fate, how can we found the new Troy of which Panthus spoke? It is dangerous to trust the gods as we know to our cost. Their ways are not our ways. They answer in riddles and their wisdom is inscrutable. Sometimes they seem to play cruel tricks upon us, punishing the righteous and sparing the guilty. Yet is it not still more dangerous to ignore their guidance and disobey the divine purpose? I cannot interpret the oracle, but I shall try to obey it, knowing that time will show me its inner meaning. I do not beg you to cast in your lot with me; the choice is yours. Now that winter is almost upon us it is too late to leave these shores; but as soon as summer comes, my father, son and I will set forth on our journey in obedience to the god's command.'

For the first time my father had spoken with the authority of a leader, and I revered him. He had not as yet my grandfather's unquestioning faith – that was not to come till later. Such pious submission to the gods was in his case an act of rare courage, and this was sensed by all his followers. Henceforth their admiration for him knew no bounds. 'Pious Aeneas', 'Father Aeneas', such were the names by which they showed their love for him, while my grandfather became known as 'Father Anchises'.

Early next summer we set sail on the appointed day after sacrificing to the gods. In obedience to an omen, our twenty ships followed the coast northwards past the blackened ruins of Troy, gaunt and bare upon her hilltop; all of us wept to think that we were abandoning her to her desolation. There too was the well-remembered plain where Scamander and Simois flowed into the sea, with its thickets of tamarisk, its elms and willows. How peaceful, how radiant in its beauty it lay beneath the evening sun; how unbelievable to me that this deserted pastoral countryside had witnessed scenes of carnage

[43]

and deeds of heroism such as the world had never seen.

Perhaps my father sensed my thoughts, for he called me to him.

'Look, Ascanius,' he said, pointing, 'that is where Hector led the attack on the Greek ships; and there, beside the rushes near the river bank I fought Achilles and lived to tell the tale. I have seen that river red with the blood of Trojans he had slain.' His voice trembled and he fell silent, staring before him. 'Why did the gods desert us,' he murmured to himself, 'and why did they spare me? Hector and Deiphobus were better men than I.'

He looked at me and his face softened. 'Perhaps it was because of you, Ascanius,' he said, 'perhaps you are destined for greater things than all of us. Perhaps my divine mother will care for you better than she cares for me.'

'Does she not care for you?' I asked.

My father hesitated:

'I do not know,' he said. 'She has not spoken to me since the night Troy fell. She bade me think of my family, not of Troy; and yet she let me lose my wife.'

'That was long ago,' I said, meaning to console him.

My father smiled sadly:

'So it must seem to you, my son, and you do well to say so. This is no time for homeless fugitives like us to brood upon the past. You will escape from it more quickly than I with all my memories. But some day, when we have reached our goal, and I can think of it without repining, I will tell you the story of Priam's Troy and of those who died for her in vain.'

He stretched out his arms to the shore in a gesture of farewell. The sun sank behind Tenedos, and a breeze sprang up. Far off the evening star shone faintly in the darkening sky.

Each night, two hours before sunset, we beached our ships on some sandy shore protected from sea-winds, where fresh water was to be found. Sometimes parties would be sent into the woods with spears and bows in search of game; sometimes we would eat the fish we had caught during the day. In bad weather we slept on board – each rower at the foot of his bench and my father on a bed by the mast, over the hold in which our treasure was stored. Before we left Antandros, rich gifts had been pressed upon us by the kindly people of the coast, and we were no longer short of gold and provisions. Yet my father would leave nothing to chance. The food and wine we carried with us were strictly apportioned, and reserves never allowed to run low; as for bartering, only he could sanction it, just as it was he alone who decided where we should beach our ships. When disputes arose, or quarrels over women, no one but he could settle them. Soon almost all the men without wives had taken a concubine: even an ill-favoured ageing woman was better than none, for often enough she was all the more eager for love, and readier to mend her lover's clothes or care for him when ill. Of the women in our ship, only Caieta would have no truck with other men; partly this was due to her devotion to my father and myself: even more so perhaps to her sense of dignity and pride.

How jealously she guarded her privileged position, turning savagely upon any who attempted to usurp it. It was she who cooked for my grandfather and ourselves, washed and mended our clothes, helped my grandfather to dress, laid out the simple bed upon which he slept, kept a watchful eye on all I did, looked after me if I fell ill. She guarded me like the apple of her eye. Her homely peasant face, her forthright manner, her brusque possessiveness, were infinitely reassuring until I grew older and began to chafe against my subjugation. It was Andromache who shook Caieta's ascendancy over me, and Dido who broke it. But all this lay in the future; for long I was to remain the docile tractable child that Caieta expected me to be – even though I soon learnt to row, to swim, to fish, to steer a ship or trim a sail. Atys was the only boy of my own age on board our ship, but my friendship with him was slow to ripen. Caieta's jealousy was such that she actively discouraged it; nor would she allow Epytides to take charge of my upbringing although my father had appointed him my guardian. I must depend upon her alone.

It was the wind and the current, not my father's purpose,

[45]

which drove us north towards Thrace. Yet despite my grandfather's warning to obey the oracle and sail westwards, he made no attempt to change our course, for he was reluctant to believe, since wind and current bore us there, that Thrace was not our goal. Its king had been Priam's ally. It was friendly territory with gods similar to ours; moreover the land was rich and lay not far distant from Troy.

Our voyage was calm with no dissenting omen, and as we neared the shore light fleecy clouds spread out in the radiant sky above us like an opening sheaf of corn. A happy augury we thought it. We were wrong.

King Lycurgus received us well, and granted my father land upon the coast to found a city. We thought our troubles ended; only my grandfather remained unhappy. There was no sign from Heaven of the gods' displeasure, but he could not believe that we were meant to settle there, and doubted the king's friendship. Priam had sent a store of gold to Thrace soon after the siege of Troy began to deny it to the Greeks if Troy should fall; where was this gold now and where was the envoy who had brought it? Priam had reclaimed the treasure later, he was told: Polydorus, Priam's son, had returned to fetch it and take it back to Troy. The answer, garnished with detail, seemed plausible enough. Yet my grandfather's uneasiness remained despite the courteous explanation.

At length the morning came when the two white oxen were harnessed to the holy plough that was to trace the outlines of our city's walls. My father prayed aloud to the gods that they should bless our project and sacrificed before us all to Zeus the Almighty, his mother and Apollo. Then he took the plough in his hands, urged forward his team, and began to follow the circuit. Suddenly a cry came from my grandfather who was watching from a near-by mound.

'Stop, Aeneas! Stop, before it is too late.'

My father, astonished and mortified, obeyed. He began to speak, but my grandfather cut him short. I could see that he was greatly agitated.

'This site is accursed,' he said vehemently. 'I can feel it.'

There was a general cry of horror.

'How do you know this?' asked my father, faltering. My grandfather did not answer.

'You can take away those oxen,' he said to Ilioneus, 'and you, my son, will cease your ploughing and start to dig – here where I am standing.'

He motioned to some by-standers to fetch implements, and we set to work clearing away the bristling undergrowth. Then my father and his helpers began to excavate the sandy soil beneath.

'You will not have to dig far,' said my grandfather sombrely, and as he spoke my father with an exclamation unearthed something and held it up. It was a shattered skull.

'Yes,' said my grandfather slowly, 'that is the skull of Polydorus, Priam's youngest son, murdered by Lycurgus for the sake of Priam's gold. I felt his spirit groan as I stood here unknowingly upon his grave. Lycurgus gave you this land to bring misfortune on us.'

We gave Polydorus a fresh burial, and set up an altar to his departed ghost, decking it with branches of cypress, the tree of death, while the women stood around with loosened hair as the rites prescribe: we offered libations, laid his spirit to rest in its tomb, and called aloud his name in token of farewell. Then with one accord we made haste to depart from this wicked land.

My father was deeply disheartened by this miserable end to all his hopes. Nearly three years had passed since Troy had fallen. We had wasted the whole autumn and winter in Thrace as a result of his faulty judgement. He had done wrong to disregard the oracle: yet, since even my grandfather was still baffled as to its meaning, how was he to obey it? Whither should we sail? Should we return to Antandros and begin our journey anew despite the discontent that this would cause, or should we sail westward from Thrace itself even though this would take us towards Greece?

'We shall do neither,' said my grandfather in answer to my father's anxious questions. 'We must sail south to Delos, the sacred isle anchored in the midst of the sea. There Apollo was born. There we will ask for guidance once more, and the oracle's ambiguity will be resolved.'

My father looked at him with awe and gratitude.

'Would that I had your wisdom, father,' he said.

'Wisdom grows with age and communion with the gods,' replied my grandfather simply. 'The time will come when you will guide your son's steps as I am guiding yours.'

The knowledge that we were rejecting the polluted soil of Thrace for the holy soil of Delos gave fresh courage to everyone. My father soon recovered his confidence, the oarsmen sang as they rowed, and all went cheerfully about their tasks. Even my grandfather seemed rejuvenated as he told me of the birth of Apollo, and the sacred isle he loved so well.

'This is the story that men tell,' said my grandfather. 'Almighty Zeus fell in love with Leto, who some say was born of the Titans, those primeval gods whom he had driven out of Heaven. Others say she was a goddess of the Phoenicians called Lat, who brought the palm tree and the olive from the east. But when Juno, Queen of Heaven, learnt that Leto was with child, she sent the serpent, Python, to pursue her all over the world. To save her, Almighty Zeus changed her into a quail, and the south wind, which bears us thither now, bore her to the floating island of Delos where the serpent could not reach her. At first Delos feared to allow her shelter, thinking that Leto's son would be ashamed to have been born on a rocky and desolate isle, and would thrust it down with his foot into the depths of the sea. But Leto promised that he would love and honour his birthplace, and there, after grievous birth-pangs, she brought forth Apollo beneath a palm tree on the summit of Mount Cynthus, while the earth shook with joyful laughter at his birth. The goddesses who had come to watch over Leto during her delivery bathed the divine child in limpid water and swaddled him in a fair white veil bordered with gold; but when they had fed him on nectar and ambrosia, the infant god exulting in his strength burst his swaddling clothes and called for his lyre and silver bow. Then he arose and walked upon Mount Cynthus, rejoicing in his birthplace, and ever since, by his decree, Delos has been immovably fixed in the sea. Part of the year he spends in a mysterious land far to the north, bathed in perpetual light, where peace reigns eternal and the happy people whom he rules never cease from singing his praises. But every spring he comes to Delos, sometimes, they say, as a dolphin, and sometimes in a chariot drawn by swans, and when he comes, the isle shines golden and blossoms in the sunshine of his favour.'

My grandfather stopped. I could see that he was deeply moved.

'Tell me more,' I said eagerly.

'There are many stories about Apollo,' said my grandfather, 'for he is the god of all that is creative in Man. He is the protector of travellers, of colonizers, of the founders of new cities. He is the enemy of all that is noxious to mortals – the rats and locusts that devour their food and crops, the diseases that afflict them. He is the god of order and harmony who inspires just laws and guides men to act rightly. He is the mouthpiece of Almighty Zeus. What his oracles declare, Zeus himself commands.'

As he spoke, the capricious wind which had abandoned us sprang up astern, and a strong gust bellied out our sails. The haze that hung over the horizon dissolved, and Delos topped by its verdant mountain came into view. Soon Palinurus our helmsman had steered us safely past the barren islet sacred to Hecate, between the treacherous reefs and into the little port where pilgrims moored their ships. My father, impatient to reach land, leapt into the clear water and began to wade ashore; then he turned and came back to the ship.

'Forgive me, father,' he said, 'it is you, the leader of us all, who should be the first to reach the shore.'

With glad hearts we lifted my grandfather over the gunwale on to my father's back. For each of us my father's act of filial piety had a deep significance. It showed his humility for wisdom greater than his own; it symbolized the inseparable unity between father Aeneas and father Anchises. How could the god ignore their joint appeal? How could they fail to interpret the answer he would give them? No sooner had we reached the shore than our unvoiced prayers seemed to be granted. Anius the priest-king of Delos came himself to meet us, and to our amazement greeted my grandfather as an old friend. It seemed that they had met in those far-off mild and golden days before the siege of Troy, and we ragged homeless exiles were received as honoured guests.

When we had bathed ourselves in fresh water, and feasted at his palace, my grandfather told Anius our story, dwelling upon the words used by Panthus and the oracle at Patara. The king listened attentively.

'First we must offer sacrifices to Apollo to see if he is willing to answer your questions,' he said, 'and then, before entering the sanctuary, you must purify yourselves.'

He himself performed the customary sacrifices for us. For three days we abstained from wine, and for one day we fasted. Then early on the following morning he led us to the sacred pool where we must purify ourselves.

'One drop of water suffices for the virtuous man,' he told us solemnly, 'but not even the Ocean can wash the sinner clean.'

The sun had not yet risen over Mount Cynthus as we followed the path through the grove of olives that grew around the ancient temple. No one spoke; all was hushed; no wind stirred, no bird sang.

My father signalled to most of our company to remain outside in the colonnade that surrounded the walls of the sanctuary. Then, taking my grandfather by the arm and motioning to Achates and myself to follow him, he led us into the holy building.

For a moment we stood awestruck in the eerie twilight. At length my father spoke, and his voice resounded strangely in the gloom.

'Give us a home of our own, great Apollo. We are weary. Give us a city with walls that will endure, where our children

All the next day and the following day we skimmed through the multitudinous laughing waves, past Paros and mountainous Naxos amongst whose vineyards Dionysus dwells. Island after island seemed to emerge as if to gaze at us as we threaded our way through the Cyclades over the wine-dark sea. So lovely was the scene, so happy the crews of our ships as they strained at their oars in rivalry while the boatswains called the time, that I gradually forgot my resentment at leaving Delos.

'On to Crete! On to our home,' called the sailors to each other. But the journey was longer than expected and we were troubled by cross-currents. The evening of the fourth day found us still at sea with land no longer in sight. We had lost our bearings. The wind had dropped, the weary oarsmen had fallen silent. Over us there floated like a cloud a vague oppressive feeling of foreboding.

It was then that I saw it rise suddenly out of the sea. 'Look,' I shouted, catching Caieta's arm, and as I spoke the great fish leapt into the air in a swift arc and plunged beneath the waves.

'It is a dolphin,' exclaimed Caieta. 'Quick, waken your grandfather.'

'No,' I said. 'I know what it means. It means Apollo is with us.'

It was the first time I had defied her. She was about to make an angry retort when two more dolphins burst out of the sea close beside the ship, drenching us with spray as they fell back into the water. Some of the women screamed, and my grandfather awoke.

'We must follow them if we can,' he told my father when he heard what had happened, 'perhaps they will lead us to Crete.'

'The sun will set within an hour,' said my father doubtfully.

'But the moon will rise,' answered my grandfather. 'Let us pray for a wind to help us.'

For some time we lay becalmed and almost motionless for my father had told the crews to ship their oars to save their strength. But the dolphins were in no hurry to leave us. One after another appeared, sometimes leaping out of the water, sometimes circling round our ships. Then just as we had begun to eat our evening meal before the sun set a breeze sprang up astern.

'Lower the sails from the yard-arm,' shouted my father. His order was repeated on the other ships – not a moment too soon, for the force of the wind suddenly increased and we found ourselves scudding rapidly southwards.

All night we ran before the wind across the moonlit sea while the dolphins frolicked around us. Frightened though they were, most of the women and children eventually fell asleep despite the groaning and pitching of the vessel.

Disregarding Caieta's protests, I went to where my father stood beside the helmsman, a tall erect figure silhouetted in the moonlight, his cloak flapping in the wind. He put his arm about me and drew me to him. Neither of us spoke, but each was conscious of the bond that had been forged between us. Dimly I realized that he had begun to count upon me not as an obedient child but as his son and heir. So we stood until sleep overcame me and my father laid me gently on his palliasse beneath the mast.

When I awoke, daylight had come. The ship was rocking gently on the water and gulls were wheeling overhead uttering raucous cries. I saw my father coming towards me; his eyes were red from the salt spray and lack of sleep.

'Land, Ascanius,' he said pointing, and I saw that we were moored in a sheltered creek flanked by enormous cliffs.

'Is this Crete?' I asked eagerly. My father nodded.

'The gods have brought us safely home at last,' he said, 'even though hardship may await us. This is the land from which our forefathers were driven by famine, the land to which Apollo has twice bidden us return.'

'Twice?' I repeated.

'Have you forgotten what the oracle said to me at Patara?'

I gaped at him stupidly.

'It said that we must sail westwards till we came to a land where we would eat our own platters.'

'But that cannot be true, father,' I cried. 'We have plenty of food. The oracle must have been playing a trick on you. You yourself said the gods sometimes played tricks upon mortals.'

My father gave me a little pat on the shoulder.

'You are wise beyond your years, Ascanius, even if you do not understand what is in my mind. I trust you to tell no one of this conversation – not even your grandfather.' He looked at me anxiously.

I nodded, suddenly aware how worn and tired his face was. A wave of pity for him swept over me.

'Father,' I said awkwardly, 'why don't you have a woman to look after you and make you happy?'

'A woman?' he repeated. 'Why should I need a woman? Caieta looks after me. I have known her all my life.'

'I don't mean Caieta,' I said savagely. 'I mean a young woman – a concubine: like the other men.'

My father smiled. 'I have not the time, Ascanius, and I have other things to think of. What kind of leader would I be if I were no different from the others?'

I was abashed and silent.

'Be patient with Caieta,' my father went on. 'Even if she is a tyrant she is a devoted one, and you are my only son.'

He turned abruptly and left me.

Not even my grandfather knew from which part of Crete our ancestor, Teucer, had come, but Anius had advised us to land upon the east coast of the island, not too close to the powerful city of Cnossus. The King of Cnossus had taken part in the expedition against Troy, but Anius had heard that on his return he had been expelled from his kingdom by his rebellious subjects and forced to flee overseas. Five different peoples, we had been told, lived on the island of Crete. The Greeks, whom we must avoid, were most strongly established in Cnossus and the west; the original inhabitants, the true Cretans, lived mostly in the hills to the east. There too stood Mount Dicte, birthplace of Almighty Zeus.

We knew that we had landed in eastern Crete, but no one could tell whether the reaction to our coming would be friendly or hostile. Wherever we were destined to settle ultimately, we were sure to remain upon the shore where we had landed for several days. As soon as we had offered thanks to the gods for our safe journey therefore, my father gave orders for us to beach our ships in such a way that they formed a bulwark against possible attack. A palisade of sharp sticks was quickly erected and a ditch dug around it. Look-outs were posted on the cliffs, and two parties under Ilioneus and Achates were dispatched into the neighbouring hills to spy out the land and hunt for game. My father himself supervised the unloading of such stores as we needed, selected the sites where huts were to be built, and traced out the sacred precinct of our camp where altars would be set up.

All of us were tired and hungry, but the thought that this was the land where we were destined to settle gave us courage, and we worked with a will till noon. We had begun to eat our midday meal when Ilioneus and his men returned with an abundant supply of game. They reported that they had followed the coast westwards through the thickly wooded hills until they had come to a shrine, but had met no one.

The afternoon wore on but still there was no sign of Achates, and my father had begun to grow anxious when a look-out upon the cliff-top shouted that he could see him and his followers descending the brow of a hill. Soon afterwards they emerged from the woods on to the beach exhausted and footsore. My father ran to meet them and warmly embraced his favourite companion.

'We bring good news, father Aeneas,' said Achates, 'but first if it please you let us eat, for we are faint with hunger.'

With his customary kindness my father left Achates and his men to eat their meal in peace. Not one question did he ask until they had rested and recovered their strength. Then Achates spoke once more:

'Father Aeneas,' he said, 'your capital awaits you.'

My father looked at him quickly.

'You mean that other Trojans have landed here before us?'

Achates shook his head. 'I mean we have found a deserted city where we may make our home.'

'A deserted city?' repeated my father in astonishment.

The man drank greedily without speaking. When he had finished, my father began to question him slowly and patiently, relying this time on single words and signs. Gradually our prisoner became more responsive and in a short time my father had learnt much that was of value.

We were some two days' journey to the east of Cnossus. The deserted city was called Gournia. Long ago it had been built by Cretans; then a sea-people, Greeks perhaps, had settled there after it had been damaged by earthquake. The city had been subject to Idomeneus, King of Cnossus; its governor had treated the Cretan peasants cruelly, taking from them as tribute most of their crops and livestock, and making them toil for him like slaves. They had prayed to the Great Goddess whom they worshipped to help them in their misery; and then, a year ago, as if in answer to their prayer, the whole population of Gournia, men, women and children, had sailed away with all their goods and chattels. Perhaps they had fled from the impending wrath of the Great Mother; at all events they had gone.

My father, realizing that Achates and his men must have been taken for enemies, tried to explain that we hated the Greeks also. Then, when he saw that he had been understood, he asked a final question like an archer drawing his bow at a venture.

'Teucer?' he said slowly and distinctly.

To our astonishment the name produced an immediate reaction. The man repeated the name correctly, indicating that it was the name of a king; then, after a sweeping gesture embracing the surrounding countryside, he pointed up the valley towards the deserted city. There could be no doubt as to his meaning. Once there had been a king called Teucer who had ruled in these parts, and Gournia had been his capital.

My father gave a shout of joy, released the bewildered peasant from his bonds and loaded him with gifts. Now at last he felt sure that Gournia was our predestined home. The same day, at a solemn ceremony of thanksgiving in the square before the palace, he renamed it Pergamea after the citadel of Troy.

Pergamea, Pergamea! How well I remember your terraced houses ranged haphazard along your winding alleyways and narrow cobbled streets. Like Troy, the town lay straddled across a hill; but there the resemblance ended. Our new capital was little more than an overgrown village clinging to the skirts of the only palace it possessed. Here there was no temple, only a single-roomed shrine that stood to the north of the palace. Evidently the rulers of Gournia had been its only priests. Later we learned that religious ceremonies and ritual dances had been largely held in the spacious palace courtyard in honour not of Zeus but of the Great Mother. All this was strange to us. Even stranger was the absence of a citadel and the inadequacy of the walls which encompassed only part of the town. Fortunate people, never to have lived under the shadow of war! We with our memories of the tenacious siege that Troy had endured could never have been content with such pitiful defences. The very name Pergamea proclaimed my father's intention of turning his capital into a fortified stronghold.

The days passed quickly for there was much to be done. We set to work at once extending and strengthening the wall. We sowed our barley before the spring rains ended, cleared the olive trees of their vegetation, trained the straggling vines. The Cretans, wary at first, became more friendly when they saw we meant no harm. From them we acquired goats and other livestock. Soon we were bartering with them briskly, and beginning to learn their language and religion. Some of our younger men took Cretan wives.

None came to molest us. My father, tireless as ever, fired us with his confident enthusiasm. Each morning when I awoke, I would run to the window of my room and look down the rocky valley to the broad sweep of bay lying placid and gleaming in the sun. Only a short distance below I could see the stretches of sand upon which our ships lay beached, stripped now of their masts and sails. Here there were no fierce cross-currents and howling winds such as we had known at Troy. Even the surrounding hills were gentle and serene.

And then, with terrifying suddenness, the weather changed. Day after day the remorseless sun poured out upon us the vials of his wrath. The streams ran dry, the crops withered and rotted away, even the vines turned sere and yellow. Syrius the dog-star brought further evils on us. One by one the goats sickened and died of a mysterious illness. Our houses were infested with fleas and scorpions. Worst of all a horde of starving rats descended upon the town and attacked our store of provisions. Then they too began to die; their corpses lay about the streets in hundreds, battened on by myriads of flies.

It was the rats no doubt that brought the plague. Exhausted by all their ordeals, hollow-cheeked with hunger, our people could not resist. Each day brought a fresh toll of victims. Desperately my father prayed to Apollo and Zeus to save us from the plague and send us rain. His prayers were unavailing. At last my grandfather told him he must struggle against the Fates no longer. The gods had plainly not intended Pergamea to be our home. If we remained there, all of us would die, possibly of starvation, certainly of the plague. Our only hope was to return to Delos and consult the oracle once more before it was too late.

With a supreme effort my father mastered his feelings of bitterness and despair. Calmly he announced the decision to our sadly diminished band of followers. Some cursed the gods, crying that they would rather die than wander any further; a few of the women wept hysterically; but most listened to his words in a stony silence. Confidence in his leadership had been cruelly shaken, but even those who murmured against him admitted his selflessness and courage.

With heavy hearts we cremated the last of our dead and said farewell to Pergamea. As we passed through the half-finished gate when the heat of the day was over, dragging the carts that bore our meagre possessions, the sight of the parched and barren fields where we had toiled in vain moved us to bitter tears. Forlorn and listless we assembled on the beach, re-membering how we had landed there confident that our wanderings had ended. Now there were only oarsmen enough for thirteen ships; many of the women and children too had died of the plague. My father ran his eye over the remnant of our company, counting us one by one. Carefully he examined our ships, consulting their depleted crews as to which we should leave behind us. Patiently and kindly he bade them choose their own captains and shipmates and rearranged each complement of passengers. Not a detail was overlooked or left to chance; not an angry word escaped him. Finally when all was ready he addressed us.

'Let us blame no one for what has befallen us. Remember how Teucer himself set sail from these shores. We are no decadent or dying race; we are the living symbol of the Troy he founded, whose gods we carry with us. Time means nothing to the gods, but let us take courage from the thought that however long the night, Apollo has promised us a glorious dawn.'

My grandfather said a simple prayer; then, after eating our evening meal, we loaded our stores and embarked. The hawsers were cast off, the crews inserted the oars in their grommets, hauled up the masts and hoisted the sails. A gentle wind carried us away from the shore. By the time that dusk had settled over the water we were far out to sea.

Because of the overpowering heat, my father had planned that we should sail by night and beach our ships under shelter by day. Above all he feared that we would find ourselves becalmed at sea under the remorseless glare of the sun. Each ship carried four days' supply of water collected with infinite pains before our departure. Not a drop was to be drunk without each captain's permission, for the watering places we had visited on our journey south might now be dry. Indeed Delos itself might be afflicted by the drought, but that was a possibility my father could not guard against and would not contemplate.

His precautions were to prove justified, but not in the way he expected. On the second day, as Thera came in sight, a

that all of us men, young and old, took our turns at rowing, keeping the time as best we could. It must have been late in the afternoon that my father roused me from an exhausted sleep. His face was grave.

'Your grandfather is very ill,' he said. 'Caieta is with him. She says that if we do not make land soon he will die of fever.'

I gave an exclamation of horror and sprang to my feet; then I stared at my father in astonishment.

'But there is land, father,' I said, pointing to a rocky escarpment to starboard, 'and look, there is a harbour with ships riding at anchor. What is that city yonder? Where are we? Surely this cannot be Delos?'

'No,' said my father. 'It is not Delos. That town is called Buthrotum. Palinurus came here many years ago. We have been driven far off our course. We are nearing the coast of Epirus to the north-west of Greece.'

I looked at him uncomprehendingly.

'Then why can't we land?'

'The King of Epirus is Pyrrhus,' answered my father slowly; 'Pyrrhus, who murdered Priam in cold blood before my very eyes. What kind of reception will we get, do you think, if we land at Buthrotum?'

'We could try to disembark further up the coast, or on that island opposite,' I said doubtfully, indicating Corcyra. My father shook his head.

'There is no other suitable landing place within easy reach. Your grandfather is too old and frail to endure more hardship. Unless he is given comfort and shelter, even my divine mother cannot save him.'

'Pray to her,' I said quickly.

My father hesitated: 'She never answers me.'

'Then I will do so.'

I shut my eyes and recited the rubric my grandfather himself had taught me, but this time I prayed to her as I had once seen her in a dream – a goddess of infinite beauty and grace who loved me with a tenderness such as I had never known.

At length I opened my eyes.

'We are to land at Buthrotum,' I said.

My father looked at me with a terrible intensity.

'You are sure, Ascanius? You are telling me the truth?'

I nodded: 'Yes, I am sure. Grandfather will live. All will be well.'

My father gave a heartrending sigh.

'If only I could believe it,' he murmured to himself. 'But I will trust her, yes, I will trust her – perhaps for the last time.'

He rested his hand on my head for a moment and stood up.

'Steer for Buthrotum, Palinurus,' he shouted, 'and you, oarsmen, pull on your oars as if your lives depended on it.' He seized an oar from an exhausted youth, and setting a quicker time began to row with all his might.

We had reached the harbour entrance before any ships could be launched to intercept us, but I could see a crowd of people gathering rapidly on the shore. A troop of soldiers ran along the mole, halted and trained their bows on us. My father signalled to Achates to take his place and leapt on to the stern beside Palinurus.

'Who are you?' shouted their officer, in a strange barbaric Greek.

'Trojans,' cried my father proudly. 'I am Prince Aeneas. We crave your hospitality.'

The officer gaped at him in amazement. For a moment I thought he was going to give the order to shoot, then, re-luctantly, as it seemed, he ordered his men to lower their bows and shouted to us where to moor our ships. One of his men was sent racing back along the mole to the shore where more and more soldiers were assembling.

My heart sank. The women's faces were grey with fear while from all our ships the men looked anxiously to where my father stood, waiting for the order to arm themselves.

'If we are doomed to die, let us do so fighting,' shouted Ilioneus.

My father shook his head and raised his arms in the air to tell us to be silent and make no move. By now we had reached the spot where we were to anchor. The crowd upon the shore had mostly fallen silent and were watching us intently from behind the row of armed soldiers.

My father turned to me:

'Come, Ascanius. Let us go together.' He leapt into the shallow water and began to wade ashore. We reached dry land together. Side by side we advanced towards the dense crowd, uncertain what would befall us, when suddenly a woman wearing a rich cloak pushed her way through the soldiers and ran towards us, calling our names. I heard my father gasp with astonishment. The next moment her arms were around my neck and she was weeping hot tears as she kissed and hugged me.

'Don't you recognize me, Ascanius? Don't you recognize me?' she was crying.

Dazed and weeping also, I shook my head.

'I used to bring my son to play with you. How like him you are. Surely you remember him?'

I looked at my father in bewilderment and saw that tears were rolling down his cheeks.

'Of course you remember Astyanax,' he said gently. 'This is his mother, Andromache.'

IV

My father had feared that by landing at Buthrotum we would be delivering ourselves into the hands of Pyrrhus, the pitiless enemy of all the Trojan race; instead we had been welcomed with open arms by the widow of the greatest of all Trojan heroes. Surely, I thought incredulously, she must have been sent to Buthrotum in direct answer to my prayer.

Within an hour, under her gentle supervision, my grandfather and all our sick and injured had been carried ashore by the very soldiers we had expected to attack us. However doubtfully they eyed us we knew that for the moment we were safe. But how did Andromache come to be queen of a hostile people in a town so far from Troy?

Strange unpredictable reversal of fortune such as even the gods but seldom operate. When Troy fell, Andromache had fallen into the clutches of Pyrrhus, son of the man who had slain her husband. Astyanax had been taken from her, and with barbarous cruelty she had been compelled to watch while Pyrrhus hurled him from the walls to his death.

Andromache had become almost demented with grief and suffering. Pyrrhus had made her his concubine; she had borne him two children in bitterness and shame. But her fellow-captive, Helenus the priest, forbade her to kill herself. Sooner or later, he said, the gods would deal with Pyrrhus as he deserved: as for herself, although she had lost for ever the husband and the son she loved so deeply, there would be others of her race for her to cherish and protect: for their sake she must live.

She had listened to Helenus, weeping with anguish and

despair, but she had obeyed him. Eventually disaster had overtaken Pyrrhus. Thanks to the advice of Helenus, who had the gift of prophecy, he had returned safely home from Troy. After his arrival he had taken a Greek princess to wife and Andromache had been contemptuously allotted to Helenus: but Pyrrhus's wife had proved barren and cursing the gods he decided to repudiate her. Soon afterwards he had been ignominiously murdered by a temple attendant, and part of his kingdom had passed to Helenus as a reward for his services. The former slave of Pyrrhus had become his heir.

My father had listened to Andromache deeply moved but in silence. We were sitting in the courtyard of the palace on the morning after our arrival, beneath a cloudless sky. A short distance below, partly visible through the spacious colonnade, our ships and a multitude of smaller craft lay bobbing on the calm expanse of the lagoon we had entered the evening before. Beyond the mole stretched its marshy indented banks alive with colonies of water fowl. To the west, separated from the mainland by a narrow strait, the mountains of Corcyra rose steeply from the sea, their peaks wreathed in a gossamer veil of mist.

My father had told Andromache our story briefly the previous evening, and she had wept at our misfortunes. But she had realized at once that my grandfather was gravely ill, and insisted on nursing him herself. After embracing me once more she had quietly left us. My father asked her for news of Helenus.

'He has gone to the oracle at Dodona, far inland in the mountains,' she answered. 'Early each autumn he goes there on a pilgrimage. He is a good man but . . .' She hesitated.

'I remember Helenus well,' said my father warmly. 'He is both good and wise.' He looked at Andromache's unresponsive face. 'But you were married to Hector,' he added gently.

'No one will ever replace Hector for me,' said Andromache. 'He was not only a hero. He was the noblest man who ever lived. Helenus and I have raised a cenotaph to him in a grove beside a stream we call Simois – just like the stream we knew

[69]

at Troy. But here the weather is harsher, the hills more barren; our Simois has run dry.' Her voice trembled. 'For as long as there was water I could imagine I was there with Hector. But now I know it's only a stony dried-up water course like any other, and each time I remember that Hector's cenotaph is empty and his bones lie far away . . .' She was silent trying to master her tears.

'Dearest Andromache,' said my father, 'your life is not over. You are young still. You have found a new home after all your ordeals. Your husband is a king and Hector's brother. Perhaps you will find happiness in the children you will bear him.' He laid his hand gently upon her arm.

'Never,' cried Andromache. She shrank away from my father shuddering, her body tense with fear. Then, seeing his astonishment, she added hesitantly – 'Forgive me, Aeneas. You mean to be kind, but since Pyrrhus ravished me I cannot bear that any man should touch me.' She was clasping and un-clasping her hands convulsively as she spoke. Suddenly she burst out: 'He took me by force the night after he had murdered Astyanax. No, he was not drunk: he was sober – sober and smiling. My skin was white and smooth, he told me, and my flesh was tender; he said he meant to enjoy my body as Hector had done.' She gave a great cry of anguish. 'Oh, Hector, my mind has remained true to you if not my body. Only a god could have given the exquisite pleasures you gave me. To think that Pyrrhus should have shared your enjoyment! To think that he forced me to bear him children! I felt defiled as if I had been daubed in filth. He even made me suckle them, suckle them from the breasts that fed Astyanax.' She buried her face in her hands.

The expression of horror and pity on my father's face had given way to one of rage, when suddenly as if she sensed his murderous fury, Andromache looked up.

'No, Aeneas,' she said. 'Do not wish for Pyrrhus to come to life. He is better dead. And do not curse the gods; that is what he did.'

'Andromache,' cried my father, 'how can I comfort you?

Will these wounds never heal?'

Andromache shook her head.

'No, they will never heal,' she said quietly, 'but already
you have brought me something infinitely precious. You
have brought me Ascanius. Now he is here I feel Astyanax is
alive again.'

For the first time my father could abdicate from the leadership
the gods had thrust upon him. Even had my grandfather been
able to tell us our destination, to leave Buthrotum while he
lay ill was out of the question. For weeks he hovered between
life and death; no doubt it was Andromache's devoted care
that saved him. By the time he had begun to recover his
strength, autumn was far advanced. Still there was no news of
Helenus. My father's sense of duty to the gods made him
suggest that he too should go to Dodona to consult the oracle
before winter set in; but Andromache dissuaded him. The
way was difficult and dangerous, she said, for those who did
not know it: why this impatience when the gods had granted
him a respite from his wanderings? Why not await the return
of Helenus whose knowledge of the future was greater than
any man's? My father needed little persuading; thankfully,
gratefully, he banished all thoughts of the future from his
mind.

No longer hemmed in by the narrow confines of a ship,
and partly freed from Caieta's jealous surveillance, I found that
I was almost my own master. While the fine weather held, I
swam and wrestled with my companions on the beach, snared
water fowl, climbed the neighbouring cliffs, went hunting with
Achates and my father. Sometimes I would talk to my grandfather as he lay in his little room next to Andromache's own,
and he would tell me stories of the gods; sometimes I would
help him to walk when his fever was past and he had begun
to hobble about once more; sometimes I would talk to Andromache while she sat at her loom, weaving me an embroidered
cloak. Frequently Caieta would find a pretext to interrupt us,
but Andromache was never angry. Occasionally she would

gently come to my rescue; more often she would whisper to me that Caieta was right and I must go.

'Poor woman, she cannot but be jealous,' she would say, for I had told her that Caieta had lost her husband and children long ago; 'besides, Ascanius, you are beautiful – almost as beautiful as Astyanax.'

Applied to myself the word seemed scarcely relevant. I would have preferred her to say that I was fleet of foot, agile and strong. It was truer of Andromache, but her beauty was incorporeal, strangely evasive, an almost spiritual emanation that neither challenged nor stirred the blood. It is not so much her long tapering fingers that I remember, or the delicate curve of her throat and breast, as her quiet melodious voice, her perennial gentleness tinged with sadness. She had withdrawn from the contest with life; to fight for anything was now beyond her. I knew that it gave her infinite happiness to have me with her; but she never acted as if she had a claim upon me. Often I would feel her following me with her eyes as I left her, and sometimes she would ask me almost shyly if I would kiss her. Half enjoying, half resentful of the pressure of her arms about me I would do so. Was my father jealous of me? Sometimes I wondered. I sensed that though indifferent to other women less nobly born he both pitied and desired Andromache. If I replaced Astyanax might not he replace Hector? Apart from that one occasion when he had laid his hand upon her arm I never saw him touch her. Yet little by little I watched him falling under her spell.

It was the spell of the past. Day after day they would visit Hector's cenotaph and perform the Rites of the Dead before the empty mound of green turf. They would talk endlessly of him, of Priam, of my mother, of Troy itself and of the many other Trojans they had known. My father would describe a brooch my mother wore which Andromache remembered; she would describe some childish toy that Hector had given his son. Together they would climb in imagination the steps to Aphrodite's temple, or follow the course of the turbulent Scamander; by different routes they would set out on imaginary journeys to meet by a shepherd's hut, a wild fig-tree, a ruined wall. My father would laugh like a boy when he had reached their chosen destination, and Andromache's eyes would shine with a shy gladness. Then a constraint would fall between them and they would relapse into a melancholy silence, both pursuing their private dreams.

Andromache represented the past. Helenus stood for the future. On the day he returned everything changed under the influence of his powerful intelligence.

Helenus was only a small man, greying and partly bald; but he dominated us all from the outset. He embraced Andromache formally rather than with affection, and greeted us with a courtesy devoid of false effusiveness. He had been informed of our arrival long ago – though not, it appeared, by Andromache; not only this, but he had heard of our adventures and knew the exact number of our company. Was it his agents in Buthrotum who had told him this? Was it his undoubted gift of second sight? We never knew.

What was immediately apparent was the respect in which Buthrotum held him. To many he must have seemed at first an interloper sprung from an alien race, but precisely because he was not a hero he was a far abler ruler than Pyrrhus, with an interest in trade and a wish to maintain friendly relations with other cities that his predecessor had altogether lacked. He had learnt to speak the local dialect; he had been tireless in visiting the outlying parts of his kingdom and administering justice. Above all he was a seer.

The first evident sign of his influence was a change in the attitude of the local population towards us. Andromache had been able to procure from them no more than a grudging indifference; our food, shelter and clothing were provided entirely by herself. Now all this changed. The women became more liberal with their favours. Boys and young men began to fraternize with us. For the first time we were given active assistance with the repair and upkeep of our ships. The reason for this sudden access of friendliness soon became apparent. Helenus had promised that we would leave as soon as winter was over. He had already chosen our destination for us. The land for which we must steer was Italy.

'Italy,' repeated my grandfather, staring at him blankly. It was obvious that the name meant nothing to him. 'Has this land no other name?'

'It is also called Hesperia,' answered Helenus.

My grandfather started.

'Hesperia; the western land,' he murmured.

'Some give the name to another land that lies still further west,' said Helenus cautiously, 'a land that stretches to the Pillars of Hercules beyond which lies the eternal Ocean.'

My grandfather did not answer but sat still with closed eyes.

'But Teucer came from Crete and it was he who built Troy,' interjected my father.

'Teucer came from Crete,' agreed Helenus, 'but Teucer married the daughter of Dardanus after he had landed on the plain of Troy. Dardanus is our ancestor as well as Teucer.'

My grandfather suddenly spoke in rising excitement.

'The oracle at Delos, Aeneas, do you remember? The god called us Dardanians not Trojans. At the time I thought nothing of it. Now I can see my foolish oversight. There were three tribes – Dardanians, Ilians, Trojans. You and I are of Dardanian stock and Dardanus, not Teucer, is our ancestor. Troy was our adopted city not our birthplace. Fool that I am to have misled us all.'

'But we are the guardians of the gods of Troy,' cried my father, 'and Hector himself committed them to our charge. Where did they come from if not from Crete?'

He looked at Helenus, who shook his head.

'I cannot tell you yet,' he answered, 'but this I can tell you now. Dardanus came not from Crete but from Hesperia.'

'Must we always be in doubt?' cried my father; 'can the gods never speak plainly?'

'To some they speak more plainly than to others,' said Helenus. 'But even if we fail to understand them, we must never cease to listen. We ignore them at our peril. The worst of all human follies is presumptuous pride.'

[74]

I saw that he was thinking of Pyrrhus.

'But why have the gods been so cruel to Andromache?' I cried impulsively. 'She is not insolent and proud.'

My father and grandfather glanced at me in surprise; only Helenus seemed to regard it as normal that he should be questioned by a child.

'You do well to ask that question, Ascanius,' he said, looking at me gravely. 'I see you love her.'

I nodded.

'Almost as if she were your mother perhaps?' He glanced at my father as he spoke.

'No,' I answered. 'She is not strong enough. The gods have broken her. Why? She is good and kind and gentle.'

'She is all that you say, Ascanius, but there is one thing you must understand. It was not the gods who broke Andromache. The fatal flaw was always there. She loved her husband and her son too much.'

My father stirred uneasily, remembering Andromache's terrible outburst of grief.

'Surely you do not mean she deserved to lose Hector and Astyanax?' he asked almost angrily.

'Not that she deserved it,' answered Helenus, 'but that to love so passionately is a kind of challenge to the Fates, an unconscious provocation of the gods. The gods are jealous. No mortal may belong to us utterly, body and soul; no mortal may take complete possession of our hearts.'

I shivered, sensing obscurely that if this were true even the sweetest of human emotions savoured of impiety. How could one ever hope to propitiate these jealous watchful deities, ready to punish us even for an excess of love?

Helenus had said we should steer for Italy as soon as winter was over; he had not told us our eventual goal. Each night he studied the stars that presided over my father's destiny, waiting for the required conjunction. At last the moment came. Crowned with a wreath of laurel he led my father into Apollo's temple bearing the gods of Troy.

All morning they remained there behind closed doors, and when at last they emerged from the dim interior into the light of day I saw that Helenus was weak and bewildered from his prophetic trance; for this had been no short and cryptic pronouncement such as the oracles had made. The names of unknown places had fallen from the seer's lips – places that would guide my father on his journey. At last he had been told where it lay, this land from which both Dardanus and the gods of Troy had come. Latium was its name; a people called the Latins dwelt there, and it lay on the western coast of Italy, south of the river Tiber. We would know when we had reached it because there, after landing, we would unwittingly fulfil the oracle by eating our platters. Not far from our landing place my father would find in a wood a huge white sow with a litter of thirty offspring; this was to be the site where he should build his capital, and there it was to remain for thirty years. Then I, his son, was to found a second capital inland among the hills.

How deeply convincing it was, this artless revelation of how the gods would guide us. This time no room seemed left for human misunderstanding. My pulse quickened at the thought that I too would have my part to play. My grandfather, supremely confident that our trials were over, was eager to be gone. Our followers whose faith in my father's mission had been sorely shaken, greeted his rousing words with enthusiasm. Helenus himself urged us not to miss the first favourable wind, appealed for volunteers to bring our crews up to strength, furnished us with new weapons, oars and tackle, and loaded us with gifts. Even Andromache seemed happy for our sakes; and yet I sensed that there was something wrong.

Was not Helenus almost too eager to be rid of us? Why had I heard his voice raised in anger and found Andromache in tears? As for my father's exuberant optimism, was it perhaps a pretence?

It was the night before our departure. Helenus had feasted us all magnificently in his banqueting hall on a rich variety of fish and game. We had dined off golden plates and drunk from fine goblets – loot from Priam's palace which Pyrrhus had brought home with him, little foreseeing how it would pass into Trojan hands once more. I sat upon a stool beside Andromache, sharing her table and telling her excitedly about the marvels we would see upon our journey. There was an island called Sicily which we would visit, where an enormous mountain reared its head into the sky belching forth rocks and smoke and fire; and on its lower slopes, I had been told, there lived a race of one-eyed monsters.

Andromache listened to me fondly, her eyes never leaving my face. When at last I fell silent, she leant across from her couch and took my hand.

'Come, Ascanius, you must try on the cloak that I have woven for you.'

I had forgotten about it in my excitement at leaving, but rose obediently and followed her.

The cloak lay draped over a chair beside her loom. I looked admiringly at its rich and delicate embroidery, and putting it on strutted about the room conscious that I was a prince and proud to imagine myself almost fully grown.

Suddenly I became aware that Andromache was watching me with a curiously intent expression in her eyes. I stopped confused, realizing that I had not thanked her for her princely gift, and mumbled shyly that I would remember her each time I wore it.

'You are growing so fast that it will soon be too short for you,' said Andromache sadly. 'Soon you will be as tall as Helenus. How old are you, Ascanius?'

'I think I am eleven,' I answered after a pause.

'Yes, you are a little older than Astyanax would have been. How I shall miss you!' She hesitated: 'I too will have something to remember you by, but it must remain a secret between us. Would you like me to show you?'

I nodded, mystified.

'Come here,' she said softly.

I went to the chair where she was sitting. Taking my hand she slipped it between the draperies above her girdle.

[77]

'There,' she whispered, 'feel it, Ascanius. Move your hand slowly over my body.'

I had seen women naked often enough, but this was the first time that I had felt a woman's naked body. I let my hand travel over its soft rounded smoothness, suddenly conscious of its alluring beauty. How could I have failed to realize that Andromache had a body?

'How beautiful you are,' I murmured almost involuntarily. Then suddenly the truth dawned upon me and I withdrew my hand quickly. I looked at her dumbfounded.

'Yes,' she said smiling, 'that is your brother, Ascanius.'

'My brother?' I repeated incredulously. 'Does Helenus know? Does my father know?'

'Your father does not know and must not know, but Helenus knew at once. He told me the child would be a boy.'

So Andromache was no different from other women. A sudden anger gripped me.

'But you said you could not bear to let a man touch you. You said you would never have another child.'

'Why are you so shocked?' asked Andromache in surprise. 'Is it because of Helenus? He was angry at first, but he wants a son and knows he cannot give me one. He does not love me. What does it matter to him who the father is?'

'No, it is not because of Helenus,' I mumbled.

'Then are you jealous because I made your father happy?' asked Andromache, gently stroking my hair. I moved away quickly out of her reach. Was I jealous? I did not know. I only knew that somehow she had betrayed me.

'Did you enjoy it – being my father's concubine?' I blurted out.

She gave a little gasp and shook her head.

'Then why did you **do** it? What must Hector think of you?' I saw with satisfaction that I had wounded her.

'I did it because of you, Ascanius,' she said unsteadily. 'I wanted a little Ascanius to remember you by. Was that so very wrong of me? Hector would understand.'

[78]

I was silent, pitying her loneliness, but anxious to escape from it.

'No, it was not wrong,' I said at length more gently, 'but why must my father never know?'

'Because he does not want to leave Buthrotum,' said Andromache simply. 'He says that here at last he is at home. He does not love me, but he is happy sharing my memories – reliving the past. If he were tempted to stay and disobey the gods . . .' She shivered. 'Besides there is your destiny, Ascanius – yours as well as his.'

Yes, I thought resolutely, nothing must be allowed to stop him. Anything was better than to linger on here in Buthrotum, living on stale memories.

I bent and kissed her cheek.

'Goodbye, Andromache,' I said, 'I hope . . . I hope the gods will allow you to be happy.'

When I had reached my room, I took off the cloak and looked at it – this touching specimen of futile love and labour.

'It is a child's cloak,' I said angrily to myself, 'but I am a child no longer. I will give it to Atys when we are on board.'

I blew out the lamp and lay down, gazing up into the darkness, thinking of my destiny. It was the future that mattered – not Andromache.

Never will I forget our first sight of Italy on the day after we left Buthrotum – the dim hills and low coastline of Apulia far off and faintly illumined by the first flush of dawn. But Helenus had forbidden us to land there. When we had crossed the narrow stretch of sea between Epirus and Apulia, and rounded the promontory sacred to Minerva, we were to sail south-westwards towards Sicily, avoiding the Greek settlements on Italy's southern coast. Once, driven by racing currents, we beached our ships on the shore below Mount Etna and saw the giant mountain vomiting into the sky a swirling cloud of pitch-black smoke, lurid with red-hot ash and balls of flame. That night we lay in the woods, sleepless from the thunderous uproar, while the moon and the stars were blotted out by the murky fog above.

Next day a wind from the north caught our sails and we sped southwards past the low rocky island known as the Isle of Quails, past the spring of Arethusa that gushes forth fresh water upon the shore. Henceforth our journey was to hold no terrors for us. Even the southernmost tip of Sicily, a turning point dreaded by the most intrepid mariners for its off-shore winds, projecting rocks and hidden reefs, seemed to survey us kindly as we skirted its craggy cliffs. Day after day we steered steadily westwards beneath a benevolent sun. In western Sicily, Helenus had told us, we would find a friendly people, the Elymians, who worshipped Aphrodite. If Apollo had been our guide, Aphrodite had been our protectress. There at Drepanum we could rest awhile from our journey in a harbour girt about with islands where our ships would lie protected as if encompassed by her arms; and near-by on Mount Eryx there stood a sanctuary dedicated in her honour.

It is difficult to say whether it was my grandfather or my father who was the more impatient to reach Drepanum. Our long journey from Epirus had been so evidently favoured by the gods that my father's early misgivings had soon been dissipated like mist in a valley caught by the rays of the sun. If he still regretted Buthrotum he showed no signs of it. Of Helenus he spoke often and with admiration, but only seldom of Andromache and even more rarely of the past. He had recovered not only his confidence in our future but also his faith in his divine mother. Forgetting her long silence he dreamt of renewing the almost mystical communion with her he had felt before we fled from Troy.

My grandfather's attitude was less simple. He had never spoken of Aphrodite, only of Zeus and Apollo whose commands we must obey; and yet he began to talk with longing of how we would visit Eryx after reaching Drepanum, almost as if Italy were no longer our goal.

Drepanum in north-western Sicily was indeed far further

from Latium than any of us then realized. The little town squatted upon a narrow spit of land shaped like a sickle, its harbour facing southwards. Later, when we returned there, I saw that this direction was symbolic. Drepanum faced Africa and turned its back on Italy, far away to the north and east. From the moment we arrived there the Fates must have been prompted to draw us towards Carthage. Why did Helenus say nothing of this? Did he not foresee it? Was it Aphrodite's doing? Did Almighty Zeus consent, or was even he powerless to prevent it? I ask myself these questions even now.

But for all its remoteness Drepanum was to prove less alien than expected. On the previous day we had sighted fishing boats, and that night beacons had been lighted along the coast. Perhaps we were taken for pirates; at all events news of our coming had preceded us. As we approached the little port soon after dawn we found the whole population already astir. There were no soldiers as at Buthrotum, and no ships big enough to try conclusions with us, but a number of smaller craft were patrolling the harbour entrance. As we neared it we were hailed from the shore by a rough-looking burly man clad in a bearskin and wearing a crown of boar's tusks. His stentorian voice carried easily across the water, and we realized with astonishment that he spoke a language akin to ours.

'We are Trojans,' my father shouted back, delighted and amazed.

The reaction was immediate. The king himself ran along the diminutive mole to greet us as we glided one by one through the harbour entrance. His followers rushed to help us beach our ships. By the time we had begun to disembark, we were surrounded by a swarming crowd of fisherfolk and peasants.

These were the Elymians mentioned by Helenus in his prophecy; and as he had forecast they had welcomed us as friends. But how was it that this distant people knew our language? Helenus had never spoken of a Trojan settlement in the west.

It was Acestes, their king, who told us the story while we

travelled in a convoy of carts to his capital high above Drepanum. His mother, daughter of a nobly-born Trojan, had been sold into slavery by Priam's tyrannical predecessor. With Aphrodite's aid she had escaped from her masters to western Sicily. She had married the king of this primitive race of fisherfolk who worshipped Aphrodite as goddess of the sea; she had taught him and their son her language, and she had spread it among their subjects. In gratitude to the goddess she had built the sanctuary upon Mount Eryx. Already, Acestes's mother had been deified; soon, when Aphrodite's doves had flown away and returned once more, he would found a new city in her honour.

'Her doves,' repeated my grandfather, his eyes shining. 'I remember . . . I remember her doves at the sanctuary of Paphos in Cyprus. I was a young man then. How long ago it seems!'

My father looked at him in surprise: 'You never told me you had been to Paphos, father,' he said.

'They say that she was born there,' added my grandfather dreamily, 'born from the waves.' He sat still with eyes closed, as if unconscious of our presence, reliving the memories of his far-off youth.

The sanctuary of Aphrodite lay only a short distance from Acestes's mountain capital. It was not a roofed building such as we had known at Troy. Sacrifices took place upon an altar under the open sky surrounded by an enclosure. Until far into the night the fires were kept burning; but when the dawn came there were no ashes, embers or half-burnt logs, no traces of sacrificial blood. Each day before the dawn when Aphrodite's star appeared, the altar was decked with fresh flowers and herbs drenched with morning dew, for wherever Aphrodite walks grass and flowers spring up beneath her feet.

We had sacrificed and given thanks to the goddess. We had implored her continued protection on the journey that lay ahead. My father's face was serene and happy; my grandfather seemed lost in a dream. We stood upon a hillock overlooking the sanctuary. Around it fluttered hundreds of doves calling to each other in the clear blue sky. No bird of prey, Acestes told us, ever came to disturb them. It was as if all living things knew that this was Aphrodite's home.

My grandfather stood watching them silently. This was the day when they were expected to fly away. Each autumn they did so as if upon a pilgrimage.

'Where will they fly to?' he asked Acestes. 'To Paphos?' There was a note of longing in his voice.

Acestes looked doubtful. 'No one knows except the goddess herself,' he said, 'but they fly southwards as if towards Africa.'

'Towards Africa?' said my grandfather in surprise. 'But where is Africa? What people lives there?'

'Phoenicians have settled there,' said Acestes briefly. 'Sometimes their ships visit Drepanum.' From the hillock upon which we stood below the summit of Mount Eryx he was staring out across the great expanse of ocean towards the unclouded horizon. A warm breeze caressed our cheeks fitfully like a playful goddess. Far below, clustered together like beehives, lay the houses of Drepanum with its harbour no larger than a rockside pool.

'There is Africa!' he shouted suddenly, seizing my father's arm. 'Can you see it, Aeneas? Can you see it, Ascanius? – that faint grey outline on the horizon far beyond those islands?'

We saw it simultaneously, that tenuous outline, so insubstantial, so remote that I could scarcely believe that it was really land inhabited by creatures of flesh and blood. We glanced at each other with an inexplicable excitement.

'I can see nothing,' said my grandfather. His voice trembled slightly. 'Let us go home.'

We returned to the cart in which Acestes had brought us to the sanctuary, my grandfather leaning heavily upon my father's arm. All the way back to the simple rustic building Acestes called his palace, he sat hunched and motionless, apparently asleep; but as we came to a halt in the bare earth forecourt with its quacking ducks and muddy pond, he suddenly spoke. Acestes who had been summoned elsewhere had already disappeared.

'It is because of the Phoenicians that her doves fly to Africa. They call her Astarte.' There was a long pause and then he added softly, 'Paphos was Phoenician too.'

My father lifted him out of the cart and set him carefully upon the ground. To our dismay he reeled and nearly fell.

'You must rest,' said my father earnestly. 'I fear you are not well.'

My grandfather gave a slight smile.

'Yes, carry me to my room, my son, and bring Ascanius too. There is something that I must say to both of you.'

With an anxious face my father lifted him into his arms and carried him to his room. Slowly and carefully he lowered the frail body on to the low wooden bed opposite the window, and drew across the goatskin hangings to shut out the bright sunlight.

'Wine,' whispered my grandfather. His face was very pale. I poured wine into a rough earthenware goblet and held it to his lips. He sipped it slowly. A faint flush crept into his waxen cheeks, and he smiled at me.

'Ascanius, the cup-bearer,' he murmured.

'I will fetch Acestes. He is a skilled physician,' broke in my father who was growing more and more uneasy.

My grandfather shook his head.

'No one,' he said distinctly. 'Not even Acestes.'

'But you are ill, father. He will know what to do.'

'I am not ill, Aeneas,' said my grandfather simply, 'I am dying.'

My father made a gesture of horror.

'I came here to die, my son. When the doves fly away my spirit will go with them. I was not meant to go as far as Italy. I always knew it.' He stopped. 'Give me some more wine, Ascanius,' he said in a faint voice. 'There is little time and I have little strength.

'Now listen, my children,' he went on in a stronger voice when he had emptied the goblet.

'Your mother, Aeneas . . . Aphrodite allows me to tell you

[84]

A great sigh came from the bed – a sigh of relief, of happiness. Then there was silence.

'He's gone,' whispered my father. He was staring fixedly before him, and I realized that for him my grandfather's death was perhaps the cruellest blow of all.

V

My grandfather's sudden death cast a deep gloom upon our followers. Even the children wept with genuine sorrow, feeling he was their grandfather as well as mine. But we had lost more than a familiar figure; we had lost without warning our spiritual leader too. His death before we had reached our destination seemed an evil omen. A precious link with the gods had suddenly snapped. How could we be sure they would continue to look kindly on us now my grandfather was gone? Latium was still far away, and Helenus had never said when we would reach it. Now it seemed further off than ever, this distant land of which we knew virtually nothing. How many unknown dangers still awaited us? My grandfather's calm faith had offered reassurance; now this reassurance was gone.

My father was more exposed than any to these doubts and fears, but if he secretly shared them he did not show it. He saw, however, that the longer our followers remained in Sicily the greater their forebodings would become. This time he displayed none of the desperate grief he had shown after my mother's death. His sole concern was to act as a leader should. As soon as the funeral ceremonies were over he bade us prepare to sail for Italy at once.

Our destination was Cumae to the south of Latium: there dwelt the Sibyl, Apollo's priestess, whose guidance my father must obtain. It was the one certain landmark that Helenus had pointed out in a future still shrouded with mist. No doubt my father never forgot the glorious future that awaited our descendants, but this was a prospect that can have brought him little joy. Each reminder that he was the chosen instrument of Zeus merely added to his crushing burden of responsibility – not only to the gods but to myself.

Acestes warned him that autumn was a dangerous season, but my father paid little attention. If the gods meant us to go to Italy, weather and winds were their concern not ours. He would sacrifice to Aphrodite for a calm voyage even though she had taken away his father. To have failed to do so would have been an impious act, and to the Elymians she was goddess of the sea. But how could he sacrifice to Juno at Aphrodite's sanctuary? He would obey his father and placate her after our departure – not before.

We embarked in drizzling rain. Acestes, kind host that he was, had loaded our ships with casks of good red wine, and now he stood there on the beach bidding each one of us farewell. Those of our followers who had chosen to remain stood in the forefront of the crowd, the men shouting words of encouragement, the women mostly weeping. Some had lost heart; some felt too old to travel further, preferring to settle amongst a people who spoke a language they could understand. Many of the women were young but weary of interminable journeys and casual concubinage, anxious only for a husband and a home. Perhaps it was mostly for us they wept as they stood there holding their children in their arms. Once they had believed, like us, in my father's mission. Now this perpetual quest for a divinely-appointed homeland had come to seem a lunatic adventure. They dared not say so, but I saw it in their eyes.

Acestes at least did not think so, but he warned my father once again of the many treacherous rocks that lay along the coast, and of the pirates who haunted the Aegatian Islands. Twice they had raided Drepanum, hoping to catch its people unawares. To the north-east lay another group of islands, home of Aeolus, god of the winds. In summer, all save the gentlest were pent up in an enormous cave like caged beasts; but when autumn came Aeolus would let them loose and they would rush across the ocean roaring like lions in search of prey.

My father listened but was not deterred. Acestes had been the best of hosts but he could endure to stay with him no longer after my grandfather's death. Our ships were in good repair and manned by experienced crews. Not only were we well armed and ready to deal with pirates, but there were fewer women and children than ever before. As for the autumn winds – he shrugged his shoulders: if we encountered storms we must make for shelter in one of the many natural harbours described to him by Acestes. At least we would be following the coast, not sailing across the open sea as during our voyage from Crete.

Acestes shook his head. 'It may be less easy than you think,' he said gruffly, 'but since you are bent on leaving, I will say no more.' He embraced us with brusque affection and strode away. Our ships, their hulls repitched, had already been hauled from the beach into the water; gear, passengers and crew were all aboard, the oarsmen at their benches sitting to the tholepins. Palinurus had taken up his position on the helmsman's bench. Suddenly a vague presentiment gripped me.

'Father,' I said, 'is it so important that we leave today?'

He looked at me in astonishment:

'Why not? Everyone is embarked, the sea is calm, the wind is favourable. Tomorrow they may not be so.'

I hesitated: 'The visibility . . .'

'Is good enough,' interrupted my father impatiently. 'The rain has already stopped, there is no mist at sea – only in the hills.' He looked at me intently. 'What is the matter, Ascanius? We have sacrificed to Aphrodite, we have poured libations to Poseidon – each captain has done so. Has Acestes frightened you with his stories of Aeolus and his winds?'

'No,' I said doubtfully, 'but he knows this coast better than we do.'

My father gave a short laugh.

'If we followed his advice we would stay here till the spring. That I will not do.'

'Not until the spring,' I said earnestly, 'only until tomorrow.'

'Why, Ascanius, why? Is it an omen or a dream? Did Aphrodite tell you so?'

I shook my head, groping in the obscurity of my mind for enlightenment. None came. Eventually I looked up at my father, awkward and embarrassed.

'I am sorry, father,' I mumbled. 'Perhaps it was only an echo of what Acestes told us.'

My father smiled wearily.

'I am always the first to hear when anyone is frightened,' he said. 'Others have the right to show they are afraid. I have not.'

We climbed into the ship, and I reluctantly took up my position next to Caieta in accordance with my father's wishes.

'What were you saying to your father?' she demanded as we drew away from the shore.

I looked at her defiantly and did not answer.

Our oarsmen rowed steadily even after we had left the harbour for there was little wind. Many of the passengers, especially the women, sat watching sadly as Drepanum slowly receded from sight, and even the looming shape of Mount Eryx became blurred and indistinct in its floating veil of mist. Then, as we rounded the peninsula, the sun came out and banished their melancholy. Everyone's spirits revived, and the oarsmen began to sing. Gradually we all took up their chant, steady but rhythmical in time with their stroke. We sang of a sea-nymph beloved of Poseidon, and of how he had pursued her seated upon a dolphin. She had concealed herself behind a curtain of waving seaweed that hung across the entrance to a cavern far below the sea, but Poseidon saw the glint of golden hair through the undulating seaweed, and knew that she was there. He prodded it teasingly with his trident, and naturally she was frightened and tried to swim away; but Poseidon caught her by her golden hair and drew her gently to him. Soon she forgot her fears, and lay with him as he desired in the cavern below the sea.

By the time the familiar song was finished, we were happy and carefree once more. For the first time since my grandfather's death I saw my father smile. A gentle breeze sprang up from the south. In each ship the mast was quickly set up and made fast with forestays, the sails and sailyard hoisted. To our south and west the Aegatian Islands rose steeply out of the sea. For some time we sailed in close formation with look-outs posted. We sighted several ships but they kept their distance. So we continued northwards past one rocky headland after another, each thrust out precipitously into the restless waves; and in between lay small half-secret inlets studded with rocks and backed by frowning cliffs, the abode of countless sea-birds. Never have I seen a landscape more awesome and more beautiful.

We had made good progress and our crews were relaxed and cheerful. More than two hours of daylight still were left us. We were rounding a massive promontory that jutted northwards like a gigantic finger. On its further side, Acestes had said, lay a broad and spacious bay where we could safely beach our ships and spend the night. And then it happened. As if at a signal from Almighty Zeus the horizon darkened and storm clouds gathered overhead. Rain began to fall hesitantly at first then with remorseless steadiness. A tremendous clap of thunder echoed through the sky. The next moment a howling blast from the north-east burst upon us lashing the sea to fury. Great waves began to break over our bows, and our ships were soon lurching wildly in a turmoil of seething water. It was impossible to keep head to wind or steer for land. There was nothing for it but to furl sails before they were torn to tatters, and try to ride out the gale.

With infinite difficulty our ships changed course. All of us, even the crew, cried out in terror as our ship wallowed broadside on in the path of the advancing waves. Precipices of water seemed to surge up one after the other and swoop down exultantly upon us. Each time we waited tensely for the deafening brutal crash as another monstrous wave broke across the gunwale. The protecting wicker screens were smashed or carried away; men, women and children were flung headlong from their places; there was the sickening sound of snapping oars and rending wood. Somehow I seized hold of Caieta and staggering and stumbling guided her to a less dangerous place. Everywhere was awash and littered with broken spars or shattered cargo. The mast leaned over drunkenly, half-torn from its step, but temporarily at least we had escaped from the trough of the waves. The height of the stern where Palinurus and my father sat afforded some protection. Though still at the mercy of the sea, we were no longer threatened with instant death.

All night the gale continued with relentless violence; but at length the rain ceased, the sky cleared and an angry moon glared down upon us through the racing clouds. No land was now in sight. His face tense with anxiety my father made his way forward to see if any were missing or injured. On his instructions we set to work baling; we plugged a gaping fissure in the bows, repaired as best we could the damaged mast. It was not easy. We were cold, hungry, drenched to the skin. All the time the wind shrieked in the rigging, and the ship rolled and lurched beneath our feet. My father worked with the rest of us, barefoot in the swirling water. Once he was nearly pitched overboard and only saved himself by clinging to the tackle. His face showed no fear; perhaps he was indifferent whether he lived or died. Only one other ship could still be seen tossing and plunging on the angry sea. For all we knew the remainder had long since foundered in the heaving tumultuous expanse that hemmed us in on every side.

Suddenly the wind slackened. My father made his way astern, took the helm in place of the exhausted Palinurus and shouted that we were to hoist the sail. The other ship followed suit. It was then that I saw it to starboard – a line of jagged reefs like a spine scarcely protruding above sea level, almost submerged in churning water. I shouted to the crew, then ran to tell my father. We signalled to the other ship by every means we could, but no one seemed to see us. Powerless and horrified we watched her in the moonlight heading for the reefs. A great wave reared up behind her and drove her full tilt on to the rocks. The prow disintegrated like a broken egg shell. A second wave came crashing down upon the stern hurling the helmsman head-first overboard, rending the ship apart, flinging its crew, its gear, its cargo haphazardly into the sea. For a brief moment we saw men swimming desperately in the surging water, and one or two women trying to cling to spars. Then a third wave descended upon them vengefully and gulped them down like a ravenous monster. Nothing was left. The friends and companions of all our wanderings had gone.

A groan burst from all our crew. My father's face was rigid as if carved from stone, his eyes were wild and staring. Suddenly he sprang up and shook his fist at the sky.

'Hear me, you gods in Heaven, hear me!' he shouted. 'You, Almighty Zeus, you, Apollo, is this the way you guide us? You, Aphrodite, is this how you protect us? I renounce the mission you have forced on me. I swear that I'll be pious Aeneas no longer. You have taken away my wife; you have taken away my father; you have murdered my comrades. Why did you let me live? Why did you not let me die in battle on the plain of Troy, or meet my death fighting the night I lost my wife?'

For a moment he was as terrible as the god of war in his demonic fury. Then he saw me, and the anger went out of his eyes. He put his hand on my shoulder.

'Was it because of you, Ascanius? Was it because of you?' he muttered.

'You told me once the gods expected great things of me,' I said, looking at him steadily.

'When did I say that?' he asked bewildered. He passed his hand across his face.

'It was after we had heard the oracle at Delos.'

My father gave a bitter smile.

'I remember. We had just set out for Crete, confident in our glorious future. How disappointed I was when you answered that all you wanted was a home and a mother. Now the gods have cheated both of us; but at least I tried to give you a home in Crete, and Caieta is better than nothing. Or have I failed you in everything?'

He looked at me anxiously, and I felt a deep pity for him.

'No, father,' I said, 'you have failed no one, but if you lose heart and curse the gods then all of us are lost.'

My father did not answer, but sat staring out across the sea.

'Yes, I must trust them,' he said at length as if to himself. 'I have no choice.' He looked at me. 'You are a good son, Ascanius. I am proud of you. May the gods treat you more kindly than they have treated me.' He paused. 'Go and lie down now,' he added gently, 'and pray to Aphrodite for me as you did before.'

I picked my way over the huddled bodies and scattered debris and found a space amidships in a pool of water. I had scarcely begun my prayer when sleep came down upon me like a shroud.

I must have slept for hours for I awoke to find the sun shining upon my face out of a halcyon sky, while gulls hovered and wheeled around the mast above my head. It was already past noon. I sprang up and saw land some distance ahead. There was still a heavy swell but the storm itself was over. Palinurus had replaced my father at the helm, and most of the crew were listlessly astir. How haggard, bedraggled and woebegone they were! There was scarcely one of them who had escaped injury during the storm. Our store of food had been largely ruined by the waves: the barley loaves were sodden, the curds and cheeses drenched with salt water. Many of the casks were broken. We were too hungry to care. No one, not even Palinurus, seemed to know where we were. I went to find my father. He lay stretched out close to Caieta fast asleep. I saw a large bruise on his forehead and another upon his cheek. As I bent over Caieta she opened her eyes and looked at me.

'Was it you who moved me here, Ascanius?' she murmured. I nodded.

'Why? Did your father tell you to move me?'

'No,' I answered.

'You are becoming too independent,' she muttered crossly, 'why couldn't you leave me alone?' Then she added pathetically,

'Help me to sit up, Ascanius. I have hurt my arm.'

'Poor Caieta,' I said, trying to prop her up against a beam.

She winced with pain. 'Be more careful, Ascanius – I am an old woman. Now fetch me some wine.'

I found an unbroken cask and returned with a cup of wine and a piece of sodden bread. She munched it slowly with her few remaining teeth, then sipped at the cup, her eyes half closed. A faint tinge of colour seeped into her flaccid grey cheeks.

'I should have stayed at Drepanum,' she mumbled. 'How can I look after you if my arm is broken?'

I sighed and did not answer, remembering how I had begged my father to leave her behind. With others he could be stern; with Caieta he was incurably soft-hearted. Yielding to her indignant protests he had let her come with us and left me in her charge. She seemed to guess my thoughts, and opened her eyes to look at me.

'Perhaps I will die, and then you will be rid of me,' she said bitterly. 'You don't love me any more. It was Andromache – she stole you from me. I always hated her.'

'I do love you, Caieta,' I said with an effort, 'but I am almost a man now.' Suddenly a wave of anger swept over me. 'You treat me as if I were still a little boy,' I shouted. 'You stop me having friends. You had Atys moved to another ship. You question and you scold me. Why can't you leave me alone?'

She began to sob hysterically.

'How can you be so cruel, Ascanius? What would you have done without me all these years? I have loved you and looked after you as if you were my child.'

I glanced quickly towards my father's recumbent figure, tempted to wake him and appeal for his help. No, I could not do it; I must not add to his responsibilities. Besides, he would prove a broken reed as so many times before. I looked at Caieta with her injured arm, angry no longer, guiltily conscious that I had wounded her.

'I am sorry, Caieta,' I said humbly.

She stopped weeping and slowly began to dry her eyes with

[96]

a fold of her dirty dress. Then she held out her other arm.

'My little Ascanius,' she said softly. Reluctantly I bent and kissed her.

'You are all that I have,' she murmured, her arm still around me. 'Do you remember those toy soldiers you used to play with?'

I nodded, embarrassed. 'I left them behind at Troy.'

'I still have one. I carry it with me everywhere. It makes me feel you belong to me.' Her eyes closed: 'You are a good boy, Ascanius. You'll not forget your Caieta, will you? Let me sleep now.'

Thankfully I left her, and returning to Palinurus told him my father was asleep.

'No need to wake him yet,' he said briefly. 'It will be a good hour before we make land.'

I looked at the unfamiliar indented coastline.

'Do you think it is Sicily?'

He shook his head. 'I'll swear I have not seen that coast before. Perhaps it is some other island.'

'Could it be Italy?' I asked hopefully.

'No, it can't be Italy. We are heading southwards. Look at the position of the sun, Ascanius.' He grinned at me, showing his strong white teeth, and I was no longer ashamed of my foolish question.

I scanned the horizon hoping against hope to sight one of our ships.

'Do you think any of the others have survived?' I asked bluntly.

Palinurus looked grim. 'They may have survived,' he answered. 'Achates, Ilioneus and the rest, they're all good seamen, but whether we will ever see them again – that's another matter.'

We were both silent, thinking of our drowned comrades. Perhaps, I thought gloomily, all of us were doomed to eventual destruction. We might be set upon as soon as we had landed. Did the gods really mean us to reach Italy at all?

'It is no use trying to understand the gods,' said Palinurus suddenly. 'They intervene for no apparent reason, and then leave you to shift for yourself. Some day Poseidon will have had enough of me and I will be drowned at sea.' He gave a short laugh.

'Why did you join my father then? Don't you believe in his mission?'

'I used to believe in it,' said Palinurus, tugging at his short dark beard, 'but if I follow your father still it is because he is a hero. It has become his mission and yours, not mine. All of us feel the same.'

He saw the troubled look upon my face and tried to explain:

'Listen, Ascanius. I am a mariner. I have sailed all over the Aegean. I have travelled as far as Egypt and Phoenicia. Often I have sailed through the Hellespont, far into the Euxine Sea. No one knows better than I the hardships and dangers awaiting all who risk their lives and fortunes on the ocean. I was one of the first to join your father. I knew the old Troy would never rise again, but I believed in the vision of a second Troy with all my heart and soul. I was eager to take part in so glorious an adventure. Led by such a hero, I felt sure it could not fail. We have had our full share of hardships and danger, but what have they brought us? Cruel loss and bitter disappointment – nothing more. For more than five years we have wandered from shore to shore always in search of an ever-receding goal. When we set out there were five hundred of us. Now there are only thirty left and Italy is further off than ever. It is not your father's fault, Ascanius. I love him and admire him more than any man alive, but he is unsuccessful, always unsuccessful. He is one of those heroic but unlucky men who are always doomed to fail.'

My heart sank. 'What should he do then?' I asked apprehensively.

'Abandon all thought of reaching Italy. Forget the oracles and prophecies. Forget their promise of a glorious future. Risk the displeasure of Almighty Zeus, since he not only withholds his help but even seems to thwart us. Give up these wanderings, and settle wherever he can.'

[98]

He stopped suddenly. My father was standing beside us.

'So you think I should give up, Palinurus? Well, let us land first and see what fortune brings.' He spoke with a forced cheerfulness that deluded neither of us. 'Do you recognize this coast?'

Palinurus shook his head.

'Three of the oarsmen are injured,' my father went on, his eyes vainly following the horizon. 'You will have to lend a hand, Ascanius. Where is Atys?'

'He was moved to another ship,' I said, looking at him.

My father avoided my eyes.

'I think Caieta has broken her arm,' I added.

He sighed and said nothing. I left him, sorry that I had spoken.

By now we were nearing the coast. Before us lay a deep inlet, flanked by an island that jutted far into the sea acting as a breakwater against the ocean's swell. The water within this sheltered haven lay miraculously still. We glided in past the twin cliffs that stood like sentinels on either side, and were enveloped at once in an atmosphere of peace. To raise our voices seemed almost a sacrilege. We rowed slowly, dipping our oars silently into the tranquil water. The distant roar of the surf belonged to another world.

The narrow inlet opened into a bay backed by a forested mountain, dark but not menacing, mysterious and gravely beautiful; and at its foot, close by the beach with its border of trees, there was a cave from which ran a rivulet of pure fresh water that splashed idly upon the rocks before burying itself in the sand.

Wearily, but with unutterable relief, the crew furled and stowed our sail, and lowered the mast into its cradle as we neared the shore stern first. We ceased rowing. My father from the bows cast out the anchor stones. With a familiar rasping of sand against wood we grounded upon the beach. I leapt out with the shore lines and made fast. Oh the joy, the unspeakable joy, of feeling dry land beneath my feet!

My father and I carried Caieta ashore, and fashioned a splint for her arm. In less than an hour it would be dark. Palinurus and the crew collected tinder and quickly kindled a flame. Soon three fires were blazing on the beach. The women fetched the cooking pots, and those who were not injured began to grind corn in order to bake bread. But it was meat that we needed above all.

'Fetch your bow and arrows at once, Ascanius,' said my father, and led the way into the wood, making for an open valley that lay between us and the mountain. Luck and the wind were with us. As we emerged from the trees we saw below us in a glade a herd of deer peacefully grazing in the setting sun. My father pointed to a noble beast with magnificent branching antlers. 'Once he is down the rest will stampede,' he whispered. 'Let us shoot together.'

'Apollo, guide my arrow,' I muttered to myself, raising my bow and taking aim. Tired and hungry though we were, our aim was true. The stag fell gasping, with two arrows in its flank. We shot and shot again at the wildly careering herd, but the light was fading fast and we were lucky perhaps to kill a second smaller deer. Stumbling in the darkness beneath our load we made our way back to our followers gathered around the blazing fires.

A faint cheer went up when they saw us.

'A fit son for a hero!' cried Palinurus, patting my back. There was a murmur of approval. I glowed with pride. Never before had I been bracketed in this way with my father.

We all set to work flaying the carcases, hacking off the meat, cutting it into steaks which we spitted and roasted over the fire. Our mouths watered with anticipation. We were so hungry we could hardly speak. Never have I tasted food more appetizing than that venison we ate upon the beach – no, not even in Dido's luxurious palace with its spacious kitchens.

When we had eaten our fill and the meal was cleared away, we sprawled out upon the grass beneath the trees while my father spoke briefly to us.

'My friends,' he said, 'we do not know where we are, nor what the morrow will bring, but let us thank the gods that we are safe from the storm. Let us ask them to protect those of our comrades who may be alive, let us mourn for those who are dead. No one laments their cruel fate more bitterly than I. This is no moment for me to speak of the future. It is the present that concerns us now. I say only this: "Grieve for our lost comrades, but be of good courage. The storm through which we have passed may be the harbinger of better things." '

Even then I realized the skill as well as the sincerity and courage with which he spoke. He had said nothing to antagonize those who had no confidence in his mission, but he had said nothing that could make them think he had repudiated it. He had not minimized our grievous loss, but neither had he exaggerated it. Above all he had given us new hope.

I lay upon my back, looking up at the earnest stars. Presently the moon rose over the shoulder of the mountain behind us, casting its glittering light upon the calm waters of the bay. From far off came the muffled roar of breaking waves. The night was strangely warm and scented, almost breathless. I felt as if we were enclosed within a different world.

A figure came towards me and lay down silently nearby.

'Father,' I whispered.

'Yes, Ascanius?'

'I love this place. I wonder where it is. I could stay here for ever.'

'So could I,' he murmured.

'We must have been meant to come here. It must have been waiting for us all the time. Perhaps it is the beginning of a new life for us.'

'I would like to think so, Ascanius,' he answered slowly. 'Pray to Aphrodite. She seems to listen to you. Then it may come true.'

VI

I was awakened by an insistent whispering close to my ear. The voice was sibilant and breathless. I sat up at once as if in answer to an urgent summons. It was still night, but the sky was pale and translucent and I sensed that dawn was stealthily approaching. The moon had almost set, the dying fires glowed dimly, but I could see the looming black silhouette of our ship near-by upon the beach. From all around came the sound of stertorous breathing. Somewhere a woman moaned in her sleep, muttered some incoherent words and then was silent.

'Father,' I called softly, thinking that it had been he who had spoken to me, but there was no reply, and I realized from his regular breathing that he too was fast asleep. I rose to my feet, looking cautiously around me, remembering that exceptionally no sentries had been posted. As I did so I heard a whisper close behind me.

'Go to the cave.'

I turned sharply. There was no one there. I trembled with sudden fear, knowing that the voice was supernatural. The cave would be dark, and I was afraid to go there; but I was even more afraid to disobey. I thought of waking my father and taking him with me, but somehow I knew that I must not do so, that I must go to the cave alone.

I groped for my sword, strapped it around my waist, and drew my tattered cloak around my shoulders. Then picking my way through the sleepers I set out for the further end of the moonlit beach. Behind I felt my monstrous shadow stalking me like a prey.

The splashing of the stream on to the rocks below the cave

had seemed innocent by day; now it sounded loud and menacing. In my nervous haste I had not thought to light a torch. Now, as the dark entrance yawned before me, I cursed myself for a fool. For a moment I hesitated, dreading to go further, longing to retrace my steps. An unseen hand seemed to propel me forward; yielding to its pressure I went in.

The cave extended far back, deep into the mountain. At first I groped my way forwards slowly, following the stream into a winding tunnel. Gradually as I advanced I became aware of a distant luminous glow ahead which grew steadily stronger. Then suddenly the tunnel ended and the darkness vanished. I found myself in an enormous circular chamber illumined by a ghostly radiance and hewn as it seemed from the living rock. Far above my head hung myriads of stalactites suspended from the vaulted roof. An unearthly light streamed from the walls glistening with quartz and crystal. The air was full of muffled echoes and whisperings, and the rustle of unseen wings.

I stood still, gazing, awestruck and dumbfounded. Before me in the midst of the cavernous chamber, surrounded by a carpet of white sand strewn with shells, stood a massive rock shaped like an altar, and from its summit rose high into the air a single upright flame. As I looked, it swooped and darted its head towards me like a serpent. Trembling I cast myself prostrate upon the sand, sensing that the flame was sacred, the visible manifestation of some jealous goddess, and that to be touched by it was death.

What did this goddess require of me? Had I been summoned here to die? My eyes screwed shut for fear of seeing what must not be seen, I began to mumble panic-stricken prayers, imploring her forgiveness, begging to know her name.

'Open your eyes,' whispered a voice high above me in the soaring vaulted roof. Slowly and apprehensively I did so. The flame rose quivering and erect once more, and now I saw that before the altar stood a second smaller rock, flat and shaped like a bed, and on it lay two wraith-like beings locked in a passionate embrace. As I stared at them they faded before my eyes, the flame went out and everything grew dark.

I cried out in terror: 'Spare me, Aphrodite. Have pity on me,' but out of the darkness came no answer, only a mocking laugh. I was suddenly engulfed by a terrible sorrow which I could not explain. It was as if something infinitely precious had been lost by my own fault beyond recall. I thought my heart would break for grief and for despair. Then for the last time I heard the voice coming from far away.

'I am not Aphrodite. I am Asherat-of-the-Sea. I raised the storm that brought you here. Go back to your Trojans but say nothing of what you have heard and seen.'

I opened my eyes and saw my father staring down upon me. I looked at him uncomprehendingly, unable to speak, then raised myself slowly on my elbow. The sun was rising over the mountain top. The bay lay rippling gently before my eyes. I was safe amongst mortals once more.

'You have had an evil dream, Ascanius,' said my father gravely.

Had it been a dream? I was not sure. The terror and the haunting sense of loss were still alive within me.

'You called out a name,' said my father, 'the name of a goddess – Asherat. Did she speak to you?'

I shivered, reluctant to answer. 'She hates us,' I said eventually with an effort. 'Who is she?'

'She is a goddess of the Phoenicians,' said my father slowly, 'but we know her by another name – Juno.'

I trembled, recalling my grandfather's warning. Was it too late now to try to placate this terrible goddess, the bitter enemy of Troy?

'Tell me your dream, Ascanius,' said my father earnestly. 'Are you sure that she hates us?'

'She forbade me to tell you,' I said quickly; but was I sure that Asherat hated us? She had raised the storm against us, but we had been guided to a safe haven. We had lost our comrades, but we were still alive. Was all this her doing? Suddenly I remembered that my father was half-Phoenician.

'Are you sure that she hates us?' my father repeated.

I looked up at him, struggling to formulate an answer.

'No, I am not sure, but I think she means to stop us from reaching Italy.'

My father gave a sigh. 'As for that,' he muttered, making a helpless gesture. He stood staring at the ground. Finally he looked up.

'Can't you tell me any more, Ascanius?'

'Only that this place must be sacred to her,' I said, stifling the tremor in my voice. 'I think she guided us here.'

My father nodded: 'We will sacrifice to her now, and ask her to protect us and our lost companions. Then when we have eaten, you and I will start to search for them along the coast.' He stopped, and gave me a searching glance. 'But you do not look well, Ascanius. Perhaps you had better stay here with Caieta.'

I leapt to my feet. 'I am quite well,' I said angrily. 'I want to come with you.'

'You look tired and pale,' retorted my father. 'If only Achates were here he could have come with me.' I saw that he was about to reproach himself for having given the command of one of the missing ships to his favourite companion, and that unless I acted promptly, my father might choose some member of the crew to take his place.

'Why do you treat me like a child?' I shouted, swaying slightly on my feet. 'I am twelve years old; I must learn to be a leader.'

For the first time I had asserted myself against my father. I do not know which of us was the more shaken. I did not dare to look at him, but stood there with eyes downcast, uneasily conscious that my head was swimming. At length I looked up and saw him smiling at me with pride and affection.

'You are right, Ascanius,' he said simply. 'I must not try to guard you from every danger. It is time I learnt to forget that you are my only son. Of course you may come with me.'

An hour later we set off together to climb the mountain from which we hoped to have a view of all the surrounding coast. Our only arms were our bronze-tipped hunting spears.

Now that we had sacrificed to Asherat, the dream had receded into the background of my mind. Our meal had given me fresh strength and I felt confident once more. We climbed steadily through the woods, following a narrow winding track made no doubt by deer. The mountain's slopes were carpeted with fallen leaves that glowed golden beneath the autumn sun. At last we emerged upon the summit. There in a glade surrounded by wild olive trees stood a solitary stele bearing an inscription beneath a sign shaped like a crescent moon.

We stared at it for a moment, unable to make out its meaning, then crossed the glade to a gap in the trees. To the west the ground fell away precipitously; far below lay a great semi-circular lagoon bordered by marshy land and almost cut off from the sea by a long irregular sandbank. Here and there we could see a few fishing boats. Not far off stood a group of huts made of interwoven reeds. Two ships were moored near-by; but we knew from the shape of the prows that they were not ours.

We saw now that we stood upon a promontory, for to the east the coast curved abruptly southwards in a succession of exposed and inhospitable beaches. The shore, at first flat and bare, merged gradually into sand-dunes, then rose yet higher in sheer red cliffs projecting eastwards, forming another headland beyond which we could not see. Not a ship was in sight.

My father was silent, observing the lie of the land and estimating distances.

'I think we are on an island,' he said at length. 'If I am right its southern coast begins not far beyond those cliffs. Let us follow this track through the woods but keep a look-out for islanders.'

We advanced cautiously, our spears poised ready for use. Once we heard distant shouts, then closer at hand a great threshing in the undergrowth made by some wild beast. We waited silently till all was still; then suddenly, as we rounded a bend in the path, we saw a figure coming towards us through the trees.

'It's a huntress,' whispered my father. 'Perhaps there are Amazons on the island.'

The girl had already seen us, and seemed to be alone. She came straight towards us without a trace of fear. Over her shoulder were slung a bow and quiver. Her hair flowed loose about her shoulders, her dress was kilted up above her knees. Her arms and her right breast were bare.

'I have lost my companions,' she said in Greek. 'Have either of you seen them?'

'Do Greeks live on this island?' asked my father astonished.

The girl laughed. 'This is not an island. This is Africa. No Greeks live here.'

'Yet you speak Greek,' said my father suspiciously.

'So do most Carthaginians,' retorted the girl. 'Traders like us learn many languages. I speak Numidian too.'

'Who are the Carthaginians?' asked my father peremptorily.

The girl's eyes flashed. 'And who are you who ask me all these questions? What is your name? Where do you come from?'

'I am called Aeneas the pious,' he said with bitter emphasis. 'My son and I are refugees from Troy. A storm drove us here.'

'From your speech, if not your dress, you are a man of noble birth,' said the girl more gently. 'Have you no followers?'

'Before the storm we had seven ships,' said my father tonelessly. 'Now we have one. One ship was wrecked upon some rocks, and all hands lost. What happened to the others we do not know.'

'You must go to Carthage,' said the girl. Her eyes flickered sympathetically over our faces. 'Perhaps Queen Dido will have news of your other followers.'

My father hesitated: 'Who is this Queen?' he said doubtfully.

The girl smiled: 'You have never heard of Dido the Phoenician who founded Carthage? But she will have heard of you.'

My father looked at her in astonishment.

'Go now,' she went on without further explanation. 'Carthage lies only a short way from here over the brow of that hill. If any mortal can help you now, surely Dido will.'

She began to move away:

'Wait,' cried my father.

The girl stopped and looked at him inquiringly.

'Your name,' he said, stammering a little in his eagerness for an answer. 'You have been kind to us but you have not told me your name.'

'It does not matter who I am,' she said abruptly. 'Farewell, pious Aeneas, farewell, Ascanius.'

Once more we heard distant shouts echoing through the wood. When we looked round again the girl had vanished.

'She knew my name,' I whispered. 'Was she a sorceress?'

'Or was she a nymph or a goddess?' said my father gravely. 'Perhaps we will never know – unless,' he paused, 'unless it was Dido herself.'

He looked up into the sky. The sun had disappeared behind grey clouds, but high above our heads we saw an eagle flying southwards in the direction that the girl had pointed.

'It is a good omen,' said my father resolutely. We quickened our pace. Soon we had reached the brow of the hill and there, spread out below, lay Carthage.

Even now I can feel the awe and excitement with which I first saw it – this new city with its great walls and buildings rising visibly before our eyes. Upon the slopes immediately beneath us lay orchards, fields and gardens dotted with reed huts – a kind of rural suburb from which Carthage drew its food. Later I learnt that its name was Megara. The city proper stood further off, close to the shore, upon a hill that faced eastwards overlooking the sea. To its south lay another lagoon such as we had already seen. We were upon a peninsula that seemed to ride like a ship at anchor, and Carthage was its prow. My father caught his breath.

'And this was founded by a woman,' he muttered. 'What a woman she must be!'

We followed the sandy path downwards through fruit trees and vineyards into a valley, crossed a turbulent stream by stepping stones and made our way up the further slope. Some women washing clothes called out as we passed, but no one else appeared to notice us. Everywhere we saw people hard at work. Some were digging, others were picking fruit or working in the vines. From the huts came the smell of cooking and the sound of sizzling oil. Half-naked children played in the dust outside.

By now our dusty path had become a broad track leading uphill to the city. Hundreds of workmen were toiling at the half-completed walls. A great wooden crane, temporarily motionless, towered into the air above the massive gate. Beyond it a newly paved street, flanked by tall houses, climbed to a market place alive with people.

My father hesitated. 'We will be challenged if we go any further,' he said, looking uncertainly at our spears. As he spoke, there came from within the city the deep reverberating boom of a brazen gong. There was a pause, then the clangorous roar of the gong resounded through the air once more. At once, people everywhere stopped work and stood or knelt in total silence. For the third time the gong sounded, and suddenly a great cry of 'Asherat' seemed to come from all over Carthage. The next moment the city came to life again. The workmen climbed down from the walls; the crowd in the market place began to disperse. It was the hour of the midday meal. A mob of labourers, artisans and peasants came surging down the street bound for the open gate.

My father grabbed my arm. 'Quick, let's take our chance,' he whispered urgently. In the huddle and confusion we slipped past the guard and found ourselves inside the walls.

We followed the street uphill, skirted the almost deserted market place, and entered a vast unpaved quadrangle surrounded by stately buildings. In its centre grew a thick grove of ilexes and from their midst rose a great temple approached by a flight of steps. At the top, beneath the porch and before the brazen entrance doors, there stood an ivory throne.

We sank down under the shade of the trees within sight of the doors, and ate our scanty meal. No one saw us. The great square seemed empty, the temple closed or deserted. Tired out

I lay down and fell asleep.

I was awakened by a confused murmur of approaching voices. I looked round for my father. To my alarm he had vanished. Quickly I made for a near-by tree – the largest ilex of them all. Perched upon a protruding branch, but hidden from sight, I watched attentively. A great crowd of people were coming towards the temple. As they neared the steps they fell back on either side, and from their midst emerged the most beautiful and regal figure I have ever seen.

How can any words of mine do justice to Dido's incomparable grace and beauty as I first saw her on that afternoon? She was dressed in a voluminous purple cloak, richly embroidered and fastened by a brooch shaped like a crescent moon. Upon her fair hair, parted in the centre and gathered back to reveal the delicate curve of her temples, rested a crown of exquisite workmanship, set with pearls and ornamented by twin doves with furled wings. From the jewelled girdle about her waist hung a large seal that lay like a pendant upon the skirt of her robe, swaying against her thighs as she walked. I watched her mount the temple steps with graceful assurance, and saw that she was tall and slender like a poplar. Turning she seated herself quickly upon her throne beneath the porch, flanked by her retinue and facing her subjects below. As she looked down, her dark eyes moved slowly over the crowd as if to identify each one of them, and her lovely face shone with a calm maternal pride. Beloved Dido – how happy you were then!

A herald called for silence, and instantly everyone was still. Then Dido spoke. What she said I did not understand, but later I learnt that each time her people assembled she used to pray aloud to Asherat to guide her judgement. Her prayer finished, the herald announced new laws and regulations for the city's welfare, and after each announcement the Queen asked the opinion of those present. Twice the discussion amongst the crowd was animated, and lots were cast as to who amongst them should undertake some common task, but for the most part each proposal met with evident approval. The Queen's voice was clear and gentle, and she never raised it. The final decision was always hers and accepted without question.

For more than an hour I sat watching her, absorbed and fascinated. Then suddenly one of the Queen's attendants leaned forward and whispered something to her, pointing across the square. She looked up surprised. Following her glance, I saw a detachment of soldiers advancing towards the temple escorting a bedraggled group of men. An inquisitive crowd brought up the rear. And then my heart leapt for joy, for amongst the group I recognized Ilioneus and Achates.

But where was my father? Suddenly I was afraid as to what might have happened to him. For a moment I was tempted to climb down from my hiding place and go in search of him, or run to meet Achates. He and his fellows were certainly under guard, but I could see now that they were not in chains.

Before I could act, the Queen had called out something to their escort. The crowd opened up before them. Achates and the other Trojans were led forward to the foot of the steps. I waited breathlessly for her to speak, half afraid that she would be stern and angry with them.

Then I heard her lovely voice as calm as ever:

'Who are you?' she asked quietly in Greek. 'Where do you come from?'

A rough and confident voice answered her – the voice of Ilioneus.

'We are refugees from Troy, your Majesty, the followers of King Aeneas. We were bound for Italy but a storm drove us upon your coast.'

The Queen started:

'King Aeneas?' she repeated. 'Do you mean Prince Aeneas, the hero, the son of King Anchises? Where is he now?'

'The gods have been unkind, your Majesty. We lost sight of his ship during the storm, but if he has reached this barbarous land, your people have no doubt driven him away.'

The Queen flushed.

'We Phoenicians do not treat strangers thus,' she said stiffly.

'Then why did your people try to drive us from your beaches and burn our ships? Do they not know the sacred laws of hospitality? Are we not even allowed to lay up and repair our ships?'

An angry murmur ran through the crowd, not so much at the words as at the tone of the speaker; but the Queen paid no attention. She called for the commander of the escort and questioned him. When she turned to Ilioneus again she was visibly embarrassed.

'I grieve that you have been so unkindly treated,' she said. 'I grieve that you have lost your noble king. I will send messengers everywhere for news of him. Ours is a new kingdom surrounded by marauding tribesmen; some of my people have never heard of Troy. Forgive them their hostility to strangers; we have our enemies too.

'But now,' she went on in a stronger voice, 'you can forget your troubles. I welcome you to Carthage as my guests. All Trojans shall be welcome here, whoever they may be. We will search for your king; we will repair your ships as if they were our own. You may stay here until the spring, or settle here for ever; the choice is yours. You shall be our partners, sharing this kingdom with us on equal terms. There shall be no difference between Trojans and Carthaginians. Whether you sail for Italy or stay with us in Carthage, be sure that I will help you and protect you in every way I can.'

Even now I feel a sense of awe at the humanity and generosity of Dido's speech. If I close my eyes, I can still hear the echo of her clear sweet voice saying those simple but momentous words that came straight from her heart.

Ilioneus began to thank her gruffly, but before he had finished there was a disturbance at the edge of the crowd. It was my father, head and shoulders above everyone, pushing his way forward. As he reached the steps, the sun came out from behind a cloud and shone upon his noble face and auburn hair.

'Here is our King!' shouted the Trojans.

The Queen looked at him in amazement.

'Are you indeed King Aeneas?' she asked, her dark eyes fixed upon him.

My father came forward and bowed to her.

'Forgive me, your Majesty, for thrusting myself before you in such unkingly fashion. Once I was Prince of Dardanus. Now I am a king without a kingdom, as meanly dressed as any homeless wanderer; but beggars such as we cannot be choosers.'

'No guest is more welcome than one who has suffered misfortune,' said the Queen. 'Tonight there will be a banquet in your honour. No, do not protest. I long to hear of your heroic deeds, your hardships, your adventures. I too am an exile from my native land. And your followers here; they too shall feast with us. My servants will see to all your needs and theirs.' She paused. 'But what of your followers who are left upon the beaches?' she went on. 'It is too late to bring them here tonight, but at least we can see to it that they are well fed.' She gave a series of rapid orders to the scribe sitting beside her, then stood up. 'Dear guest, it is growing late and I have other matters to attend to. Your sick and injured shall be brought here tomorrow. In Carthage we have many skilled physicians. And now I must leave you. Is there anything more that you have to say to me?'

'Only to assure you of our undying gratitude, sweet Queen,' said my father solemnly. 'We, alas, can never repay your loving kindness, but if there is any justice among the gods, if goodness such as yours means anything to them at all, may they reward you as you deserve.' His voice trembled.

I could see that Dido was deeply moved. She put out her hand instinctively towards him. He fell upon his knees and kissed it. Everyone was silent. Then very gently she withdrew her hand and placed it upon his head.

'May the gods watch over you and your followers,' she said.

Slowly she descended the steps followed by her retinue. The crowd parted reverently before her and began to disperse. Our fellow-Trojans gathered round my father embracing him, watched by some officials who had been deputed to look after us. The light was beginning to fade. Stiff and weary I scrambled down from the tree. Our spears were still lying on the grass. They seemed to belong to a different world.

'Here is young Ascanius,' cried Ilioneus, giving me a bear-like hug. My father looked at me dazedly as though he had forgotten my existence.

'Where have you been, Ascanius?'

'I was up a tree. I saw it all; I heard everything. But you, father, where did you go? I could not find you.'

'On the other side of the temple are some frescoes,' said my father slowly. 'I saw them. I looked closely at each one of them. Do you know what they are?' His voice shook. 'They are frescoes of the siege of Troy.'

We stared at him incredulously.

'All that heroism, all that grief, all that suffering, she wanted to commemorate it here in Carthage. I saw Troilus fleeing from Achilles. I saw Hector's lifeless body. I saw the mourning women of Troy. I even saw myself. It was as if Troy itself had been brought to life again. Why should a foreign queen, who never shared our misery, have done this thing?'

'Because she is a woman and admires heroes as women should,' said Ilioneus gruffly.

My father shook his head.

'No,' he said quietly, 'it is because she grieved for our sorrows long before she saw us. It is because her compassion is limitless.'

VII

The Queen's palace stood upon the summit of the hill over-looking the sea, but we were taken first to the high priest's house where we were to be lodged. When we had washed, and dressed ourselves in the clothes provided, we were escorted by torchlight to the palace and led into the banqueting hall where Dido and the chief men of Carthage were already awaiting us. An usher announced our arrival.

At first I was too bewildered by our sudden incursion from darkness into the opulent splendour of Dido's marble palace to take stock of my surroundings. I only remember the wonderful blend of tiredness and well-being that pervaded my whole body, cleansed of its accumulation of dust and brine, as I and my fellow-Trojans followed my father into the warmth and comfort of the banqueting hall. Everyone except the Queen rose as we entered. Preceded by the usher we made our way past massive ornamented tables surrounded by Carthaginian nobles to where the Queen was reclining in the centre upon a golden couch covered with cushions beneath a purple canopy. Her face lit up as we approached.

'Welcome under my roof, dear guests,' she said. 'How happy I am to see you.' Then her eye fell upon me. 'But who is this lovely boy? Why have I not seen him before?'

'This is my only son, your Highness,' said my father, pushing me forward. 'His name is Ascanius.'

'Your only son,' repeated the Queen, looking at me. 'You are lucky, my lord. He is as beautiful as Adonis.' She put out her hand and stroked the faint down upon my cheek. 'How old are you, Ascanius?'

'Twelve, your Majesty,' I mumbled shyly.

'Then you are almost a man, Prince Ascanius, and shall have your own banqueting couch. I shall put you here beside me so that we can talk. I am sure you have much to tell me.'

How can I describe the impact of those simple discerning words spoken with such grace and friendship to me a mere boy? I knew that for her I was a person in my own right, not merely my father's youthful son, not just a child to be made much of and then ignored. I felt a great love for her sweep over me like a wave.

A couch was brought forward for me. Our companions dispersed to their various places at other tables. My father moved to the place of honour on Dido's other side. Servants brought silver ewers to each one of us, with bowls in which to rinse our fingers. They distributed soft napkins on which to wipe our hands. They brought us slices of bread in baskets. We Trojans gaped in amazement at such luxury and refinement, remembering the crude masculine simplicity of Acestes's palace where no one had belched and spat more vigorously than our host, and how even at Buthrotum we had wiped our fingers upon our bread and thrown the pieces to the dogs. Here there were no dogs, and the floor was of polished marble. Here there were no dirty slouching serving-men, but clean unobtrusive man-servants and serving-maids, each with an appointed task.

The Queen poured a libation, and prayed to the gods. A whole variety of shell-fish and salads was brought in and set upon the table, followed by thick slices of tunny served in a rich sauce. The tunny was succeeded by a number of different meats – kid cooked in sweet wine, roasted gazelle, and wild boar flavoured with cumin.

I ate slowly, overwhelmed by the quantity and richness of the food, surreptitiously watching the uncouth manners of my fellow-Trojans. Of all of them only my father seemed completely at ease. Out of the corner of my eye I saw the delicate Dido talking to him with civilized assurance. I noticed that she ate sparingly. Sometimes I felt her steal a glance at me, and guessed that she had been questioning my father about the kind of life I had led. Suddenly she leaned across to me.

'How old were you when you and your father fled from Troy, Ascanius?' she asked gently.

'I was five,' I answered.

'Poor boy. You must have forgotten what it is to have a home and a mother. Do you still miss her?'

I considered. 'Not now. It is too long ago.'

Other women less perceptive than Dido might have found my answer callous. She accepted it as a statement of fact.

'Then who has looked after you since?'

'Caieta, my father's old nurse,' I said awkwardly.

'But she must be an old woman like Barce, my husband's nurse,' said Dido quickly. I sensed her disapproval, and looked at her gratefully but mystified.

'Then is there a King of Carthage?' I blurted out.

Dido shook her head. 'I am alone, Ascanius. I brought Barce to Carthage with me because otherwise she would have been murdered. But my beloved husband died long ago before I fled from Tyre.' Her lovely face was suddenly pensive and sad, and she was silent for a moment. Then she gave me an enchanting smile. 'The gods did not bless us with children, but I have a younger sister, Anna. Tomorrow you will see her.'

She turned to my father once more. He began to tell her haltingly how amazed and moved he had been to see frescoes commemorating the siege of Troy upon the walls of Asherat's temple. What had inspired her to choose such a theme?

'Admiration for your courage, and pity for your sufferings,' said Dido quietly. 'Your tragic story, my lord, has echoed all over the world. But there is much that I do not know,' and she began to question him about Hector, himself and other Trojan heroes. Reluctantly at first, then with growing animation, my father began to tell her of his own part in the fighting. She listened intently, drinking in every word, plying him with eager questions: how tall was Achilles; what was the colour of Hector's hair; what had been the name of my father's charioteer or the points of his horses? But she was not only interested in the warriors. She asked about life in Troy during the siege, about the women and children; and as she listened her compassion shone from her eyes. At last she said:

'Dear guest, I must question you no further, but grant me this favour. When the feast is over, tell us all the story of how Troy fell, of your miraculous escape, of all your wanderings. We fellow-exiles must share both our happiness and our sorrow.'

'But your lot has been far happier than ours, sweet Queen,' said my father reluctantly. 'You are rich; you have reached your journey's end; you have founded a new and prosperous capital. Your name will live for ever. You, a woman, have succeeded in your mission. The gods have smiled upon you as you deserve. Whereas I, a man, have failed.'

'Yet you have been luckier than I in one respect,' said Dido. 'The gods have given you a son.' She looked at me as she spoke.

'So beautiful a queen cannot lack suitors,' murmured my father.

Dido smiled. 'Yes, it is true. I have several suitors. Your late host, King Acestes, for one.'

'Acestes?' repeated my father. 'But he never spoke of you or Carthage. He never even told us he had been to Africa.'

'Perhaps he chose not to speak of it,' said Dido lightly. 'You should have seen him, dear guest, stalking into my audience chamber in his bearskin, wearing his crown of boar's tusks. As for his bodyguard, I have never seen such a bunch of ruffians.' Her voice trembled on the verge of laughter.

My father gave a broad smile.

'He expected me to leave Carthage,' she went on, 'and to go to live with him in a shack on Mount Eryx. Poor man, I must have hurt his pride. I am afraid I gave him short shrift.' She paused, and continued more seriously: 'I have other suitors too, but I make little account of any of them except the Numidian, Iarbas. He is my neighbour and could be dangerous. Sometimes I am almost afraid of him.' She stopped abruptly.

Her face had become grave. My father looked at her with concern.

'Perhaps I am less fortunate than you think, dear guest,' she added. 'Iarbas is a barbarous savage to whom women are no more than chattels. His people are fierce and warlike and far more numerous than mine. Besides, we Phoenicians are traders not warriors. Iarbas has grown rich through trading with us. Now that he has seen how Carthage prospers, he has become greedy for our wealth. His kingdom borders mine. I have tried to play for time until our walls are completed, but he is beginning to grow impatient. If I refuse to marry him, he will certainly attack us.'

I listened with growing alarm.

'Then what will you do?' I asked impulsively before my father could speak.

The Queen turned to me with gentle authority.

'I have prayed to Asherat to protect us, Ascanius,' she said simply. 'Somehow she will do so. This is her city. She guided me to this very spot; she showed me the site where I should build a temple in her honour. We dug there and found a horse's skull; and then I knew.' She stopped, her dark eyes fixed upon me.

'What did it mean?' I asked breathlessly.

'It was the sign she had promised, the sign that Carthage was destined to become the capital of a mighty and prosperous empire.' She spoke solemnly and with supreme confidence. My father stirred uneasily, but Dido did not notice.

'I think . . .' I began hesitantly, uncertain whether she would think me presumptuous, 'I think that Asherat may have meant us to come to Carthage.'

My father signed to me to say no more, and broke in at once:

'Tell me more of the goddess Asherat, and the other Phoenician deities, your Highness.'

'Asherat is the Queen of Heaven,' said Dido. 'Her symbol is a crescent moon. She is the Mother Goddess of us all, the goddess of marriage and fruitfulness. She is the goddess of the sea. She is my patron. She has preserved me from every danger. But she is not alone. We worship other gods in Carthage too. There is Melkart, the god of Tyre, whose priest my husband was.' Her voice trembled slightly. 'There is Astarte, his consort, the goddess of beauty and love. Her symbol is the evening star. Each year her doves fly here from Mount Eryx.' Tears stood in her eyes. 'Forgive a woman's tears, dear friends. I loved my husband deeply. Sometimes I feel that only love is good, but only misery is true.' She broke off and looked away, trying to master her emotion. My brain was awhirl. So it was to Carthage that Aphrodite's doves had flown on the day that my grandfather had died! Not only this, but she as well as Asherat was the protectress of Dido's city.

I could see that my father was as startled as I. I thought of the mysterious huntress who had guided us to Carthage, of whom he had forbidden me to speak. Must she not have been a goddess? The conviction grew upon me that it had been Aphrodite. I glanced quickly at the Queen. She had recovered her composure, and was looking around the hall. For the first time I was able to study her beauty unobserved, as she reclined upon her couch, the light gleaming upon her golden hair. Her face was a delicate oval, her cheeks faintly flushed. She had used no harshly-coloured cosmetics. I could see the tracery of a tiny vein beside the gentle curve of her temple. I looked at the graceful arch of her brows, the shapely nose with its sensitive nostrils, the sweetness and gravity of her mouth; the chin was both delicate and firm. My eyes travelled slowly down the whiteness of her throat adorned with a filigree necklace, lingered upon the exquisite curve of her shoulders, and came to rest upon the star-shaped brooch that fastened the bosom of her flowing gold-fringed dress. Below I could see the soft rounded outline of her breasts. She must have felt my glance as if I had touched them, for suddenly I felt her gazing at me. I reddened, and raised my eyes bashfully to hers. A long look passed between us.

'Poor boy, you are so tired,' she said softly. 'You shall come here beside me when I have poured a libation to the gods.'

By now everyone had finished eating. The Queen made a signal. Servants removed the plates and dishes, placed great bowls of wine, honey-cakes and fruit upon the tables, and lit the glistening chandeliers. At once the great hall was ablaze with light. A Babel of conversation sprang up. A servant brought the Queen a goblet of gold encrusted with jewels. She filled it carefully to the brim from the garlanded bowl upon our table, and then rose to her feet.

'I call first upon the gods of our Trojan guests. Some say it was Zeus who created the laws of hospitality. May he make this joyful occasion a day our descendants will remember. May Dionysus, the god of wine, fill our cups with rejoicing, for the whole world dances when there is friendship. May bounteous Asherat, our protectress, give us all her blessing and bind us together so that we become one people. Fellow Carthaginians, I call upon you; show your goodwill to your guests, welcome them to your hearts as if they were our kinsmen.'

She poured a wine-offering on to the table, then raised the goblet and touched it lightly with her lips. A Carthaginian noble stood beside her waiting to receive it: she passed it to him smiling, with a challenge. Entering into the spirit of her words, he seized the goblet with both hands and made as if to drain it. Everyone laughed. One after another the Carthaginians drank to us. For a moment the Queen stood watching, elated and happy. Then she lay back upon her couch and beckoned to me. I looked at my father questioningly. He nodded. My heart pounding I crossed to her couch and sat down awkwardly beside her. She drew me back so that I leant against her thighs, and put her arm around me.

For a moment I was tense with shame and embarrassment. What would our companions think to see me petted like a child? Did not the Queen realize she was making me look a fool? But almost at once a delicious drowsiness settled upon me. I felt numbed by sleep. My eyes closed, and my head drooped upon Dido's shoulder. Seeing this she made room for me and drew me closer to her so that I should be more comfortable.

'Now you can go to sleep,' she whispered, 'and no one, not even your father, shall disturb you. Lie still and close your eyes. A minstrel is going to sing to us.'

How tenderly Dido held me in her snow-white arms. How fragrant her body was; how sweet her kisses. From afar off, as it seemed, came the long-haired minstrel's mysterious song of the birth of the sun and moon and stars. Then I heard the Queen's voice close by, asking my father to tell them all his story. A profound hush fell upon the whole gathering. Slowly at first, and sorrowfully, he began to describe the fall of Troy. I could hear Dido's heart beating as she listened intent and motionless. When he spoke of how he had lost my mother, his grief almost overcame him. I felt Dido press me close to her, murmuring some sweet endearment. Drowsily I snuggled up to her; and so I fell asleep, my cheek against her breast.

VIII

The next day I was ill, and by nightfall I had a raging fever. No doubt it was the Queen who arranged that I should be moved to the palace where her sister, Anna, could look after me. My only recollection of the days that followed is of a series of confused and shifting nightmares: Pyrrhus pursuing me through the streets of Troy, brandishing a gigantic sword; my father and I being hauled like prisoners before the judgement seat of Almighty Zeus; the remorseless face of an unknown goddess, her lips set and stern, her eyes flaming. As my fever gradually subsided, I became dimly aware of the various people who appeared and reappeared in the room – the swarthy bearded physician who came to examine me, Anna's handmaid Imilce, Anna herself, short, slight and dark-haired, utterly unlike her beautiful sister, and lastly my father and Dido, sometimes separately, sometimes together. But I found that I was too weak to speak to any of them. At best I could only raise an uncertain smile.

It was Anna whom I saw most frequently; either she or Imilce seemed to be always with me. It was she who gave me my bitter-tasting medicine, who placed cold compresses upon my forehead, who wrapped more clothes around me each time that I was seized by a violent spasm of shivering. As the days passed, and my strength slowly returned, I began to appreciate her utter selflessness; and then, one day as I lay watching her moving about, I saw that she was lame. The sight of that limping thin little figure began to haunt me. I realized that I still knew nothing about her except that she was Dido's younger sister. I could see that she was a fully-grown woman; but I sensed in her something curiously virginal, as if she were scarcely conscious of her sex and had never thought of marriage. She was not so much shy as naturally self-effacing. All her kindness to me had been tinged by a certain reticence. Now that I was once more capable of conversation I meant to penetrate her reserve. Most of all I wanted her to talk to me of Dido, whom I had seen so seldom. I had begun to think of her endlessly. Even to hear her name mentioned would bring her closer to me.

'Tell me about the Queen's husband,' I said suddenly. 'Was he the King of Tyre?'

Anna looked startled.

'No, he was the high priest of Melkart, the god of the city. His name was Sychaeus.'

'Then why is she called Queen Dido?'

'Because she was Queen of Tyre,' said Anna. 'She ruled it jointly with our brother. But Dido has not always been her name. It is the name the Numidians gave her when we first landed here, and now her subjects call her by it too. It means "newcomer". She liked it; she felt it showed she was beginning a new life and had turned her back on Tyre for ever; that is why this city is called Carthage. In our language it means "new capital".'

For the first time Anna's voice was charged with emotion. I knew now that if she had seemed so curiously impersonal, so withdrawn, it was because all her thoughts were bound up with her sister.

'You love her,' I said.

Anna nodded. 'Yes, I love her, Ascanius. She is dearer to me than the light of day. For me she is not Dido, Queen of Carthage: she is Elissa, my sweet sister, who saved me from death at our brother's hands. But why am I telling you this? You are only a boy, and to you we must seem little more than strangers. What can it matter to you that Dido saved my life, that her husband was foully murdered? A nobler man never lived: but if only she could forget him!'

She buried her face in her hands.

'I love her too, Anna,' I said.

She raised her head and looked at me in silence.

'I guessed you did,' she said eventually, 'even though you scarcely know her. Over and over again you called out for her during your fever.' She paused, searching my face with her eyes. 'Yes, I will tell you her story, Ascanius. You are old enough to understand; and since you love her what harm can it do?'

Much of what Anna told me was utterly strange to me. How different her life from mine! She began by telling me of the Phoenicians, a race of seafarers and merchants, who lived upon a narrow strip of coastal plain hemmed in by mountains. They were too numerous to support themselves by agriculture. Trade was their life blood, she said; without it they would have perished. She spoke of their journeys to distant lands – to Ophir where they found gold and spices and sandalwood, to Tarshish, far to the west, which was rich in silver and tin. She spoke of their trade in ivory and cedarwood and precious stones, of the fine linen that came from Egypt, of the copper from Cyprus, of strange long-armed crouching animals shaped like men, and of the birds with resplendent plumage which had strutted like potentates in her father's garden at Tyre. She told me of the other cities of Phoenicia – of Byblos, once the greatest of them all, where Astarte had been worshipped since the dawn of time, of Sidon sometimes the friend and sometimes the enemy of Tyre. She spoke of the great rival powers of Egypt and Assyria, each of them striving to dominate Phoenicia, of a people called the Hebrews, formerly Tyre's allies, who worshipped one single god and hated all other religions. She spoke of the craftsmanship of the Phoenicians – of their skill in shipbuilding, of the purple dye that they made from shell-fish, of their carved ivories, of their gold and silver work. She described the city of Tyre upon a rocky island close to the shore – its many-storeyed houses, its workshops, wharves and warehouses, its two ports and spacious anchorage girt about with reefs to which ships came from the four corners of the earth.

Her father, the king of this rich and thriving city, ruled also over part of Cyprus. Of his three children Dido was the oldest. Pygmalion, his only son, was the fruit of a second marriage, but it had always been Dido whom he had loved the most. She had inherited all the beauty of her mother, a Cypriot princess; not only this, but she had the intelligence of a man. The young Pygmalion was vicious and degenerate, but the long-established law of succession made it impossible to exclude him from the throne. After much anxious thought, the king hit upon a solution. Dido and Pygmalion were to succeed him jointly, and to keep his son in check, Dido should be married to Sychaeus, his friend and counsellor, the chief man of the kingdom.

The marriage was not only political; it was also a marriage of love. From her childhood, Dido had revered Sychaeus. Now she fell passionately in love with him, with all the ardour of her generous nature. No other man existed for her, although he was far older than she. She never sacrificed her independence of judgement, but in all other respects her one thought was to make him happy and to enjoy with him to the utmost the delights of conjugal love. Her only grief was that their union was childless.

Her married happiness was to prove short-lived. Soon after her marriage her father died and Pygmalion, spurred on by Sychaeus's enemies, began to intrigue against her. He had always regarded his sisters with jealous hatred, but he hated Sychaeus still more. A carefully prepared campaign of slander was built up against him. Paid agitators denounced his wealth as ill-gotten gains acquired by tyranny and extortion. He was accused of having a hand in the late king's death, and of plotting to murder Pygmalion. He was accused of being in secret league with Tyre's enemies. Any calamity was attributed to Melkart's wrath at his impiety. Dido was too widely loved for any direct attack to be made upon her, but she was represented as no more than a figurehead. The gods had never meant a woman to reign over Tyre; it was a further reason for their anger.

The population of Tyre included many foreigners – a discontented turbulent riff-raff of refugees and runaway slaves who had come to the already overcrowded island to escape from the mainland or in search of work. Sychaeus had many enemies even among the Senate – men who begrudged him his power and envied him his marriage to a young and wealthy queen. They took care to inform the mighty King of Assyria of Dido's beauty, promising that Pygmalion would hand his sisters over to him as concubines in return for his support.

When all was ready, Pygmalion and his allies struck. A riot was organized amongst the foreign population. Agitators demanded an assembly of the people. Pygmalion consented to the demand at once without informing his sister. A tumultuous mob occupied the Senate-house, clamouring in the people's name for Dido's deposition.

Sychaeus, though taken by surprise, was undismayed. He knew that most of the Tyrian population were loyal to him and Dido. He had troops at his disposal; but Sychaeus was a man of peace and Dido hated bloodshed. They sent troops to restore order, and declared the assembly illegal; but they took no action against Pygmalion. They still hoped for a reconciliation as a means of resolving the crisis. In an evil hour for themselves they granted him a safe-conduct to their palace, where Anna also lived.

It was night. Pygmalion arrived apparently without an escort, accompanied only by a single servant. He expressed regret for the turn that events had taken, and disavowed the assembly's riotous proceedings. Sychaeus called upon him to make a solemn covenant with him as proof of his sincerity. Pygmalion readily agreed. Sychaeus led him before the altar of Melkart: the two men purified themselves, offered sacrifices, and swore upon the altar that they were reconciled. Then Pygmalion drew his dagger and stabbed Sychaeus through the heart.

The two men had been alone, for women were not admitted to Melkart's sanctuary. No one had witnessed the sacrilegious crime. Rushing to the palace entrance, Pygmalion shouted for help, claiming Sychaeus had attacked him. The signal was preconcerted. A mob of foreign soldiers dressed as Tyrians poured into the building: the palace guard was taken by surprise and offered no resistance. Anna and Dido were immediately seized and taken to Pygmalion's palace where they were shamefully confined like common prisoners. With deliberate cruelty Pygmalion separated the sisters and refused to see them, leaving Dido in agonized uncertainty as to her husband's fate.

It was Dido who discovered they were to be sent to the King of Assyria. She swore that she would kill herself rather than submit to the slavery of a harem; but her chief thought was for her sister. She had managed to conceal some of her jewellery and bribed one of her foreign guards to carry a message to Anna. Soon a system of communication was established between them, and Dido learnt for the first time that her husband had been murdered. So touching was her sorrow that her guards took pity on her. They swore they would serve her rather than her husband's murderer. They conveyed messages for her to the outside world. Although some of her husband's supporters had fled into exile, there were still many who had remained in Tyre itself. A plot was hatched to rescue her before Pygmalion could carry out his shameful purpose. To rescue Anna was more difficult for she was confined in a room on the top floor of the palace, but Dido refused to flee without her sister. Eventually a second plan was agreed upon. Anna's former handmaid, Imilce, was a servant in Pygmalion's palace: with the help of the guard she smuggled a long strip of linen to her mistress. Both sisters were to escape simultaneously whilst Pygmalion was banqueting below. A ship would be waiting to take them to the mainland. There they would be met by their many supporters who preferred exile to Pygmalion's tyranny and subservience to Assyria. Together they would sail to Cyprus.

Dido escaped successfully; but before Anna had reached the ground, her improvised rope gave way. She fell and broke her leg. Dido refused to leave her, and but for the help of Imilce and Sychaeus's steward, all would have been lost. At last, with infinite difficulty, they reached the ship, their flight still undetected. On the mainland their supporters were already awaiting them, their ships loaded with treasure. Pygmalion had hoped to lay hands on all his sister's fortune, but much of it had been concealed from him by Sychaeus's faithful steward. With tears in her eyes, Dido thanked them for their loyalty. They swore that they would follow her wherever she led them. She offered a sacrifice to Melkart, and weeping, invoked the shade of her dead husband. Then, saying a last farewell to her native city, she bade her company embark. In the pale light of dawn, with the star of Astarte gleaming faintly from afar, their fleet of forty ships set sail for Cyprus.

At Kition, the chief Tyrian city on the island, Dido found that she was still recognized as Queen. But to remain there would be to invite attack from her brother, to inflict upon its people the horrors of civil war. A less magnanimous ruler would have thought only of revenge no matter what the cost. Dido saw further: she had lost her beloved husband for ever. Nothing she could do would bring him to life again. Only by turning her back upon the past could she hope to allay the cruel ache of loneliness. She must not take up arms against her brother; rather she must put herself beyond his reach. All her thoughts and energies must be devoted to some new and memorable enterprise to the benefit and glory of her race, such as would be pleasing to the gods and her dead husband's shade. She resolved to found a second Tyre in Africa beyond the confines of the civilized world. South of Crete the Greeks were active; but further to the west, on the route past Sicily to Tarshish, only the Phoenicians had penetrated.

From Tyre the journey was long and hazardous. For such far-reaching expeditions special ocean-going ships were used. Sometimes they never returned; often they were absent for three or more years. Their cargo of silver, iron and tin was of enormous value; the merchant princes of Tyre had waxed fat upon the profits. But if a second Tyre could be established on the African coast near Sicily, how much surer and more lucrative this traffic in precious metals would become.

Dido had never travelled further west than Cyprus; but like most Phoenician women she was highly educated. She had learnt to speak Greek and Egyptian fluently. She knew where Crete was; she had heard of Sicily. She had spoken to mariners who had sailed to Tarshish, and knew of the anchorages they used along the African coast. She knew too of the scattered Phoenician trading posts that had sprung up there – palisaded encampments upon a spit of land near some lagoon or estuary, consisting of a few beached ships and daub and wattle huts. No one had founded these humble settlements; they had come into existence as ports of call. If Tyre sank into decline, and the trade with Tarshish ceased, they would dwindle away and die.

Tyre was rich and prosperous, but exposed to constant dangers from her powerful neighbours. In Africa there would be no such threat. The coast was wooded and almost un-inhabited, the population in the interior primitive pastoral nomads. But, barbarous though they were, they were not unfriendly to traders. Moreover, the land was reputed to be fertile; wild fruit trees grew in abundance, and the woods were filled with game. To find a good natural harbour, to buy land from a local chieftain, to found a second Tyre – why should it not be possible if the gods gave their blessing? Dido herself was rich, and many of her followers were men of substance who had brought their households with them. To recruit fresh labour in Cyprus should not be difficult – quarrymen, masons, smiths, craftsmen of all kinds, soldiers and mariners, shepherds and tillers of the soil. Thus the vision of a great enterprise began to take shape in Dido's active and far-seeing mind. But she said nothing of it to anyone save Anna until she was sure that it was favoured by the gods.

Dido had lost none of her reverence for Melkart and Astarte, the patron and patroness of Tyre; but to pray to them had become painful to her. Since her marriage to Sychaeus, they had been for her the symbols of their conjugal love. To think of them now was to remind herself of the pleasures she and her husband had enjoyed together. Her thoughts turned more and more to another deity, worshipped as the Great Mother by all Phoenicians – Asherat, the Queen of Heaven and Lady of the Sea. It was she who was invoked by mariners; ships were often dedicated to her. Not only this, but she was a queen and the special protectress of women. From the outset, Dido identified Asherat with her secret enterprise. No sooner had she landed at Kition than she went to Asherat's temple and offered sacrifices. She prayed silently for protection against her brother, for a sign that the goddess favoured the ambitious plan that was forming in her mind. The days passed; Dido visited the temple daily at sunrise, but said nothing of her purpose. Then one morning as she was leaving the palace, she found the High Priest waiting for her. He was in a state of great excitement. Asherat had appeared to him in a dream and told him the Queen's plan. She had bidden him accompany her with his wife and children, promising her protection. The widowed exiled queen was destined to be the foundress of a great and powerful city, more prosperous even than Tyre. The goddess herself would guide them on their journey. She had shown him the site upon a hill beside a lagoon, to the south of some high red cliffs. They were to land and dig at a certain spot where they would find a horse's skull; there they were to raise a temple in honour of the goddess, and round it they should build their city. She would remain in their midst; she would watch over their queen and defend her from her enemies.

Overjoyed, Dido hastened to the temple and poured out her heart in gratitude before the altar. Then she summoned her followers, and with the High Priest beside her, told them of her divinely-sanctioned plan. It was greeted with enthusiasm; one and all regarded it as a sacred enterprise. Many of the population volunteered to join her; others offered goods and ships and treasure. For the first time since her husband's death, Dido was happy. But she did not allow her happiness to cloud her judgement, and organized her expedition with care. It was to sail to Crete before turning southwards towards Africa, and thereafter it would follow the coast. But the journey would be long and possibly dangerous; she and her followers might meet with opposition from the Greeks, from pirates, from unfriendly Africans. They might run short of food or water. Until the site had been found, and a preliminary settlement established, no one must come with her whose presence was not necessary. Some of the volunteers were turned away together with many of the women and children. It grieved Dido to act thus; but she promised that she would not forget those whom she left behind, and that as soon as she could she would send for them. So greatly was she loved that there was little murmuring. In the late spring she set sail with half her fleet.

The journey was miraculously uneventful. Dido had chosen only experienced seamen, many of whom had some previous knowledge of the African coast. They seldom had difficulty in finding watering-places. No ships were wrecked or lost because of storms. Such hardships as they encountered were cheerfully shared by all. Above all their feeling that they were fulfilling a sacred mission never left them. Had this been an ordinary commercial venture, few of Dido's company would have accepted her as their unquestioned leader. For a woman, even a queen, to lead such an expedition was unprecedented. But in the eyes of all her followers Dido was more than a beautiful and courageous woman. She had become the living symbol of Asherat. Her person was sacrosanct. They revered her and obeyed her as if she was a goddess. Several of her nobly-born followers were bent at first on marrying her. Quietly but decisively Dido dismissed all such proposals. Her body she told them belonged to her dead husband: as for Anna, she should only marry when and how she chose.

It was upon her crippled younger sister that Dido lavished all her tenderness. She was repaid by Anna's limitless devotion. Anna was her only confidante, the only person to whom she could speak freely of her inner doubts and hesitations, of her moments of overwhelming loneliness. Anna was no leader but she was not lacking in shrewdness. She defended her generous-hearted sister from exploitation, she protected her from futile or trivial questions. As her father's favourite child, Dido had been brought up surrounded by comforts and luxuries. She was quite unused to the hardships of a long sea voyage. She endured them bravely but they exhausted her too. There were times when she found the close contact with rough seamen utterly repugnant. She never showed her feelings. Only Anna, less sensitive than her delicately-nurtured sister, knew how much their coarse behaviour and crude language could revolt her. Unobtrusively, she would act as Dido's unofficial spokesman. The Queen was tired, she would inform the crew, and her health was delicate; if they wished to please Asherat, they must show more consideration for her. It was an appeal that never failed.

In the early autumn they called at a Phoenician trading post, and learned for the first time that they were not far from their goal. Further to the north, they were told, beyond a mighty promontory and a solitary mountain with a peak like a pair of horns, there lay an anchorage called by the Africans 'Kakkabé', which answered to their description. The name meant 'Horse's skull' though none knew why it had been given to such a spot. The surrounding country was inhabited by a fierce people called the Numidians. Ships had often called there but no one had ventured to found a settlement although the soil was fertile.

After giving thanks to Asherat, Dido took on board with her a Phoenician who could speak the Numidian language. Four days' sailing took her fleet safely round the windswept promontory into a broad gulf that stretched westwards as far as the eye could see. Upon its further shore she could dimly make out in the autumn sun the sheer red cliffs of which the High Priest had spoken. With rising excitement, they hoisted more sail and pressed on. Gradually the great lagoon to the south came into view. A short distance away, overlooking the sea, stood a gently rounded hill. Dido was unable to speak for emotion. She could only point and look inquiringly at the Phoenician she had brought with her. 'Kakkabé,' said the man, nodding his head and smiling. Anna flung her arms round her sister's neck. For the first time since she had left Cyprus, Dido wept for joy.

They sailed into the lagoon and beached their twenty ships. When they had disembarked, the High Priest sacrificed to Asherat before them all. The solemn ceremony was scarcely finished when they saw two bands of horsemen converging upon them at the gallop. With scowling faces the tribesmen surrounded Dido's company. Their leader rode arrogantly forward. His voluminous woollen white mantle was fastened to his head by a golden band. Beneath his mantle he wore a lion skin to emphasize his rank. Upon each of his muscular arms was a massive ivory bracelet. He carried a light javelin in his hand. The leather belt about his waist bristled with darts. It was the Numidian king, Iarbas.

Ignoring Dido, he asked the High Priest angrily in faulty Punic why he and his followers had landed.

'It is for our Queen to tell you,' said the High Priest.

Iarbas stared at her in amazement.

'What sort of a people are you who have a woman as your leader?' he said at length, eyeing her insolently.

'We have come to trade with you,' said Dido quietly. She ordered Imilce to bring her a gold cup, and presented it to Iarbas.

He snatched it rudely from her.

'What else have you?' he demanded.

'First I wish to buy land and build a settlement; then we will trade with you.'

'I will not sell land to strangers,' said Iarbas abruptly, 'but you can pay me tribute for it.'

Dido shook her head: 'I will only buy it. No one lives upon that hill. Your people are neither fishermen nor seamen. What use is this coast to you?'

Iarbas leered at her.

'I bought my wives for oxen,' he said slowly, 'and I will sell you an oxhide of land. You may choose the spot yourself.'

'I accept your offer,' replied Dido. 'Name your price.'

Iarbas weighed the gold cup in his hand.

'Ten of these cups.'

'Produce your oxhide,' said Dido, 'and I will produce the cups.'

Iarbas was patently uneasy.

'We will settle the matter tomorrow,' he said awkwardly.

'No,' said Dido with quiet authority. 'If you wish to have the cups, and if you wish to grow rich by trading with us, it must be settled today.'

Iarbas hesitated, biting his lips, but his greed was too strong for him. He shouted an order to one of his men. An oxhide was produced and spread out upon the ground. Dido examined it carefully.

'Now, my lord,' she said, 'you and I will swear by my gods and yours, here before our people, that we will observe the agreement we have made, and that neither we nor our subjects will molest each other.'

Iarbas began to bluster.

'What is the matter, my lord?' asked Dido. 'Do you not want to trade peacefully with us? Do you mean to break our agreement?'

Iarbas flushed. 'Where are the cups?' he demanded in a thick voice.

'I have ordered my steward to bring them to you as soon as you have sworn your oath. They are the same as the cup I have given you, but if you wish, they shall be weighed before you accept them.'

She had established complete ascendancy over him. Iarbas swore his oath in a loud voice, first in Numidian then in Punic. Dido followed suit. The cups were produced and weighed. Iarbas formally accepted them. Now that they were in his possession his manner became almost genial. He authorized the Phoenicians to build a temporary camp near their ships. Looking at Dido meaningly he spoke of his wish for close relations with them. At last he brusquely took his leave. With unutterable relief the Phoenicians watched him and his horsemen gallop off in a cloud of dust.

Dido was pale and exhausted after her long ordeal, but she was anxious to set the minds of her followers at rest. As soon as the Numidians had vanished, she called them together and explained what she had done. Her aim had been to buy land; in this she had succeeded. Iarbas had made her pay an outrageous price. He had thought in his insolent pride that he had sold her too little to be of any value to her. He was wrong; unwittingly he had sold her enough to build a settlement. Tomorrow they would cut the oxhide into one long narrow strip. They would pray to Asherat to guide them to the site where they were to build her temple and there, on the hill, within the surrounding circle of oxhide, they would solemnly found their city. The land would be hers alone. Iarbas could not claim it. Not only this, but he had sworn not to attack them. She and her subjects would be free to build their city in peace.

It was Dido's greatest moment of triumph. A murmur of admiration spread through the crowd at the way she had outwitted Iarbas. They pressed around her, assuring her of their devotion; some knelt and kissed her hand. Never before had she been so conscious of their love.

Anna stopped abruptly.

'It is late, Ascanius. You must sleep.'

'You will tell me more tomorrow?' I asked instantly.

She smiled: 'If you want to hear it.'

'I want to see her too,' I blurted out.

Anna looked at me gravely: 'I will tell her.' She bade me good night and went out of the room.

I lay staring up into the darkness thinking of Dido, and of how she had founded Carthage. I was filled with incredulous admiration. How futile our own efforts had been by comparison. I thought of my father's misguided attempt to found a settlement in Thrace, of our disastrous failure in Crete. Dido had made no such mistakes. She had known her own mind from the outset. She had not relied blindly upon the gods to tell her what to do; she had not wasted time consulting ambiguous oracles as my father had done. She had been practical; he had not.

Suddenly I realized I had begun to question his leadership, and was shocked by my disloyalty. I remembered what Palinurus had said to me. It was true. My father had been unlucky. Zeus had never helped us as Asherat had helped Dido. But must not Asherat be mightier than he was? She had raised the storm that had prevented us from reaching Italy; she had brought us to Carthage. I feared her as the enemy of our destiny; yet she was Dido's protectress, and Dido had shown herself to be our friend. She had offered us common citizenship. She had treated us with extraordinary generosity and kindness. Her sister had nursed me through my illness. I was a guest in her palace, living in such comfort as I had never known. Tomorrow she would come to see me, and I would tell her that I loved her. I wanted to stay with her for ever. My destiny lay in Carthage. What did far-off Italy matter to me now?

IX

That night I slept deeply and dreamlessly. When I awoke the next morning the sunlight was already filtering into the room through the drawn curtains. I felt strong and well once more. Springing out of bed I went to the window.

A cold wind was blowing but the sky was radiant and cloudless. On the other side of the vast bay spread out before me a solitary mountain rose high into the sky crowned by twin peaks shaped like horns. The sun illumined its bare reddish flanks and shone upon the agitated expanse of sea. To the south of the bay ten ships were sailing in single line towards Carthage, following the flat and marshy coast. Close at hand lay the great lagoon where Dido and her followers had disembarked. Then it had been empty and desolate. Now it was alive with ships and fishing boats – some beached in rows upon the shore, some riding at anchor in the middle of the lagoon, some moored beside the long mole where fishermen were unloading their morning catch. The quay from which the mole projected was swarming with people manhandling great blocks of stone and marble from the ships tied up alongside. Massive carts drawn by oxen stood close by, waiting to transport them to the city. Immediately below the city walls more labourers were hard at work excavating an artificial harbour. From everywhere rose a confused hubbub of voices.

The sight of so much activity made me restless. As I withdrew my head, I saw Dido and my father crossing the courtyard immediately below my window. They were talking earnestly. My heart leapt at the sight of them. I had been cooped up for too long in a room, and I decided I would dress and go to meet them. But before I could move, the door opened and Anna came into the room accompanied by the physician. Despite my insistence that I felt well again, I was made to submit to a long examination. An incomprehensible conversation took place between Anna and the physician. Then Anna informed me that I might get up and dress tomorrow, but was not to go out of doors. I began to protest, but she cut me short with unexpected firmness.

'You are our guest, Ascanius, and we are responsible for you. Do you realize how ill you have been, and how thin and pale you are?'

She handed me a mirror, and I saw in its burnished surface the reflection of a white and hollow-cheeked face. I made grimace at it, and she laughed.

'At least I can tell Dido you have recovered your spirits. Later she will come to see you. But you must be hungry.'

A servant brought me some simple fare and a pitcher of wine. I ate and drank voraciously.

'Now,' said Anna, 'I will fetch your father.'

She limped out of the room, and presently I heard the sound of their voices and the echo of his long easy stride coming along the corridor. As they came in I saw that Anna's cheeks were faintly flushed and that she was smiling. She looked diminutive beside him, and he was looking down at her with an expression of protectiveness that I had never seen before. He embraced me and told me at once how devotedly Anna had nursed me through my fever, and that more than once she had sat up the whole night beside me. She listened embarrassed but not without pleasure. I thanked her awkwardly.

'It is nothing,' she said. 'I did it for my sister.' And then unexpectedly she raised her eyes and looked at my father. 'If my sister and I ever look to you for help,' she said, 'we will know that you will not fail us.'

She withdrew to leave us alone. I asked my father for news of our companions. All of them were lodged in different parts of the city, he said. Our ships were beached close by. As the

Queen had promised, they were being repaired, and damaged sails and oars were being replaced. Most of the Carthaginians were hospitable and friendly. Our people felt less at home than at Drepanum, but no one could have shown them more kindness than the Queen had done. She had taken particular trouble over the care of the sick and injured – especially Caieta who would be allowed to come to see me as soon as her arm had mended. 'But by then,' my father added, 'you should be well enough to return to the High Priest's house.'

I started at this unwelcome news.

'Why can't I stay here?'

'This is the part of the palace where the Queen lives,' said my father. 'You cannot go on staying in the women's quarter indefinitely.'

'Is that where I am?' I asked in astonishment.

He laughed. 'You are surrounded by women. The Queen, her sister, her maids. It is the most jealously guarded part of the palace. Even I was not allowed in here alone.'

Strangely it had never occurred to me that I was in the women's part of the palace, that Dido's bedchamber might be close to mine. My heart beat faster. With my mind's eye I saw her maids undressing her. I watched them as they unfastened her flowing gold-fringed robe. I saw the gleaming whiteness of her naked body, and marvelled at its beauty.

My father had stopped speaking, and was looking at me with a faint smile. I wondered if he had guessed my thoughts, and felt ill at ease.

'The Queen is very fond of you, Ascanius. I know you will not take advantage of her kindness.'

I said nothing, remembering how my head had lain upon her breast. He felt obliged to explain.

'It is because she has no children of her own. She should have married again after her husband died. She has had no lack of suitors.'

'Perhaps she has never wanted another husband,' I said defensively.

My father nodded:

'That is what she told me, and it may be so. After all she has achieved single-handed, she cannot wish to share her power. She is a born ruler, Ascanius, a natural leader. I have never met a woman like her. She has courage, wisdom and beauty, but she is childless. She says that Carthage is her child, that it is the will of Asherat that she should have no other children. If this is true, I find it very strange. For the sake of her people she needs an heir to succeed her.'

The thought had never occurred to me.

'There is Anna,' I said.

My father shook his head: 'Anna will never make a queen. She is good and kind, but the people seldom see her. She hardly stirs from the palace, the High Priest tells me, and knows little of affairs.'

I remembered that Anna looked after the administration of the palace. No, she would never aspire to anything more. All that she thought of was serving Dido. Moreover, she was a cripple. Even if she were to marry, would she ever have children?

'You see, Ascanius, I am talking to you like a grown man,' said my father seriously. 'The Queen has welcomed us with marvellous kindness. But she is in danger.'

'In danger?' I repeated quickly. 'From Iarbas?'

'Not only from Iarbas; from some of her subjects too. Several of the Senators think that she should marry him.'

I looked at him dumbfounded.

'They say it is in the interests of Carthage,' added my father gravely. 'They have not acted yet. But if Iarbas were to attack . . .'

'He cannot attack,' I interrupted, and told him of the oath the Numidian had sworn when Dido and her followers had landed.

My father listened attentively.

'What was true then is not true now,' he said.

He went on to explain that Carthage had grown far more rapidly than anyone could have anticipated. The Queen had allowed for more settlers from Cyprus, counting upon her agents there to regulate their numbers. But each year hundreds of refugees had arrived from Tyre. Dido had had compassion on them. Each year, therefore, she had had to bargain with Iarbas for more land, and each time the conditions had become more onerous. Only part of the hill upon which Carthage stood belonged to her: for all the rest, for all the land outside the walls, she had to pay tribute and acknowledge Iarbas as her overlord. Outside the city she had no right to build defences or even to demarcate the boundaries between Iarbas's land and hers. He could resume possession of all such land whenever he chose; he could cut Dido's capital off from all but a fraction of its coast and from all its rural suburbs. If he did so, the Carthaginians would be forced to attack him, for otherwise they would starve. This would give Iarbas the excuse he wanted for seizing the city itself. As he well knew, its defences were inadequate. The Queen had few trained soldiers among her subjects.

Matters had now reached a crisis. The Queen had felt obliged to submit to Iarbas's terms; but latterly his demands had become so outrageous that she had publicly protested against them. Iarbas's reaction was immediate: he informed the Carthaginian Senate that he wished to marry their queen. If she consented, all tribute would be abolished, and all Carthaginians would be free to live and trade anywhere in his dominions, provided they recognized him as king. As their overlord, he claimed a full and direct share in their prosperity. This he would obtain when Dido married him; not only this, but he would be able to enjoy the luxury of her palace, to lay hands on all her wealth. But these were not the only reasons he demanded her hand in marriage. He required, he said, some person to teach him and his subjects a more civilized way of life. Who could be better qualified to do this than their queen?

I shuddered at the thought of the fastidious Dido having to submit to the embraces of a barbarous savage who regarded women as chattels. Even if he learnt more civilized ways, and tried to treat her with some consideration, how would she be able to endure living among such a brutish people? And yet some of her subjects thought she should sacrifice herself for the good of the city she herself had founded!

'If I tell you this, Ascanius,' said my father quietly, 'it is because I think the gods sent us here to help the Queen, to fight for her if need be. I have decided to stay in Carthage.'

My heart leapt for joy.

'For ever?'

My father shook his head: 'I must not be tempted. My mission is to go to Italy. The Queen has always known it. We are Trojans, not Phoenicians. Asherat may not be our enemy, but she is not our goddess.'

'But you are half-Phoenician, father,' I cried, 'and we have been offered equal citizenship. Where else will we meet with such a welcome as the Queen has given us?'

My father sighed: 'I must not be tempted,' he repeated, 'but at least we can stay here until the spring. The Queen is clever. She has stirred up war between Iarbas and another of her suitors to gain a breathing-space. He cannot attack her for several months to come. By the time winter is over, he may see reason. Much can be done by then.'

I stared at him blankly.

'What advantage is there to Iarbas in attacking a well-defended Carthage? He may lose everything that he has gained. I have offered to take charge of all defence works; by the spring they will be greatly strengthened. The Queen is accumulating stocks of food and weapons. Soon I will start to train all citizens in the use of arms. If he attacks, he will meet with stout resistance.'

My father spoke with a fierce resolution that gladdened my heart. It was as if, without realizing it, he had made Dido's cause his own. He rose and embraced me.

'I must leave you, my son. The Queen will have finished giving audience to the merchants from Tarshish, and I must not keep her waiting.'

'Do you see her every day?' I asked, flushing despite myself.

My father nodded: 'We have much to discuss. Each day she

[143]

shows me a different part of the city.'

Perhaps he saw a flicker of resentment in my eyes, for he added reassuringly, 'As soon as Anna thinks you are well enough, you shall come with us.'

'Anna!' I repeated angrily. 'She is as strict as Caieta. Why should I obey her?'

My father's expression changed abruptly. 'You are her guest, Ascanius,' he said sternly, 'and I thank the gods that you have been in her charge. You owe your life to her. I could wish . . .' He hesitated. 'I could wish that she would come with us when we sail for Italy.'

I was stupefied.

'But she is a cripple.'

'She would make an excellent wife,' said my father slowly and deliberately. 'You remember your grandfather's last words? I shall never forget them. But you must say nothing of this to her or to the Queen.'

He went away leaving my mind in a turmoil. How well did my father know Anna? How often had he seen her during my illness? He had not said he loved her, but perhaps he would never love anyone as he had loved my mother. It had not been love but their common memories that had drawn him towards Andromache. If I had broken my promise to her, if I had told my father that she bore his child in her womb, would it have made any difference? The gods had never favoured their marriage and they had always known it. But in the case of Anna it was very different. My father knew that he was destined to marry a woman of foreign blood, and that the Phoenicians were somehow bound up with our destiny. He still thought of Italy as our eventual goal; but even if Anna loved him, would she ever leave her sister? My heart beat faster. It would be yet another reason for my father to stay in Carthage. Then I would be with Dido for ever; was not that what the gods intended?

I looked up suddenly. Anna had come into the room.

'When is the Queen coming?' I asked at once.

'I don't know, Ascanius. She has so much to do. You must be patient.' She went to the window and looked out, then drew across the sheets of talc. 'It is raining and the wind is rising. You had better stay here. Shall I tell you more about Dido?'

I shook my head. 'I would like to learn Punic. Will you teach it to me?'

Anna looked surprised and gratified. 'Of course. Dido will be pleased when I tell her.'

Why should she be pleased? I wondered. Did it mean that she really cared for me? Or did she only think of me as a beautiful boy, and the son of a hero?

I hesitated: 'Did you tell her that I loved her?'

Anna smiled: 'No, Ascanius. Your secret is safe with me. Is that why you want to learn Punic?'

I nodded: 'But there is another reason. I want to stay here. I hope my father will settle in Carthage and never go to Italy, whatever the oracles said. After all, he is half-Phoenician.'

'Your father is half-Phoenician?' repeated Anna in amazement. 'But he speaks no Punic; he knows nothing of our gods.'

'His mother was a priestess of Astarte. She died when he was born.'

'A priestess of Astarte? Where?'

'At Paphos in Cyprus.'

'Our mother came from Paphos,' said Anna. 'Oh, I am glad you have told me, Ascanius. It brings you and your father closer to us. How happy you have made me!'

Her eyes were shining and there was a flush of excitement on her cheeks.

It was the beginning of a deep unspoken friendship between us. Dear Anna. I never loved you as I loved Dido, but perhaps my debt of gratitude to you is no less great.

Until sundown Anna taught me Punic – the first of several lessons that she gave me. I was an eager learner. I had thought Punic a harsh unpleasing language until I heard Dido speak it with her incomparable grace of diction. But soon I was to master its complexities. Even on this first occasion I sensed its poetic beauty for Anna recited to me a hymn to Asherat.

'Reverence the queen of women, the greatest of all the gods:

she is clothed with majesty and power, and in her mouth is life. She is terrible in her anger. When she is present felicity is greatest. How glorious she looks, her veil drawn back from her face, her lovely form, her brilliant eyes.'

It was only after Anna had left me that my tranquillity abruptly vanished. I began to look forward to Dido's coming with an agonized impatience. The night outside was storm-tossed and moonless. The wind howled like a wild beast. Most of the room was in darkness for the oil lamp beside my bed gave off only a feeble glow. I was determined not to fall asleep. More than once I went into the corridor, hoping I would see Dido or perhaps Anna coming towards me. Everything was silent and dark. Suddenly I remembered my father had said there was to be another banquet to which many of our company had been invited. So that was it; all the Queen thought of was her banquets. I meant nothing to her. Perhaps Anna had been lying when she had said she would come at all.

I returned to my room angry and frantic with frustration, leaving the door open, bent on staying awake all night if necessary. I recited the furious reproaches I would have liked to hurl at Dido if I saw her pass my door. I had no idea where her bedchamber was or even Anna's. In any case I was too proud to look for either of them. They must not suppose I needed them; they were only women like Caieta and Andromache. And yet it was not true. How I wanted Dido; how I longed for her!

Suddenly I began to think of Asherat, clothed with majesty and power, and terrible in her anger. Had it not been she who had been the bitter enemy of Troy? We had fallen into her clutches; we were defenceless against her. I remembered her cruel mocking laughter in the dream when she had summoned me to her. It was she who had made me fall in love with Dido. Dido was a wicked temptress sent to torture me.

Outside the wind seemed to rise in a hoarse scream of anguish; and then, quite suddenly, I fell asleep.

I was back in Asherat's cave once more, but it had become

strangely smaller. A woman was coming towards me. It was Dido. Her arms were outstretched as if to welcome me, and I began to run towards her, calling her name. I had almost reached her when her whole aspect changed, and the cave became the palace corridor. It was the unknown goddess with the flaming eyes. It was Asherat herself who was trying to catch hold of me. I heard her hiss like an angry snake as she reached out her hand to grab me. Desperately I turned tail and ran. I fell. Now she was upon me; she was clutching at my throat with her powerful hands. Her nails were long and as sharp as talons. She was going to tear me in pieces. I gave a great scream and awoke. As I did so I felt a cool hand upon my forehead.

I looked up, half-conscious and still terrified, and saw Dido looking down on me holding a lamp in her other hand.

'It is all right, Ascanius,' she said soothingly. 'Your dream is over now.'

I tried to sit up. 'Where am I?'

'You are in your room at the palace.' She saw the sudden fear in my eyes. 'Don't be afraid. You are quite safe.'

I stared at her uncertainly, trying to collect my wits. What was she doing here? How did she know I had had a dream? She seemed to guess my thoughts.

'I heard you call out as I came along the corridor.'

The corridor. I shivered. Was this really Dido and not Asherat?

'Give me your hand,' I muttered.

She gave it to me. There was a golden chain upon her delicate wrist. Her ringed fingers were slender and white, the nails carefully trimmed. I looked at them in silence, then lifted her hand to my lips and kissed it. I heard her catch her breath. The next moment her arms were around me.

'Tell me your dream, my darling. Then you will be free of it and can go to sleep again.'

I hesitated: 'It was an evil dream. It must have been Asherat who sent it. I think she hates us.'

'Why should she hate you when it was she who brought you

here?' asked Dido gently. 'Is this not her city? Did I not welcome you here as friends?'

Reassured by her words, comforted by her presence, I told her my dream. She listened stroking my hair.

'It was some evil spirit that you saw,' she said at length. 'Often they come to torment us when we have been ill; but they cannot hurt us. Do not be afraid of Asherat, Ascanius. She is so good, so merciful.' She paused. 'I have a statue of her. Come, I will show you; then you will be frightened of her no longer.'

I got out of bed and thrust my feet into my sandals. She took off her voluminous cloak and wrapped it carefully around me.

'We must behave like conspirators and be very quiet,' she whispered. There was a glint of laughter in her eyes. Then she picked up her lamp, and we made our way stealthily out of the room and along the narrow corridor. My heart was thudding with excitement.

'Where are we going?' I whispered.

Dido did not answer. We passed through two archways and I saw an ornate door before us. It opened at the touch of her hand. She glided in and beckoned to me to follow. I found myself in a spacious dimly-lit chamber. The floor beneath my feet was soft with antelope skins. From the gilded beams of the ceiling hung a large silver lamp fashioned like a ship. Its faint rays cast a shadowy light upon tapestried walls and upon the white expanse of the bed that stood at the further end of the room. About it, resting upon four delicately-carved pillars of ebony, was draped a pale blue canopy embroidered with a crescent moon surrounded by golden stars. The air was warm and sweet with an exquisite scent. From beyond, through a distant archway, came the faint splash of water trickling into a marble basin.

I looked about me in awe, hardly able to believe Dido had brought me to her bedchamber. Gone were all my earlier resentment and my fear. All I could feel was a complete and absolute trust in her, and a deep consuming love. How could the goddess whom she worshipped have any terrors for me now?

She put out her hand and took mine.

'Come, Ascanius, I will show you her statue. But first we must take off our shoes out of respect for her.' Before I could do so myself, she had bent and unfastened my sandals as Caieta might have done. She loosened her fair hair so that it fell like a rivulet about her shoulders, and took off her rings. Then, having taken off her slippers, she led me by the hand to Asherat's shrine in the far corner of the room. The statue was decked with greenery and flowers, and before it burned a tiny lamp.

'Look, Ascanius,' whispered Dido, raising the lamp in her hand, 'do you see how beautiful she is?'

I saw before me the statue of a tall and beautiful woman. The veil upon her head descended on either side of her face to her waist. A row of delicate curls which had escaped from it followed the line of her forehead. She wore golden cone-shaped ear-rings such as I had seen Dido wear. Her robe, encircled at her waist by a narrow girdle, descended to her sandalled feet. Her left hand was raised palm outwards in a gesture of blessing; on her right arm, close to her breast, she bore a small child. Her lovely face shone with an expression of grave serenity, and from her whole being emanated an atmosphere of peace.

Could this be Asherat-of-the-Sea who had forced me to enter her cave on the night we had landed in Africa, and then mocked me with her cruel laughter? Could this be the implacable enemy of Troy?

'Like all the gods, Asherat has many aspects,' said Dido softly, 'but this is the one that she has always shown me and that I love the best.'

She began to intone a prayer to the goddess in a clear sweet voice. When she had finished, she turned to me:

'Now you can go back to your bed without fear of evil dreams,' she said. 'I have asked Asherat to protect you as if . . . as if you were my child.' Her voice trembled. 'Shall I tell you why I can never remarry, never have children, Ascanius?'

I was silent.

'Only Anna knows this. I swore to my beloved husband that I would never belong to any man but him. It would be a mortal sin to break my oath; but, oh, how lonely I am.'

Suddenly she began to weep.

It was more than I could bear. I found myself on my knees before her, kissing her hands, crying out over and over again, 'I love you', and begging her to let me stay. I can recall as if it were yesterday the softness and warmth of her hands under my lips, the delicacy of her fingers. I don't know what she said. I only remember her yielding to my persuasions and taking me to her bed. In the darkness she unfastened her dress, and cupping her breast in her hand held it to my lips. That night despite herself she let me become her lover.

My sweet love lay asleep beside me. How softly she breathed as the morning light slowly dawned upon her pillow and gleamed upon her fair hair. How smooth and calm and delicate her brow, how still her long lashes, how white her slender throat. How precious she was, but, oh, how fragile. She was mine now, but how could someone so young and ignorant as I protect her? Even with Anna as an ally, there was so little I could do. I must sacrifice everything for her. I must kill Iarbas in single combat. I must spur on my father to do all he could to serve her. I must become a Carthaginian and worship Asherat. I must sail the seas in search of precious things for her; I would bring her costly jewels to wear in her fair hair. She was my beloved, my queen and my goddess. She would never grow old; she would always be beautiful, gentle and gracious. How tenderly we would love each other until the last; for one night we would fall asleep in each other's arms and never awaken. But our spirits would be united for ever in the Islands of the Blest.

Alas, poor Dido, you were born under an unlucky star.

X

Thenceforth Dido gave no more banquets. Early each evening she and Anna would dine in the women's part of the palace. When she had dined she would go at once to her bedchamber where her maids would undress her. As soon as they had finished, she would dismiss them and bathe and anoint her body, sprinkling it with a sweet scent which she knew I loved. She would put on a white symar, loosen her fair hair, take off her jewels. Then, when all was quiet, she would steal along the corridor to fetch me.

What agony they were those hours of waiting after sundown. Dido had said that her maids must not know that I came to her bedchamber. I must wait until she fetched me, and even then I must not greet or kiss her until we reached her room. Although they were devoted to her, her maids could hardly fail to gossip, and soon the story would spread: her reputation would be tarnished, and her people would cease to love her: they might even cease to obey her, or to acknowledge her as queen. I knew that for her sake I must obey her implicitly, that somehow I must possess my soul in patience until the moment of ineffable joy when I could take her in my arms. Her supple body would yield effortlessly to mine as she sank back upon the bed. I would cover her with kisses, telling her how much I loved her, how much I had missed her, and she would put her arms around me whispering to me that I was her Adonis, her sweet one, her only joy. Sometimes we made love there and then; almost always we did so by lamplight so that I could see her matchless beauty. How white and graceful her body was, how delicate her flesh. Her breast was a sculptor's dream.

I had seen men and women making love so often during my childhood that to think of it as an art was at first quite strange to me. It had never occurred to me that it could call for subtlety and skill. At the outset I was as clumsy and impatient as a young bull. Gradually Dido began to teach me:

'Not so quickly, my darling. There is plenty of time. We have all night together. Love is a gift from Astarte. She is here with us in Carthage with her doves. Let us enjoy it to the utmost.'

She would take my hand in hers and show me how to caress her. As I did so, her lovely face would become transfigured, her white breast would heave in a soft sigh and her eyes would look into mine with infinite tenderness. Often she would stroke me so delicately that I could scarcely believe she was not the goddess of love. Sometimes she would guide me into her, murmuring sweet encouragements, and afterwards she would hold me close and tell me how happy I had made her. Beloved Dido, you told me so often of the joy I gave you; it was not until later I realized how seldom it can have been true.

Sometimes when we had reached her bedchamber, she would gently dissuade me from making love to her although if I insisted she always yielded.

'Don't you want me simply as a mother sometimes?' she would ask wistfully, 'just as you did when you looked at me at the banquet? I know I am not a real mother, but may I pretend to be one?'

There were times when I was so moved by her pathos and beauty that I surrendered at once to her maternal tenderness without asserting my virility. It was surely then that Dido was happiest, when I was transformed into her child.

When I think of the joy it gave her to cradle me in her arms and suckle me from her milkless breast, a feeling of awe descends upon me. I remember too her kisses, so full of love yet as fresh and sweet as dew. Never can any woman's love have been more tender than hers, more pure, more simple, more selfless and more poignant.

One night after an assembly of the people outside Asherat's temple, Dido was so tired when she came to fetch me that she could scarcely stand.

'I cannot love you tonight, Ascanius,' she whispered. 'Would you forgive me if I slept alone?'

She looked at me appealingly. I nodded sulkily. Seeing how disappointed I was, her face softened and she put out her hand.

'Come then,' she said, 'but you must let me sleep, my darling. I am so tired.'

Her head had scarcely touched the pillow before she was asleep in my arms. I lay still beside her, listening to her calm and regular breathing, gazing at her lovely face, scarcely daring to move for fear I should awaken her. In the middle of the night I felt her sweet arms about me, and heard her murmur sleepily that I was her Adonis, that she desired me. Wrapped in a golden mist of sleep we made love, and Astarte smiled upon us. As I glided into her, our bodies merged in an un-hurried rapturous ecstasy and we became one flesh. For those few brief moments nothing could sunder us for we had become immortal. My beloved was all women throughout all ages; the mystery and beauty of her body was the mystery and beauty of all Creation. She was the Gate of Life.

Only Anna knew our secret. It was Dido who told her after our first night together. Each morning, before the darkness had yielded to a twilit dawn, she came to rouse me and tell me I must go back to my room. It was hard to leave the warmth and comfort of my sweet love's breast, to free myself from the soft imprisonment of her arms. As I struggled to the surface from the depths of sleep, and hauled my inert body out of the bed, I would feel Anna watching me compassion-ately. Dido lay motionless, fast asleep. Anna would hold her lamp high for a moment so that the light fell for a brief instant on her face, and all day I could carry its image with me.

'Look at her but do not wake her,' she would whisper if I moved to kiss her. I would say a silent farewell to my darling, feeling each time that I was parting from her for an eternity. Sometimes when I had reached my room the gods were kind and sleep settled once more upon my eyelids. More often I lay awake thinking of Dido and waiting for the sunrise. The soft footsteps of her maids would pass along the corridor but I knew they would let her sleep until Anna bade them waken her. Perhaps she was still lying as I had left her; her fair hair was still spread out upon the whiteness of the pillow, her hand resting gracefully beside her head, the palm partly exposed, the fingers gently curving.

At first a desert of boredom lay before me. Each day the urge to go outside the palace grew stronger. I longed to visit my Trojan companions, to explore the city. It was Anna who warned me that if my father learnt that I had left the palace precincts he would conclude that I was well enough to return to the High Priest's house. Was that what I wanted?

'But I cannot stay here all day,' I protested. Anna looked at me thoughtfully.

'Malchus, the steward's son, is of about your age,' she said. 'You can see him every morning. Imilce will take you. But you must be here each time your father comes to see you. Otherwise he will grow suspicious.'

Not for the first time I realized how much I owed to Anna. She could so easily have been jealous of me because I was Dido's lover. Instead she was doing all she could to help me. What had I done to deserve such friendship?

I began to thank her but she quietly cut me short.

'I am helping you for Dido's sake, Ascanius. I think she needs you. I hope that I am right.'

Suddenly she burst out with passionate vehemence:

'I want her to forget her husband, to forget her vow to him. It is that which has been poisoning her life. She has been starved of love and tenderness. Now you are here to give them to her. She is so beautiful, so generous; she needs them so much.'

'She has had you to love her,' I said, wishing to give Anna her due.

[154]

'Me?' said Anna contemptuously. 'What do I matter? I am only her sister. Do you think I can make Dido happy?'

'Does no one else love her as we do, Anna?'

She shook her head: 'No one. All the palace servants think of her only as the Queen. How much do any of her suitors care for her? All they want is her wealth and her body. The Senators will be loyal to her for as long as it suits them. The people worship her as if she were a goddess. But no one seems to realize that she is a human being – not even your father.'

'But he is doing all he can to help her,' I cried.

'Because he is grateful to her for her hospitality and to me for having nursed you through your fever,' said Anna simply. 'Those are the only reasons.'

I remembered how my father had invariably referred to Dido as 'the Queen' in all our conversations. It was obvious that since the banquet their relations had become far more formal, that although he admired her courage and sympathized with her difficulties he thought of her always as a queen and a ruler. All his interest was centred on Anna. Three times he had asked me to describe her escape from her brother's palace; each time he had shaken his head pityingly at the thought of her broken leg.

'Does Dido know my father is half-Phoenician?' I asked suddenly.

Anna flushed.

'No, I didn't tell her.' She hesitated. 'It is enough that she admires him as she admires all heroes. But it is you whom she loves, Ascanius. She will always love you now, whatever happens. That has always been her way.'

I was silent, remembering how fondly Dido had kissed me when I had asked her whether she would marry me.

'I am afraid that you are still too young, my darling,' she had said. 'Let us be happy together while we can and not think about the future.'

But surely, I thought suddenly, her attitude would change when I had killed Iarbas and become a hero myself? By then I would speak Punic fluently. I was already tall and strong for my age. Each day that passed was a step closer to manhood. The thought of Dido bearing my child in her womb, of her radiant happiness in her motherhood, seemed inexpressibly wonderful. I looked at Anna. 'Can Malchus wrestle?'

She appeared startled:

'I don't know, Ascanius. Why?'

'I need someone to fight with every day. My muscles have become flabby.'

Anna hesitated:

'We will see tomorrow.'

'Why not today?' I asked angrily. 'I am not a weakling. I need exercise.'

Characteristically she did not question me further.

'Very well,' she said at length. 'But you must be sensible, Ascanius, and not over-exert yourself. If you fall ill again I shall refuse to look after you.'

I laughed, knowing it was an empty threat, and saw Anna smile at me for the first time with undisguised affection.

'How like your father you are when you laugh,' she said.

Each morning thereafter, Imilce conducted me past the guard to the central courtyard of the palace where Malchus would be waiting for me. To the rear of the palace, surrounded by store rooms, was an open sandy space sheltered from the wind. In the centre grew a palm tree. There we would exercise ourselves and wrestle with each other. Malchus was two years older than I, but I soon found that I was the stronger. Still he was not an unworthy opponent. He taught me several tricks, and sometimes he used to throw me. An amicable rivalry grew up between us. He spoke little Greek, and patiently corrected my floundering Punic; before long I was speaking it with comparative fluency and could broach the subject which most interested me. What sort of warriors were the Numidians: what weapons did they use? They were the best horsemen in the world, Malchus told me. They rode bareback without any bridle, guiding their horses by a switch which they laid between the ears. Their horses were small but sure-footed and highly mobile. The Numidians were too primitive to have chariots or armour, nor did they fight on foot as we did. They carried small round shields made of elephant hide. Their chiefs might wear sabres acquired from the Carthaginians, and all of them carried long knives for fighting at close quarters, but their favourite weapon was a light javelin. They would gallop full tilt at the enemy, discharge a shower of darts at him with deadly accuracy, and then swerve out of range, returning next time from a different direction. They were a fierce, proud and vindictive people, he added thoughtfully. I asked Malchus if he could procure some Numidian javelins for me. He nodded.

'Of course. We use them for hunting, just as they do.'

'Do you mean you hunt on horseback?' I asked in surprise, for the idea was strange to me.

He smiled pityingly.

'The Queen has fifty horses, Ascanius. She always hunts on horseback. Didn't you know?'

I shook my head, ashamed of my ignorance.

'Each time she takes me and my father with her,' he added proudly.

A wave of jealousy shot through me. Why had Dido never told me this? Did she think I could not ride, that I knew nothing of hunting? I felt Malchus was looking at me scornfully. I seized him by the waist and threw him to the ground. He caught me by the leg and I fell on top of him. We rolled over and over in the dust, fighting with real fury until at last I got my knees upon his arms and pinioned him. We were gasping for breath. My anger seeped away, for I knew he had somehow understood it, that we were closer friends than ever. We rose to our feet panting, and grinned at each other.

'I will fetch some javelins and a shield as a target,' said Malchus. 'You may be the better wrestler, but when it comes to the javelin you haven't a chance of winning.'

We attached a round shield to the palm tree, and for the next few days he trained me mercilessly. I threw one javelin after another, using either hand, first motionless then running. Each day I had to throw them from a greater distance or from a different angle. Each time my javelin missed the shield, or failed to penetrate it, he was openly contemptuous.

'Your hold is still wrong and there is not enough force behind your throw,' he would say derisively. 'These javelins are shorter and lighter than ordinary spears. You must use both shoulder and wrist. Look.' He would adjust his grip, raise the bronze shaft, and give a powerful flick to his arm with his whole body behind it. The javelin would shoot through the air and bury itself quivering in the centre of the target.

Each day I felt my skill increasing and my muscles growing stronger. Fortunately my father was becoming more and more occupied with the city's defences, and Anna was able to dissuade him from visiting me except for a few brief moments. What excuses she made I do not know, but at least they satisfied him that I was still not well enough to return to the High Priest's house, and he never learnt of my wrestling bouts with Malchus. Dido knew of them for she was quick to notice my bruises. I remember lying in her arms and boasting of my exploits. I made her feel my muscles and reminded her I was almost as tall as she was. Not one of the Trojan boys had been able to throw me in wrestling, and I was the fastest runner of them all. I had scaled innumerable cliffs. I was skilled in archery and navigation, and now I was learning to handle a Numidian javelin. As soon as I had mastered it, and learnt to ride a horse as the Numidians did, I would issue a challenge to Iarbas. Possibly he was the stronger, but I would be more agile and the gods would help me. I would certainly kill him. By the time I had finished describing my victory over Iarbas, the cheers of all Carthage seemed to be ringing in my ears while Dido herself was setting a crown of laurel on my head.

'And then,' I concluded triumphantly, 'I will ask you to marry me. I won't be too young for you any longer and you will love me all the more because I will be a hero; and we will be happy, and Asherat will give us children.'

'I could not love you more than I do now, my darling,'

whispered Dido, pressing me close to her. Suddenly I saw that tears were trickling down her cheeks.

'Dido, what is the matter?' I asked in astonishment, raising my head to look at her.

'I can't tell you, Ascanius,' she said unsteadily. 'You won't understand.'

I kissed her. 'Don't you believe that I will kill Iarbas?'

She shook her head. 'It is not that.'

'Does Anna know?'

'No one knows except . . . except my dead husband. Oh, I wish I were dead too.'

She began to weep passionately, her body racked by sobs. Dismayed, I took her in my arms and tried to comfort her. She clung to me tightly, as if for protection. I prayed to Astarte to help me drive her dead husband for ever from her memory and to cure her sorrow with love. Gradually her tears ceased. She sat up and began to dry her eyes on a fold of her symar.

'I am afraid I have not given you much happiness tonight, my darling,' she said with a rueful smile. 'Shall I hold you close to my breast? Or would you like to make love to me?'

Now I can see that her only thought was to reassure me after my evident dismay by trying to please me. Then I was too young.

'I want to make love,' I said, my desire already astir.

With a single graceful movement she took off her symar and lay down beside me, naked. I began to caress her and to cover her whole body with kisses. She lay still, smiling at me tenderly, gently complying with my every wish, yet strangely unresponsive.

When I had finished, she kissed me and asked if I was happy. I fell asleep at once, my head upon her breast. During the night I felt her moving restlessly.

'Why are you awake?' I murmured drowsily. 'Are you still unhappy?'

She pressed me against her breast. 'Don't worry about me, Ascanius. I have never slept well since my husband died. That is why I never get up till after sunrise. Go to sleep now.'

I remembered that there was something I had forgotten to say to her.

'I will need a horse, Dido, to fight Iarbas.'

'You shall have one, my darling. We will talk about it tomorrow.'

'And I want to go hunting with you.'

'I promise to take you with me.'

'I want to look after you, Dido, to be with you always. That is why I must marry you. I will tell my father that we are going to marry, then he will stay here too.'

'Don't tell him yet,' said Dido gently, 'there is no hurry. He has said he will stay until spring.'

She began to stroke my forehead with her fingertips.

'Go to sleep, my darling, otherwise you will be tired tomorrow. Close your eyes and don't worry about the future. All that matters is that we love each other. You are safe in your mother's arms now, and no one can separate us.'

The next day I spent several hours practising with the javelin. For the first time Malchus expressed reluctant approval.

'You are certainly improving, Ascanius,' he said grudgingly. 'It is time for you to start practising on horseback. Are you a good horseman?'

I described the part I had played in the tournament at my grandfather's funeral games. As I expected, he was not impressed, for the notion of games was entirely alien to him.

'But they were all boys, and there was no fighting. No, Ascanius, you will have to exercise yourself more seriously than that if you want to become a real horseman. In the meantime, the more you hunt the better.'

We had finished washing and rubbing oil on our bodies, and it was time for me to return to my room in case my father came. I walked back to the main courtyard, reflecting gloomily that if Malchus was right it would be months before I was good enough to challenge Iarbas. Nor had I ever ridden without a bridle. For the first time I realized my temerity. I was not afraid of being killed, for a hero's death is always glorious and I would be dying for Dido's sake, but I was alarmed at the prospect of being made to look a fool. Iarbas might unhorse me at the very outset, and disdain to fight me thereafter. I would become the laughing stock of Carthage. How could Dido marry me then, however much she loved me? She would try to console me, for her tenderness was infinite, but how would I survive the shame of it? And what would my father think of me?

For the rest of the day I chafed furiously at my enforced inaction, angrily contradicting Anna while she tried to teach me Punic. How long must I wait before I could go outside the palace, before Dido gave me a horse, before I could go hunting? All these shifts and manoeuvres to conceal our relationship had become intolerable and shaming. What a sickly milksop all the Trojans must think me, cooped up for all this time in the palace, surrounded and cosseted by women. I would endure it no longer. Tomorrow before dawn I would steal out of the palace and not return till nightfall. There was a private and unguarded way of which Malchus had told me, which led from the store rooms to the stables. I would take one of Dido's horses and gallop wildly over the hills and through the forests. What a panic there would be when they found that I was missing! Search parties would be sent out to scour the countryside, but I would evade them. They would report that they had found no trace of me. I imagined my father's face, tense with anxiety, Anna wringing her hands, Dido weeping: then suddenly at the thought of her all my anger vanished. How could I give my sweet love a moment's unhappiness? Had she not clung to me for protection on the previous night when I had tried to kiss away her tears? Already dusk had fallen. Soon she would come silently along the dark corridor to fetch me. My door would be slightly open so that she could see the gleam of lamplight coming from within. I would be ready waiting for her, breathless with impatience. For a brief instant she would appear before me in the doorway like a lovely vision. At once I would blow out my lamp. Neither of us would speak as in the darkness she opened her cloak and took me to her. For a moment of rapture I would feel her slender waist within my arms once more, and smell the exquisite fragrance of her body. Then she would clasp my hand in hers and lead me to the blissful haven of her bed.

That night when Dido took me in her arms I was aware of a mysterious change in her. She was as loving as she had ever been but her thoughts seemed far away. Her abstraction made me uneasy. I became all the more anxious to possess her body so that her mind should not escape me. Almost at once I began to make love to her. Sensing my disquiet, she tried to reassure me by pouring sweet kisses on me. Soon she was responding to my caresses and I knew I had made her desire me. I was consumed with love for her, and prayed to Astarte that her desire should never leave her. And then, in one horrifying instant, I realized I was failing her.

For a moment I could not believe it. We ceased moving and lay motionless. I could not look at Dido. It was as if I had betrayed her. I moved brusquely away, turned my back upon her and covered my face with my hands.

At once she blew out the lamp beside the bed and, in the darkness, gathered me into her arms. I began to weep like a child for shame and mortification.

'It doesn't matter, my darling,' she whispered, uncovering her breast. 'That is not how I love you. I have always known it.'

'But you let me make love to you,' I persisted.

She sighed and pressed me closer to her. 'You are so young, so beautiful; that you should love me seemed incredible. You brought such joy into my heart. How could I refuse you anything? – you, whom Asherat had sent to me in pity for my loneliness. I told myself that I was still faithful to my husband's memory, that it was no sin to give you what you wanted. But all the time I knew it was not true.' Her voice shook: 'I have betrayed my beloved husband, and I will be punished for it.'

By now I had recovered from my humiliation.

'Wouldn't your husband have wanted you to be happy?'

'You don't understand, Ascanius. My husband is always with me. When my father gave me to him in marriage we were united for ever. I swore eternal fidelity to him. My body belongs to him alone. It is not mine to give.'

'But he is dead, Dido,' I cried.

She began to tremble with emotion.

'Yes, his body is dead, but his poor ghost haunts my dreams. Each time I see his spectre floating in the air. His face is upturned towards me, bloodless and pale as clay. Each time he points to the cruel wounds my brother gave him. Each time I remember how shamefully he was left unburied, and know that his lonely spirit can find no resting-place. Each time he reminds me piteously of our married happiness and tells me I am his. All these years I have been faithful to him, Ascanius. No man but he has ever known me. Daily I go to my bower alone and put fresh flowers before his shrine. Each day as I stand there renewing my marriage vow, I kiss his image and greet him as his bride. Each time my heart is full of love for him, and for a brief moment he is alive again. Oh, why did the gods allow him to be so cruelly snatched from me and rob me of my happiness? But how can I be eternally faithful to him, however much I love him? What will happen to Carthage if I never remarry?'

There was an agonized despair in her voice which I had never heard before. The terrible words of Helenus came back to me. Could it be true, as he had said, that the gods were angered by those who loved too passionately? Had they meant to punish Dido as they had punished Andromache, by snatching her husband from her?

But why should she be punished now? How could it be Asherat's will that Dido should not remarry? She was the goddess of marriage and the patroness of Carthage. I thought of Andromache once more. She had not been condemned to perpetual widowhood; she had taken my father as a lover in order to have a child. 'Hector would understand,' she had said when I reproached her. Why then should Dido's dead husband torture her with reminders of her duty to him? Was not her first duty to Carthage and her people?

I took my darling in my arms and did my best to console her. Her love for me had been no sin, I said, and told her Andromache's story. She listened compassionately. Then I told her of Andromache and my father. For a moment she was too surprised to speak.

'And so she loved you just as I do,' she said at length. 'But you never asked her to marry you, did you, Ascanius?'

I could sense her smiling at me in the darkness, and knew that at last I had cheered her. She paused, and then added hesitantly, 'Did your father love Andromache?'

I shook my head: 'I do not think so. He never speaks of her.'

'And she let him be her lover although she did not love him? I could never do that. For me love is something sacred.'

She was silent for a moment. Then she put her arms around me.

'You have made me happier, my darling. I will think about what you have told me. And now there is something I must tell you.'

Gently she told me her monthly courses were approaching. For a week she would be expected to go into seclusion. If she failed to do so, bad luck would fall upon us and all her people.

'Then for all that time I will not see you?' I asked in dismay.

'No, Ascanius,' she said sadly, 'I am afraid it will be impossible.' She paused. 'You must leave the palace tomorrow.'

'You mean I must go back to the High Priest's house? But then we can never be together again.'

'I will find some reason for bringing you back,' answered Dido soothingly. 'Malchus is your friend now, isn't he? Beyond my apartments, outside the women's quarter, there is another room where you could sleep.'

I was silent, feeling as if the ground had suddenly given way beneath my feet, filled with foreboding that I was losing her.

'I will miss you too,' she said softly, guessing my thoughts. 'How empty my bed will be without you. But let us not be miserable. Tomorrow you must go to my stables. I have asked my Numidian groom to choose a horse for you and he will teach you to ride and fight like the Numidians do. He has no love for Iarbas,' she added smiling, 'so he should be a good riding-master.'

I brightened at the thought, and asked when we could go hunting. She told me that she had already given orders for a hunt to be organized in my honour, to which my father and all the Trojan chieftains would be invited.

'And Malchus will be invited too,' she added. 'If the gods grant us fair weather we will spend a carefree day together, and leave our worries behind us.' She sighed. 'How happy I will be to forget about affairs of state for once. Even in seclusion I cannot escape them.'

For the first time I realized that not once had she spoken of them to me. Even my father's name had been scarcely mentioned. Of all her work as a ruler I was totally ignorant. I knew nothing of the daily problems that awaited her, the decisions she had to take, the measures she had to initiate, supervise or sanction for the welfare of her city. She was the heart and soul of Carthage; upon her courage, skill and wisdom everything depended. Nothing of importance could be done without her: the erection of walls and buildings, the excavation of harbours, the wages paid to workmen, the trading expeditions, the negotiations with neighbouring princes or merchants from other settlements; all these and many other matters absorbed her time and energy day after day. And she, this marvellously brave and beautiful woman, had lavished unstintingly upon me, a boy of twelve, all her sweet solicitude and tender love. I saw at last all she had done for me, and I was so moved by the thought of it that I could not speak.

I felt her looking at me questioningly in the darkness.

'What is it, Ascanius?' she asked at length. 'Poor boy, are you so unhappy?'

I did not answer.

'There there, my darling, it won't be for long,' she said, misinterpreting my silence, 'and look, I have a present for you.'

She lit the lamp beside the bed once more, and took from the table a massive gold cup.

'It is the cup I drank from at the banquet, Ascanius – do you remember? I would like you to have it in token of my love.'

I have it still, that sacred relic of her. No one but I shall ever touch it; and when I die it shall go to the grave with me.

XI

I need not describe the aching sense of loss which I felt during the days that followed. It was not until I returned to the High Priest's house that I realized how totally I belonged to Dido. Never before had I experienced such longing, or been conscious of such a void within me. She had taken possession of my heart to the exclusion of all others; no one but she and Anna counted for anything any more.

At the High Priest's house I shared a room with my father. Each night while he slept I would lie awake thinking of Dido, and soon her lovely image would appear to me. Sometimes she came in her white symar and took me in her arms; sometimes I saw her lying naked upon her bed. I would feel once more the magic of her touch, and the sweetness of her kisses. The whole room would become filled with her presence, and scented with the fragrance of her body. How could my father not know that she was there? Often I would imagine that she lay close beside me, that I had only to raise my hand to uncover her fair breast. Perhaps it was the vision of her breast that haunted me the most. I would remember how my head had lain there and I had heard her sweet heart beating. Her breast was the shrine that contained her innermost being. Within that precious shrine dwelt all her love for me.

I had thought that at least I would be glad to see my fellow-Trojans again. Instead I found myself avoiding them. They had become strangers, all of them. They saw Dido and her city with an alien's eyes. None of them could speak Punic; none of them felt any devotion to Asherat. They had begun to take Dido's hospitality for granted and to criticize her people, comparing them unfavourably with the simple Elymians. In all this criticism there was a note of envy. The Carthaginians were too clever and had been too successful. No one could deny their industry and resourcefulness, their skill as mariners; but they were too knowledgeable and too sophisticated, too shrewd in their commercial undertakings, too unwarlike, too deeply absorbed in trade. No one could deny that the city was admirably governed: each craft had its fraternity to protect its interests; even the lowliest workmen had their elected representatives with a right of access to the Queen. All classes, even the slaves, were united by a sense of civic patriotism. They were proud of Carthage and devoted to their sovereign. But they had none of her breadth of vision or compassion for others. They could not understand why she had welcomed us so freely, and were apt to feel jealous of us. They had a grudging respect for my father because of his rank and reputation but his followers meant nothing to them. We were foreigners; we could not speak their language, we knew nothing of their traditions; we were homeless wanderers living on the Queen's charity, and there were more than two hundred of us.

I still knew virtually nothing of Carthage and its people but already I had begun to identify myself with them. The slightest complaint by the Trojans aroused my instinctive resentment, although I had generally the sense to hold my tongue. But what enraged me far more was the good-natured chaffing of Ilioneus and other chieftains about Dido's affection for me. They never referred to her disrespectfully, but they made me feel ill at ease. More than once they tried to question me about her and Anna. I said coldly that I had scarcely seen either of them during my illness, and took refuge in a haughty silence. My comrades were nonplussed by my indifference to them. As for Caieta, I avoided seeing her. Even my father seemed almost a stranger. My admiration for him had become tinged with jealousy. He was all that I wished to be and could not be. He was doing so much for Dido that I could never do. And yet he was quick enough to criticize her – to me if not to others.

Each morning he set off on a tour of the city's defences

with one of Dido's counsellors to supervise the works which he had initiated. He was full of praise for all she had done to develop the port of Carthage, but complained bitterly about the insufficiency of the fortifications. There were still gaps in the wall in several places; elsewhere no battlements had been erected; two of the watchtowers had been badly sited; such ramparts as there were were far from adequate; weapons of all kinds were in dangerously short supply; as for the citadel, its foundations had scarcely been laid.

'How like a woman,' he said ruefully on one occasion, 'to think that her palace is more important than her city's defences. If Iarbas were to attack now he could seize Carthage in an hour.'

'How could she know about fortifications?' I asked indignantly. 'There has been no one to advise her, and she has had so much else to do.'

My father seemed surprised by my reaction.

'The Queen has done marvels,' he said quietly, 'but her way of life is too luxurious. That is her weakness. No wonder Iarbas is afire to marry her. With all her wealth she is a temptation to any man. It is unwise of her to flaunt it when she is so ill-protected against greedy neighbours. Surely she must realize it.'

Suddenly he looked at me: 'That magnificent goblet which I saw amongst your belongings, Ascanius – what made her give it to you? I know she is fond of you, but you are only a boy still.'

I had tried to hide the goblet from him, and was taken unawares. 'She gave it to me when I left the palace,' I said flushing. 'I suppose it was because I am your son and had been her guest. You know how generous she is. Everyone says so.'

To my relief my answer appeared to satisfy him. 'She is very generous,' he agreed, 'generous to a fault.' He was silent for a moment, then added unexpectedly: 'Poor woman. She needs all her courage. Her life cannot be easy.'

True to his new policy of trying to treat me as an adult and to train me as his successor, my father pressed me to accompany him on his daily tours of inspection. He knew that Anna had begun to teach me Punic whilst I had been at the palace, and had given his cautious approval. He would not learn it himself, and I must tell no one that he was half-Phoenician; but that I should learn to speak it was a different matter. All the chief Carthaginians could speak Greek, but I still might be useful to him as an interpreter; besides there was much that I could learn about fortifications. Perhaps he thought of me also as a potential spy.

Much to his surprise I refused to go with him. Soon there was to be a hunt, I explained awkwardly: the Queen had given me a horse, and I must ride it as much as possible. My father laughed good-humouredly. He was himself an excellent horseman and knew that I lacked experience. He had heard that a hunt was being organized and was no less anxious than I that I should acquit myself creditably. He asked no further questions but left me to my own devices. On most days I did not see him again till sundown. I was relieved. I had had enough of parrying questions about my stay in the palace, of concealing my love for Dido by pretending that I had seldom seen her. How could my father talk about her so cold-bloodedly? Didn't he realize how beautiful she was? Yes, I was her child, I knew it now, for outside the compass of her arms there was only solitude. The one consolation was to ride the horse she had given me, to train myself secretly to be her champion. Only she knew my secret. I had said nothing of it even to Anna.

Each morning I went early to the palace stables where Soubas, the Numidian groom, would be waiting for me – a tawny-skinned little man with bandy legs, and eyes that could flash like rapiers. He was proud, taciturn and suspicious; but he hated Iarbas, and Dido had won his devotion by her tact and kindness. I soon realized that I could have asked for no better riding-master. Every day we went to a field not far from the palace, and there he trained me to ride as the Numidians do. Nothing escaped his vigilance. I always rode bareback, and mostly without a bridle – first on a docile mare, then on the lively bay colt which Dido had given me. I called him Aristo.

But it was the art of communication with my mount that I learnt above all from Soubas. The influence of the spoken word and tone of voice, the varieties of pressure from leg or heel, the subtle use of the switch: no other people has such an intuitive mastery of these aids as the Numidians. After a few days of ignominious failure, I found that Aristo was responding willingly to my promptings. He was spirited but obedient. Soon we were clearing obstacles without parting company.

How Dido will admire my horsemanship, I thought to myself, one evening after several hours of strenuous exercise. Perhaps even Malchus would be secretly impressed. The hunt was due to take place in three days' time and I plied Soubas with eager questions. He showed me the black charger my father would be riding, and Dido's elegant white horse. I patted and stroked him as always, imagining how beautiful she would look when seated upon his back – so beautiful that I would want to fall upon my knees and worship her. She would be gracious to everyone, but it would be upon me that her eyes would rest the longest. All day long I would not leave her side. Miraculously we would become separated from the others. Perhaps she would feel tired and I would help her to dismount. For an exquisite moment I would hold her precious weight in my arms, and then her sweet mouth would be upon mine and she would kiss me with a rapturous tenderness.

I could think of nothing but Dido, and bidding farewell to Soubas, began to make my way past the palace store rooms towards the High Priest's house. The sun was sinking beyond the distant hills like a ship in flames. As I approached the covered walk which led to the main courtyard of the palace, I saw Imilce coming towards me. I guessed that Anna had sent her to look for me, and my heart leapt for joy. I had not been able to see Anna since I had left the palace; perhaps she had a message from Dido for me at last.

I ran to Imilce and greeted her. Yes, she said, her mistress wished to see me. She led me not to the women's quarter but to a small room beside the banqueting hall. I waited there in the twilight with mounting impatience. At last the door opened and Anna appeared alone, carrying a lamp. She set it down upon a table without speaking, then closed the door and turned to me.

I embraced her impulsively. 'When can I see Dido?'

She looked at me gravely. 'I don't know, Ascanius. I am worried about her.'

I felt a thrill of fear. 'Is she ill?'

Anna shook her head. 'No, she is not ill and she is not in seclusion. But she refuses to see anyone. I have never known her like this before. It is as if she had suddenly abdicated.' She paused: 'I have had to give orders for the hunt to be cancelled.'

She saw the consternation upon my face and added gently: 'I am sorry, Ascanius, but Dido is not herself at present. She scarcely leaves her apartment. We must pray to the gods for her. She is very unhappy.'

'Unhappy?' I repeated, unable to control the tremor in my voice. 'Why is she unhappy?'

'It is not easy to explain, Ascanius.' She hesitated. 'Yes, why shouldn't I tell you? It concerns you, and you love her. Last night I could not sleep for worrying about her. All day she had stayed in her apartment and refused to admit anyone. For two days I had not seen her. Suddenly, as I lay awake, I heard her footsteps coming towards my room. At first I thought that she was coming to see me as she sometimes used to do when she felt lonely; but instead of stopping she went past my door. Cautiously I followed her, wondering where she was going. To my surprise she went along the private passage that leads to the banqueting hall. Neither of us carried a lamp, but at last she reached the door and pushed it open. There was the whole banqueting hall before us, empty, silent and drenched in moonlight. I stood back in the shadow of the passage watching her. She went up to her couch and lay down. For a moment she lay motionless, then suddenly she began to speak, and I realized she was talking to you – to you and to your father. Was she dreaming about the banquet or was she

'May I come with you?' I asked quickly. She shook her head: 'No, Ascanius. We must go alone. Our prayers will be secret, and no one must guess their purpose. You must say nothing to anyone of what I have told you. Pray and be patient; and remember, whatever happens, Dido will always love you.'

She kissed me, picked up her lamp and was gone.

That evening I noticed that my father's face seemed sad and drawn. As if by common consent we scarcely spoke to each other. During the night while I lay thinking of Dido I heard him muttering in his sleep.

For ten more days Dido did not appear in public. The postponement of the royal hunt attracted little comment; but when an assembly of the people over which she was to have presided was belatedly cancelled without explanation, a feeling of disquiet spread all over the city. Such a thing had never happened before. Everyone knew that the Queen's health was delicate, but everyone knew also how devoted she was to her people. On previous occasions, if she had been prevented from attending a meeting or public ceremony, a reason had always been forthcoming. This time no reason had been given. Nor had the Queen resumed her customary audiences. Even the Senators and her advisers were still unable to see her. Everywhere there were vague and confused rumours as to what was the matter. It was said that she was troubled by evil dreams and sleepless nights, that she would eat nothing, that she spent hours alone in her bower, that at night she roamed about the palace like an unquiet ghost. Presently the news spread that early one morning she had been seen going to Asherat's temple with only her sister for company. Soon it became known that they went there daily to ask for some favour from the goddess. What was it, this favour that they were seeking so earnestly? No one knew, not even the High Priest. Some guessed that they were imploring Asherat's protection against Iarbas. Others believed that the ghost of the Queen's dead husband was haunting her: perhaps he was calling upon her to avenge his murder. Everyone knew of her devotion to his memory, but that her brother's atrocious crime had gone unpunished.

Whatever the motive for these repeated secret visits to the temple, there could be no doubt as to its importance: otherwise why did the Queen herself take part in the elaborate sacrificial ceremonies? It was she herself, and not the priest, according to rumour, who poured the wine from the sacred dish between the horns of the white heifers that were daily sacrificed to Asherat. It was she herself who each time performed the prescribed rites and ceremonies before the altar beneath the goddess's statue. Why should she do this day after day? Was it not because she was desperately anxious for Asherat to grant her some personal favour?

The echoes of these rumours soon reached me. The High Priest himself said nothing; but at his house and at the palace I often heard the servants gossiping, and suffered torments. I prayed to Asherat; I prayed to Astarte my protectress. It made no difference. One day succeeded another without fresh news from Anna or a message from Dido; and all the time the cloud of rumour grew thicker.

My father complained that work upon the walls was grinding to a halt as a result of the Queen's continued absence. The workmen had lost heart and were slow to obey his orders. At some sites they had ceased work altogether. Scaffolding was left half-erected, the noise of hammering ceased, and great cranes towering into the sky hung motionless and silent.

By this time I was growing desperate. My father had already tried to see Anna to warn her as to what was happening. I decided to intercept her and Dido outside the temple but missed them in the darkness. I began to ask Soubas each morning whether he had been told when the hunt would take place. He always shook his head. For the remainder of the day I tried to banish thoughts of Dido from my mind by practising the use of the javelin on horseback. Aristo was obedient enough. It was my aim that was at fault. Each time my impatience made me over-hasty. Gloomily I realized that I was making little progress; and then at last, to my incredulous joy, I had a message from her. The next morning one of her maids was waiting for me as I entered the main hall of the palace. The Queen and her sister wished to see me: if I would follow her she would take me to them.

The Queen and her sister: then Dido must be well again at last. But why did both of them wish to speak to me? I remembered that I had never seen them together before, and suddenly felt uneasy. That they should both want to see me seemed a bad omen. What would they have to say to me – the Queen and her sister? The words sounded cold and formal now. Was it the Queen of Carthage whom I would see, or was it Dido? Would she let me kiss her? Would I even dare to kiss her? It was so long since I had been her lover. But now – now, I had suddenly become a frightened boy once more, as bashful and as awkward as when I had first met her. It had always been at night that we had seen each other. We had lain together by lamplight or in the sweet mystery of darkness. She had loved me then. But now, in the cold hard light of morning, we would seem strangers to each other. She would see me as I really was – a half-grown youth, ungainly and coltish, a poor facsimile of my heroic father; and she would know then that it had all been a dream; that she, the Queen of Carthage, loved me no longer.

The maid took me up the great staircase to a large room adjoining the women's quarter where Dido used to receive her counsellors. She was standing by the open window and turned as I entered. Her face was pale, there were faint blue lines beneath her lovely eyes and her skin seemed almost transparent; beneath her dress I could see the slenderness of her body. How unbearably fragile she was, and how infinitely precious.

I could not speak for love of her. I forgot about Anna, I forgot about my fears. I threw myself at Dido's feet and began to kiss her beloved hands with passionate devotion, telling her that I could not live without her. She pressed my head against her thighs without speaking. Presently I felt her fingers in my hair.

'Poor Ascanius,' she said softly, 'do you love me so much?'

I looked up at her: 'I would die for you.'

She shuddered: 'No, my darling. That you must never do. The gods have other plans for you. One day you will be a great man. Your father is sure of it. Anna and I are sure of it too. But look, you have not greeted her, and she has been like a sister to you. How can I kiss you till you have done so?'

I rose to my feet and embraced Anna shyly. Then Dido gave me an exquisite smile and took me in her arms, and I forgot everything but her once more.

'When can I come back to the palace?' I asked at length.

Dido hesitated.

'Tomorrow, Ascanius, if your father agrees,' said Anna quickly. 'Dido will ask him during the hunt. He can hardly refuse her then.'

I could scarcely believe my ears.

'Then the hunt will be tomorrow?' I asked Dido.

'Yes, my darling. Asherat has spoken to us at last. If the hunt is held tomorrow your father will stay in Carthage as she means him to do. Of course I shall obey her whatever the people say.'

'But why? . . .' I began.

'Why will the people grumble? Because they will think that I am neglecting my duties if I go hunting. Oh, I know very well what they have been saying about me. I know too that some of them do not like the Trojans. But they are like children, Ascanius: they do not understand. All this will change if your father stays in Carthage. Our two peoples will merge with each other. Your father will inspire us by his heroism to defeat Iarbas: and Carthage will go from strength to strength until she is all-powerful, invincible, the greatest and most prosperous city in all the world. All this Asherat in her goodness has revealed to me. How she will bring it to pass she has not told me. My duty is to obey her, not to question her. Perhaps you will have your part to play in making my city great and powerful. Who knows?'

[178]

Her face was alight with an almost mystical excitement. For a moment she was more than a beautiful woman; she was an inspired prophetess gazing into the future. I was conscious for the first time of her strength of will, of her heroic stature, of the power and passion of her personality. Then the light faded from her eyes.

'Now you must go, Ascanius,' she said gently; 'I have been ill for too long and have much to attend to. Anna and I wanted you to know that all is well once more. Do not fear. I will see you tomorrow. Your father will stay in Carthage. Asherat herself has promised it.' She put her arms round my neck and looked into my eyes; 'And then, my darling, you will be happy, won't you? A part of me will always be yours, always, always.'

She kissed me with a curiously grave solemnity upon the forehead. Then suddenly she put her lips to mine and kissed me with a passionate possessiveness that she had never shown before.

'Goodbye, my darling,' she said softly, 'you are very precious to me. May the gods protect you.'

XII

I spent the remainder of that day helping Soubas and his fellows to exercise and groom the horses which Dido was providing for the use of my father and other Trojans. To do so was to serve her and added to my happiness. While we worked, Soubas explained to me how the hunt would be organized. The meet was to assemble at dawn in the great forecourt of the palace – hounds, beaters, mounted huntsmen equipped with nets, the chief men of Carthage and their sons, the Queen and her retinue, ourselves. Hounds and beaters would set off into the thickly wooded hills to the west of Carthage to drive the quarry into a flat valley running northwards, where pursuit on horseback would be easy. Nets would be disposed at strategic places to catch the quarry or be used to surround a cover.

Although Malchus had already told me something of the Queen's hunting parties I was awed to hear that so many people would be taking part. I remembered the simple expeditions on foot with my father and Achates at Buthrotum – without horses, hounds or beaters. I knew that deer would be our quarry now as then: but were there not other and more ferocious animals to pursue in the vicinity of Carthage – lions and elephants for example?

Soubas shook his head: 'In my country, yes, but not here.' He gave a bitter smile. 'If you want real hunting you must go to Numidia. We hunt ostriches for their plumes, and wild asses too. They are fleeter of foot than any deer. Hunting in these parts is a tame sport.' Then his face brightened: 'But at least there are boar in the forests not far from the city. Perhaps

[180]

we will start some tomorrow. When they are roused and desperate they are as fierce as any lion.'

I looked at him thoughtfully. Not for the first time I sensed his dislike of Carthage, his longing for the great open spaces of his native country. I knew that amongst his own people he had been a minor chieftain, the owner of flocks and herds. Why had he quarrelled with Iarbas? Why had he chosen to come to Carthage a year ago and enter Dido's service in so humble a capacity? Why had he left his wife and children behind him? I had tried to discover, but his reserve was impenetrable. His gods were not those of the Carthaginians; but that he was loyal to Dido I did not question.

That night I could not sleep for thinking of her. I heard my father restlessly tossing and turning. He was dreaming again. Twice I heard him mutter my grandfather's name. Perhaps he was still haunted by thoughts of Italy. But tomorrow it would be revealed to him clearly and unmistakably that he must remain in Carthage. Something would happen that would tell him so; perhaps Asherat herself would appear to him. She had raised the storm that had brought us to Africa. She had prevailed against the wishes of Zeus himself. Our own gods had failed us. Even my father had known it, for had he not cursed them when he had seen our comrades drowning before our eyes? Despite himself he had still continued to trust them. But how could he still have faith in them once Asherat had spoken? He would know then that her word was law, that it would be folly to disobey her. He would bow to her will gladly, settle in Carthage and marry Anna. And Dido would be mine for ever. I remembered again how passionately she had kissed me. Tomorrow night we would be together again, and I would give her such pleasure as she had never known. She would know then that I was her predestined husband, and Sychaeus would haunt her no longer. Soon the High Priest himself would marry us before Asherat, and she would bless us with children. How happy my sweet love would be in her motherhood. Oh, how I loved her, how I loved her!

The morning star had emerged and was gleaming shyly as

I stole out of the High Priest's house after eating a hurried meal and waking my father and the Trojan chieftains who were to go hunting with us. From the temple precincts came the drowsy cooing of some doves. The moon had set and dawn had not appeared, but already the darkness of the night was gradually dissolving. A fresh and zestful wind blew in from the sea boisterously announcing a new-born day. Soon Aurora would leave her ocean bed, mount her golden chariot and urge her snow-white steeds into motion. Far out at sea upon the horizon a bar of glowing light would show that she was approaching. The birds nesting in the grove of ilexes would greet her with their twittering, and soon the whole city, now so inanimate, would be roused by her radiant presence as she passed in her chariot across the eastern sky.

In the stables, warm with animal heat, Soubas and his fellow-grooms were already at work by torchlight. I went to see the Queen's horse, and he whinneyed at me in greeting. I groomed him carefully with brush and comb, patted his glossy flanks, massaged his legs, inspected his hooves before handing him over to Soubas. I had not time to do more, for Aristo too must be groomed so that Dido should admire him. I was dressed for the hunt already, but must fetch my weapons from the armoury – two light javelins, a hunter's knife, my sword? – no, it should not be necessary, and the Queen's attendants would be carrying a stock of broad-tipped hunting spears; but I would take my bow and arrows.

As I was leaving the stables my father entered accompanied by other Trojans. I tried to hurry past but he stopped me and asked me to interpret for him. Which was his horse, he asked. He ran his eye over it appraisingly and asked a number of peremptory questions, not realizing that my riding-master was more than an ordinary groom. I could see that Soubas was angered by his tone although the questions were innocuous enough. I broke away from them at length, feeling that my father had made an enemy.

By the time I had reached the great courtyard before the palace dawn was breaking. Hounds, beaters and huntsmen were already beginning to move off to the accompaniment of joyous barking and the clattering of hooves upon the paving. Horses neighed to each other and tossed their heads impatiently. The crisp air tingled with excitement and the joy of life. A number of gaily-dressed Carthaginians had already assembled, Malchus and his father amongst them. I rode across to greet them. Soon the Carthaginians began to form up as if for a procession to the left of the main door of the palace. Presently my father appeared, mounted at the head of his Trojans. They took up their position on the opposite side of the courtyard facing the Carthaginians. Various retainers followed on horseback and stationed themselves near the centre; and last of all came Soubas, his hair plaited, his beard trimmed, leading the Queen's white horse, magnificently caparisoned in purple and gold; even the bridle and curb-chain were decorated with golden trinkets. Upon its back was an elaborately upholstered and richly-ornamented saddle.

I saw my father gazing fixedly at Dido's horse. Then he caught my eye and motioned to me to take up my place behind him. I shook my head. He did not know that this hunt was being held in my honour. Dido had said so although I had forgotten to remind her. I would not ride behind him. I would ride beside the Queen. Not only this but I would escort her from the palace to her horse.

The sun had risen now. It shone upon the brightly-costumed gathering in the courtyard. It shone upon the glossy white flanks and trappings of Dido's horse which stood in the centre held by Soubas. I looked up for a moment at the window of my sweet love's bedchamber, and said a prayer to Astarte. Then I dismounted, placed my weapons beside a near-by pillar, tethered Aristo to it by his halter of plaited rushes and walked across the courtyard to the main door of the palace. A hundred curious eyes followed me. I pushed my way through the group of chattering servants assembled on the steps and entered the main hall. The first person I saw was Anna with Imilce in attendance.

She started with surprise at seeing me, and drew me to one side.

'Why are you here?' she said quickly in Greek. 'Is anything the matter?'

I explained why I had come, and she smiled.

'Of course. I understand. Dido is in her bower still, but she will be coming shortly.'

So she was praying to her dead husband before setting out upon the hunt. I felt suddenly uneasy. The minutes crawled by and I began to grow anxious. Would Dido never come?

At last I saw her descending the staircase like the goddess of the chase, her hair bound up by a jewelled clasp of gold. From her shoulders hung a cloak of glowing purple with richly embroidered hem, fastened below her throat by a star-shaped brooch set with pearls and amethysts. Her tunic too was purple, and an ornamental girdle encircled her waist. She looked almost boyish in her brightly-coloured hunting boots secured to her slender legs by golden bands; but no boy could have moved with her incomparable grace.

I saw Anna's face light up at the sight of her, and Dido's answering smile. She came straight to Anna, put her arms around her neck and kissed her, her lovely face aglow with deep affection. For a moment she was oblivious to everyone except her sister. Then for the first time she noticed me standing near-by.

'Why, Ascanius,' she said smiling, 'I see you have come to escort me.'

I offered her my arm and she put her delicate white hand upon my wrist. It rested there as lightly as a butterfly might do. The crowd of attendants and servants made way for us, and we passed slowly through the door, down the marble steps, across the courtyard. I was dimly conscious of people all around us bowing or applauding, and of Dido graciously acknowledging their salutations. As we reached the centre my father came forward to pay his respects to her. He stood there towering over both of us. I knew that he was displeased with me from the way he ignored my presence. I think that Dido sensed it too for she complimented him charmingly upon my gallantry. We were standing beside her horse and she had taken her hand from my wrist. Soubas came forward to help her to mount.

'I will help you to mount,' I whispered, 'and then may I ride beside you?'

Before she could answer, my father had intervened: 'You can go back to your horse now, Ascanius. I will help the Queen to mount. Allow me, your Majesty.'

He grasped her slender waist in his great hands and lifted her into the saddle. I heard her give a little gasp. Then he bowed to her courteously and walked back to his horse.

I was too blind with rage to look at Dido, and turned away quickly to hide my face from her. I wanted to grab my father by his cloak and strike him across the face. But no, I must not do it. My father was a king and the Queen's guest. For her sake I must behave as if nothing had happened.

I walked back to my horse, untethered him with trembling fingers, picked up my weapons and mounted quickly. The cavalcade was beginning to move off now, led by the Queen and my father. He signalled to me to fall in behind them, and Dido glanced at me hurriedly as she passed. Was it pity that I saw in her eyes? Oh no, not pity, I could not bear it. 'Poor Ascanius. Do you love me so much?' She had said it only yesterday. Yes, I loved her: how could I help it? But she must not pity me for my humiliation. I would not ride with her, and I would not obey my father. I would ride with Malchus at the rear of the cavalcade.

He was surprised when I joined him.

'I thought you would be riding with the Queen's party like your father.'

I shook my head: 'I can do what I like.'

He looked at me quizzically: 'You seem to be angry about something.'

I pretended not to hear him and began to question him about the hunt.

We passed through a narrow street lined with curious people

and flanked by tall buildings, then out of the western gate. A short distance below lay orchards, fields and gardens dotted with huts. Beyond, dominated on either side by partly-forested hills, a broad, flat grassy valley stretched northwards. The sun was mounting the rooftops behind us into a clear blue sky. The wind was tugging playfully at my cloak and ruffling Aristo's mane. He was twitching with excitement. I felt my anger gradually receding. The cavalcade had begun to disperse in different directions. Malchus was eager to follow a track up into the hills. At any moment, he said, mountain goats driven by the beaters would come bounding down from the rocky summits, and hounds would be unleashed. The woods below were thick with game. I was tempted by his enthusiasm but asked where the Queen would be.

'She will stay in the valley. She enjoys hunting but she tires easily.'

I remembered how I had imagined myself helping her to dismount. Why should it not come true? Perhaps when she saw me she would tell my father graciously that he must feel free to leave her for I could escort her for a while. Perhaps I would save her from a wild boar. Even my father would admire me then.

'I want to be in at the kill,' I said to Malchus. 'I think I will stay in the valley.'

He looked chagrined and began to argue, but I would not listen. Eventually he rode angrily away. As soon as he had gone I dug my heels vigorously into Aristo's sides. He broke into a gallop. It was the first time I had ridden him outside the familiar field. Each of us felt the same exhilaration at our freedom. In a moment he was galloping with all his might, his neck stiff and outstretched. We were well into the valley now, and overtaking scattered horsemen. I could hear hounds baying on the distant heights above, and the shouts of beaters and of huntsmen crashing through trees and undergrowth. Ahead of me I could see my sweet love cantering, my father still beside her. Her purple cloak was streaming out behind her in the wind. My father seemed to loom over her on his black war-horse. For an instant I thought of joining them. But what if my father treated me like an intruder? Twice I had disobeyed him openly. I feared his cold anger, his disdainful silence. My cup of humiliation would be full. I would not ride with Dido now; I would join her later. I galloped past my father, pretending not to see him. Soon I saw high nets on either side of me drawn across intersecting tracks, but despite the baying of hounds there was still no sign of game.

Suddenly to my left some distance ahead a whole herd of deer burst through the trees at the foot of a hill, jostling each other in their precipitous flight. Leaping across the intervening bushes they made for the dusty track that I was following, and disappeared round a bend in the valley. I set off after them, proud that I had been the first to see them yet expecting to find a net across the track to bar their way.

But when I reached the bend in the valley there was no net, no living person. To my right a sandy track wound up the slope of a hill into a pine forest. To my left towered a great treeless crag shaped like a wolf's fang. Before me lay the sea.

The deer had vanished. They must have fled into the forest. It would be foolish to pursue them any further, for the forest was thick and without others to help me I would never find them. I was about to turn back when suddenly I knew, yes knew, that I must follow them. It was as if a god had spoken.

I could not take Aristo with me. I tethered him to a sapling and set off up the hill. Soon I had entered the forest and the valley was out of sight. At first progress was easy; then the track disappeared completely. Of deer there was no sound or sign. The whole forest seemed dark and lifeless. At length I halted panting, refusing to go any further. Each step was taking me away from Dido. I must return to the valley at once, jump on Aristo and ride back to her. I broke into a run, forcing my way through the densely packed pine trees, but I had not gone very far before I realized I was lost. From the knoll where I stood, neither valley nor sea was visible. The sky had turned grey, the wind had dropped, the sun had disappeared. All around I could see only forested hills.

I looked around me in desperation, searching in vain for some familiar landmark, and it was at that moment that I saw the deer once more. Yes, I felt sure it was the same herd. They were browsing in a glade some thousand paces away on the slope of a further hill. I had left my javelins with my horse, thinking they would impede me, but for stalking deer only bow and arrows were needed. I moved cautiously through the wood on parallel ground, then began to approach them against the wind, sometimes crawling, sometimes taking cover. I had almost come within bowshot when I felt the sky rapidly darkening. A sudden gust of wind lashed the trees, a jagged streak of lightning rent the heavens, and the whole herd made off in panic over the brow of the hill. From overhead came the menacing growl of thunder. The next moment the storm broke. A wild fear gripped me. The gods were angry; I must hide from their sight. I began to run blindly fleeing from their wrath.

I do not know for how long I ran, crashing into trees and quivering branches in the storm-tossed gloom, tripping, stumbling, falling; but at last I emerged in an open space surrounded by wild olive trees. The wind was howling like a beast of prey, and hail had begun to fall. There was a tremendous flash of lightning. For an instant the whole grove was lit up by its terrible dazzling brightness, and in that second I saw it. It was the stele which I and my father had seen on the day after we had landed.

I cast myself on the ground at its foot, and buried my face in my arms. If Asherat wished to strike me dead let her do so now. Here I was, prostrate before her stele. I would not move. She could do what she liked with me.

After a time I became conscious that someone was standing beside me. I looked up. It was a boy. No, it was a woman. She was wearing hunting boots and her dress was kilted up above her knees. I rose to my feet mystified, peering at her face, but it was too dark to make out her features.

'You are lost,' she said in Punic. 'Come, I will guide you to shelter.'

She took me firmly by the hand. I followed her without

speaking along a track which led downhill. Despite the gloom and driving sleet she seemed to know the path well for she never faltered. No, it was neither track nor path; it was a swirling torrent. More than once I slipped; each time she helped me to my feet. And all the time the wind roared, the lightning flickered and the rain lashed down upon the gaunt and leafless trees. So we continued, always downwards, until at last she halted on some level ground and released my hand. The wind had dropped, and I could hear the distant onrush of breaking waves.

'Where are we going?' I asked hesitantly.

'There is a cave yonder on the shore where we can shelter.'

'A cave?' I repeated.

'You will be quite safe. The Queen is sheltering there.'

'The Queen . . . How do you know?' I stammered.

'It was I who guided her there. What is the matter? Are you afraid of her because she is a queen?'

'Oh, take me to her,' I cried, and began to weep at the thought of seeing her, but my guide did not seem to notice. She set off at a rapid pace and I had to run to keep up with her.

The trees were thinning out now. In a short time we were clear of the woods and I found that I was standing on the edge of a sandy beach. The roar of the waves had become deafening. Dimly I could see the white crests of gigantic breakers surging forward to hurl themselves in seething rage upon the shore. All at once there was a vivid flash of lightning: a cavernous roar of thunder reverberated across the sky, and Stygian darkness descended upon everything like a pall. I began to call out. How could I find the cave without my guide? Had she deserted me and left me here to die? I stood there staring desperately into the darkness.

Suddenly a distant flickering light appeared. I began to make my way towards it. As I drew nearer I could see it was burning briskly. I had nearly reached it when my foot struck a rock. I stopped and groped in the darkness. There were rocks on either side of me. I listened intently. Despite the roar of the waves I could hear the faint sound of splashing water overhead. I knew where I was now. I knew and was afraid.

The rain had almost ceased, but the darkness was black as pitch. Slipping and sliding I felt my way towards the flaming light a short distance above. In a few moments I had reached it. It was a torch that had been thrust into a cleft in a wall of rock. I pulled it out and held it in front of me peering into the darkness. No one was there; but on a patch of sand at the entrance to the yawning mouth of the cave I saw footmarks, blurred by the rain, but unmistakable. There were several of them. Of course, Dido's attendants would be with her: my father too no doubt.

My darling was here then. How could I fear to go where she was? The torch had been thrust into the rock so that I could find my way to her. My guide must have gone ahead to tell her I was coming. She would be waiting anxiously for me.

All my fear left me. Half walking, half running, I advanced into the black tunnel, the torch aloft in my right hand, my feet sometimes splashing in the shallow water. Presently the stream disappeared and I saw a fire glowing a short distance ahead. Her attendants must have lit it. They would all be there, seated around it drying their clothes. How glad my darling would be to see me. She would spring to her feet, and stretch out her arms, and we would kiss like lovers.

I began to run, calling her name. Now I had reached the fire at last; but there was only one person there. It was a woman, but it was not Dido. Who was it? Her back was partly turned towards me. Then she slowly turned her head, and I saw her face and dropped my torch.

'Do you recognize me now?' she said.

I nodded, unable to speak.

'Who am I?'

'You are the huntress whom I and my father saw,' I whispered.

'And now your father is not with you. But you will see him.'

'Where is he?' I asked, trying to master the tremor in my voice.

'He is here in this cave with the Queen.'

I looked wildly around me. Outside the small circle of light cast by the glowing fire everything was in darkness, but from somewhere came the sound of movement and heavy breathing.

I made to pick up my torch but the huntress had already taken it. With a quick movement she extinguished it in the sand.

'Show them to me,' I cried.

'Yes, I will show them to you, but they are under a spell. They will not see or hear you. Look.'

She threw something on to the fire, and instantly great flames leapt up to the roof. The whole cave was suddenly lit up. No, it was not the cave of my dream, but there was the flat rock shaped like an altar, and before it on the sand lay Dido, motionless, her cloak spread out around her. A man was crouched over her, his body moving convulsively. It was my father. Oh God, he was ravishing her!

I gave a great cry, and drew my knife to kill him. The huntress caught my arm.

'Would you murder her husband, Ascanius? Would you rob her of her happiness? She is in an ecstasy. If you touch him she will die.'

'Her husband?' I gasped. 'He is not her husband.'

'They have joined hands and pledged themselves to each other here in this holy place. Asherat, the goddess of marriage, has given her to him.'

As she spoke, the leaping flames of the fire died out and darkness descended on the cave.

An immeasurable despair took possession of me. I flung myself on the ground and began to weep helplessly. Presently I became aware that the huntress was bending over me shaking my shoulder, a lighted torch in her hand. Slowly I rose to my feet.

'The storm is over now,' she said. 'Take your torch and go.'

I took it from her mechanically.

'Your horse is tethered to a near-by tree. You will see a huntsman there. You will tell him you are lost, and he will guide you to your home.'

'To my home?' I repeated.

'The palace is your home now. You will never leave Carthage. Isn't that what you wanted?'

I stood staring at her, realizing at last that she hated me.

'Go,' she repeated angrily. 'Don't you know who I am? Do you dare to defy me?'

As she spoke, her eyes blazed and her whole face seemed to shine in the darkness. I uttered a cry of terror and ran blindly from the cave. I knew who she was now. She had pursued me like a quarry and caught me in her net. I was the sacrificial victim she had chosen. She was all powerful and nothing could withstand her.

XIII

The blind ferocity of the storm, the ominous brooding darkness that followed, had spread terror all over Carthage.
Everyone had taken refuge from the supernatural violence
and sepulchral gloom. When at last the darkness lifted the
people began to emerge apprehensively from the buildings and
houses where they had taken shelter. A pallid sun shone
down upon them furtively out of a grey sky. Wherever they
looked there were scenes of devastation.

Ships had been capsized or smashed, precious cargoes had
been spilt violently into the sea, harbour installations had been
washed away or pounded into fragments by gigantic waves.
Within the city the streets were littered with rubble. Sections
of partly-finished wall had collapsed, the roofs of many
buildings had disintegrated. The palace itself had not been
spared; but worst of all the temple of Asherat had been struck
by a thunderbolt. A great hole gaped in the roof and the whole
wall on which the frescoes of the Trojan war had been painted
was blackened by fire. Asherat must be angry with her people.
She had wrought this havoc to punish them.

Presently the first scattered groups of horsemen from the
hunt began to filter back into the city through the western
gate, bedraggled and despondent, still fearful after their recent
ordeal. Others followed on foot, exhausted and covered with
mud, having lost their mounts. All through the afternoon
stragglers continued to arrive. But where was the Queen
herself? She had still not returned at nightfall. Suddenly the
whole city was seized with panic. The Queen was missing.
She had not been seen since the storm had broken. No one

knew what had happened to her.

Despite the lateness of the hour, a distraught and hysterical crowd invaded the forecourt of the palace clamouring for news of her. Presently a little figure appeared upon the balcony and tried to calm them. It was the Queen's sister. But she herself was sometimes overcome by tears, and she had nothing new to tell them except for one thing. The Trojan leader who had been with the Queen was also missing.

A wave of furious anger against the Trojans swept through the crowd. All had been well until these strangers came. They had brought ill luck upon Carthage. It was because of them that Asherat was angry. It was because of them that the Queen was lost. Their wicked leader must have abducted her. Perhaps she would never come back. Perhaps Carthage had lost her for ever.

A stentorian voice called out that the Trojans should be dragged into the streets and massacred. There were shouts of approval and a general rush towards the entrance gate. But at that moment something happened. Two figures on horseback emerged from the grove of ilexes into the moonlight, and began to ride slowly towards the palace. The crowd fell silent, and stood motionless watching them. The smaller of the two was riding a white horse. Was it really the Queen or was it her ghost? No, it was she, she had come back to them; she was alive and safe!

There were cries of joy and relief, and those in the forefront of the crowd ran forward to meet her. But when they reached her they fell back disconcerted. Her tunic was disordered, her face was streaked with mud, her fair hair all dishevelled. She was staring straight in front of her and did not seem to see them. As she and the Trojan leader rode through the entrance gate the crowd began to murmur uneasily. Was the Queen under a spell? Why did she not look at them or speak to them?

At last the horses came to a halt before the main door of the palace. She looked slowly around her as if trying to realize where she was; then she spoke in a strange faraway voice.

'I belong to King Aeneas. Asherat has united us.'

There was a stunned silence. The Trojan leader dismounted and lifted her from her saddle. As he did so her whole face lit up with an expression of rapturous joy. She put her arms about his neck and laid her head upon his shoulder.

'Carry me to our bedchamber, my beloved,' she said.

He gathered her into his arms without speaking, and moved towards the door. She clung to him tightly, her eyes closed. And then, as he stepped across the threshold, he stumbled. A cry of dismay burst from the crowd. For a moment he seemed to hesitate, looking down on her. She lay motionless in his arms as if nothing had happened, her eyes still closed, her face radiant with happiness. He hesitated no longer. Slowly and carefully he bore her across the hall, and up the marble staircase, until they disappeared from sight.

Of all that happened in Carthage on that fatal day, of Dido's and my father's homecoming, I saw nothing. It was only later that I heard of it – from Anna, from Imilce, from various Carthaginians. I have no recollection of my own return to the palace. I seem to recall Imilce intercepting me on my way from the stables about an hour before sunset, and taking me to the room that Anna had chosen for me. It overlooked a small grassy courtyard with a fountain in the centre. All my belongings were there already. I stood there staring at them stupidly, remembering how sure Anna had been that Dido wanted me to come back to the palace. She had thought that Dido needed my love. She was wrong. Dido had no need of me now. No one needed me any longer.

Imilce was very kind to me. Of course she had helped Anna to look after me during my fever, but I could not speak Punic then and Imilce knew no Greek. We had scarcely spoken to each other; but now she began to talk to me as if she knew me well. She brought me food and wine at once, helped me to take off my filthy sodden clothes, and asked me anxiously if I had seen the Queen on my way back to Carthage. Her mistress was concerned about her; so was everyone. I shook my head and managed to stammer out that I could tell her nothing, that I did not want to see or speak to anyone. She must have seen from my face that I was half-demented. I suppose she thought that the storm had frightened me out of my wits. At all events she went away and left me alone with my misery.

Next morning Imilce came again bringing some curds and fruit and barley loaves. She told me breathlessly that the Queen had returned to the palace with my father long after nightfall, saying that they were married. Her behaviour had been very strange. Everyone could see that she was passionately in love with him. He had carried her to her bedchamber, and they had spent the night together. They were both still asleep. All Carthage was seething with rumours. No one knew what to think.

'You must be glad, Ascanius, for your father's sake,' she added. 'To have a rich and beautiful wife who loves him deeply – what more could he ask for? And no one seems to have guessed that she was in love with him – not even my mistress. It is strange. They are so close, the Queen and my mistress, and yet they hide things from each other.'

She stopped as if she felt she had said too much, and looked at me uncertainly.

'What do you mean?' I asked quickly.

'I think that the Queen fell in love with him long ago, Ascanius. I think that she tried to fight against it. I think that was why she shut herself up and would not speak to anyone. No one could understand what was the matter with her; but I guessed it. I have known her and my mistress all my life.'

I stared at Imilce's homely face, remembering that she had helped Dido and Anna to escape from Tyre. She was of about the same age as Anna, but she had already been in their service during their father's lifetime. Could it be true what she had said? Was it possible that Dido had hidden it from everyone, that even Anna had never guessed it? I thought of that night when Dido had wept so desperately but would not tell me the reason. Only her dead husband knew, she had said. She had been in love with my father even then. I knew it now. I had never been more than a plaything, a pitiful substitute.

'My mistress has never understood the Queen,' said Imilce. 'She loves her too blindly. She never understood her devotion to her husband's memory. She never understood why she would not remarry. She has never realized how scrupulous and sensitive she is.' She sighed. 'I hope your father will be kind to her, Ascanius. And you are like a son to her. Often when you were delirious she would come and sit beside you and hold your hand. She was the only person who could always calm you.'

'I never knew that,' I muttered, and quickly turned away my head. When I looked round again Imilce had gone.

After I had finished my meal I felt I could stay in my room no longer. For a moment I thought of going to see Anna. No, it would be cruel to inflict my misery on her when she herself must be so unhappy. Imilce could not have realized that she loved my father. I would go and work in the stables; any work would do so long as it stopped me from thinking. Perhaps I would go to the field with Aristo and practise with the javelin. No one would talk to me there. And then, and then? Oh God, what could I ever do that would cure me of my misery? She was his now. He had taken her from me. She would never be mine again. And she loved him, she loved him.

Somehow the stables had escaped serious damage, but several of the horses were missing still, and I could see no sign of Soubas. There was Dido's horse. She had ridden him back to the palace during the night. Now she was lying in her room asleep. How beautiful she must look! I must see her. I would go mad if I did not see her. But not with my father. She must send him away. If I saw him with her I would kill him – with my knife: just as her brother had murdered her husband. No, I couldn't, I couldn't. I would be killing her too.

I found myself back in my room once more, and flung myself upon the bed. After a time I sat up and began to stare vacantly out of the window. Suddenly I heard a voice close beside me. I looked up. It was Imilce.

'What is the matter with you, Ascanius?' she said anxiously. 'Didn't you hear me speak to you? Are you ill?'

I mumbled that I was quite well, and made an effort to smile at her. She told me that the Queen had asked for news of me as soon as she had woken. She and my father had been overjoyed to hear that I was safe. Now she wanted to see me.

'Is my father with her?'

'No. She is alone.'

Oh God, what would we have to say to each other? He had lain with her. Each night he would lie with her and enjoy her beauty. How could I ever see her or speak to her again?

Imilce led me along a passage to a small and unfamiliar door a short distance away. I realized that this was another entrance to the Queen's apratment and that my room must be the one of which Dido had spoken on our last night together. I pushed open the door savagely and saw her standing there waiting for me.

My whole body seemed to crumble at the sight of her. She put her arm about me without speaking and led me into another room where a fire was burning. There were the remains of a meal upon a table, and some cushions spread out before the fireplace. She seated herself upon them drawing me down with her, and took my head upon her lap.

'We love you,' she said. 'We both love you. We thank the gods that you are safe. Your father is grieved to think that he was angry with you.'

I did not answer. She began to stroke my hair.

'When we found that you were missing we became very anxious. We started to search for you along the shore where your horse had been found wandering. Where did you go, my darling? We could see no trace of you.'

'I lost myself in a forest,' I whispered, staring at her.

'And how did you find your way back here?'

'I don't know. It doesn't matter. Tell me what happened to you. Tell me quickly.'

She saw the agonized expression on my face and questioned me no further.

'When the storm broke, all our followers scattered in panic. Your father and I were searching in vain for shelter when a huntress appeared, guided us to a cave and left us there. We never saw her face.

'The cave seemed empty, but a bright fire was burning and we could see a rock there shaped like an altar. We were thinking of you all the time, my darling, and sorrowing because we had lost you. I prayed aloud to Asherat to guide you to us, and your father repeated the words after me. He told me it was the first time he had spoken Punic. And then, looking at me all the time, he said that his mother had been a Phoenician, that Carthage had become his home and that he loved me.' She broke off. 'I cannot tell you any more, Ascanius. It was too sacred, too beautiful. We found ourselves standing hand in hand before the altar. I heard her voice. I heard the nymphs intone our bridal song.' She closed her eyes. 'Even now I can hear her voice as she gave me to him – so pure, so grave, so full of love and peace.'

Oh, how lovely she was, more lovely than any goddess. And I had lost her for ever. How cruel and wicked the goddess whom she worshipped – to snatch her from me, to lead me to that cave, to show them to me wrapped in a trance of passion. He had been crouching over her like a beast, enjoying her, grunting with satisfaction like a hog; and she – she had lain there in an ecstasy such as I had never given her. Tears of rage and humiliation welled up in my eyes. I began wildly to break free from her.

'Don't go, Ascanius,' she said softly, holding me back. 'We need you.'

'You need me?'

'You are our son, my darling. I am really your mother now. Don't you love me any more?'

Suddenly the floodgates of my misery burst. I flung my arms around her neck and wept, surrendering utterly to my despair.

I felt her kisses on my face, and sensed that she was unfastening her dress. Gently she drew down my head and began to suckle me as Astarte suckled Adonis.

'I told you a part of me would always be yours,' she whispered, pressing me close to her. A blissful illusion of peace and happiness took possession of me. Was it not enough to be just her child? Was it not enough that she was my mother? – a mother so tender, so divinely beautiful that now that I was at her breast all my pretensions to manhood counted for nothing? And at that moment I heard my father's voice calling to her, and the sound of his footsteps approaching.

I felt Dido suddenly stiffen. Quickly she withdrew her nipple from my lips, covered the breast she had given me in token of her love, fastened her dress, rose to her feet. Poor Dido, I do not blame you; but in that brief flickering instant all my illusions collapsed in ruins.

I made for the door blindly, but it was too late. As I reached it I came face to face with my father. I saw to my astonishment that he was richly dressed like a Carthaginian noble. He embraced me warmly.

'How glad I am to see you, my son,' he said. 'I thank the gods that you are safe.' Then he turned to Dido. She put her arms round his neck and looked up at him, her face alight with adoration. He put his arm round her waist and drew her to him so that their thighs merged. Her whole body yielded to his. Still standing in the doorway, he bent his head to put his lips to hers and kissed her passionately, oblivious of my presence.

'Beloved husband,' she said softly. Then she freed herself reluctantly and looked at me.

'You have told him?' said my father putting his hand on my shoulder.

'Yes, I have told him,' she said. 'He knows that we both love him. He knows that he is our son and this is his home. He knows that we want him to stay with us for ever – don't you, Ascanius?'

She put her arms around me and kissed me fondly. I stood there staring at them, unable to move.

'Our son was lost in the forest, Aeneas. That was why we could not find him. But Asherat answered our prayers and brought him safely home.'

Dido, my darling, if I had stayed I would have died from love of you. I had to go, my darling. I had to flee from you because you were not mine.

Clearly it had all been preconcerted. Young though I was I sensed it even then. She had suggested that she should see me alone to explain to me that what had happened had been ordained by Asherat. My father had agreed. I am sure that he never guessed how desperately I loved her; but that I was somehow jealous of him he can hardly have failed to realize. Not that he took it over-seriously. I was young but precocious for my age, and growing fast. Jealousy and self-assertion were to be expected of me. Dido would know how to handle me. She had the intuition, the finesse, the patience.

My sweet love had done her best. But he had returned too soon in his Carthaginian clothes, and she, only too conscious of our mutual jealousy, had been forced to choose between us. You loved us both, my darling. You never wanted to weigh us in the balance the one against the other. Each time you had to do so, you suffered because of it.

I remember how, at the banquet you gave to celebrate your marriage, your eyes sometimes rested upon me, and your face which had been radiant with happiness became anxious and troubled. You smiled at me with a shy appealing sadness: 'I cannot help it, Ascanius. I love your father passionately. I love you too, but not as I love him.' At least you never discovered that Anna loved him. Imilce was right. Anna did not understand you; but her devotion to you was limitless, and she saw at once that you were aflame with love for him.

Soon everyone saw it. You could not hide it. You embraced him passionately before all your people when you announced that he was your consort and their king, this penniless stranger of yesterday. How could they welcome this sudden mysterious marriage which no one had anticipated? How could they fail to sense that it boded ill for Carthage? The whole city knew how my father had tripped and stumbled carrying you across the threshold. You told your people that Asherat had united you, but the High Priest declined to commit himself. No mortals had been present, and everyone knew that this supernatural union had been attended by evil omens.

If Asherat favoured the marriage, why had her temple been struck by a thunderbolt? Why had the Trojan frescoes been blackened by fire? How could you have been given in marriage to a Trojan by the patron goddess of Carthage? True, he was a king; but he was a king without a kingdom, who spoke not a word of Punic. True, he was a hero; but misfortune had dogged him in all his wanderings. He was a bird of ill omen, a bringer of ill luck. Even the fact that his mother had been a Phoenician did not count in his favour; for who had she been, this mother whom he had never known? She had been a runaway priestess who had incurred the wrath of Astarte, and she had died in giving birth to him. Were not these evil omens also? Might you not die in giving birth to his child – you to whom Carthage owed its very existence? This stranger would become sole ruler of your city then. Was that what Asherat intended?

But was he not sole ruler already – in fact if not in name? Your people seldom saw you now. You seemed to have lost all concern for them, to care nothing for your city. You stayed all day in your palace like a submissive wife, embroidering a purple cloak for him to wear so that all should recognize his royalty. You thought of nothing but him – him and the pleasures of the marriage bed.

You must be mad, they said, mad or bewitched, to surrender your power to him, to shower rich gifts on him and all his followers, to give endless banquets far into the night so that all could hear once more the story of his adventures. You would lie on the same couch, side by side beneath a canopy, you would press your body to his, you would twine your white arms about his neck and embrace him with passionate devotion. Sometimes you would take his great hand in yours and kiss it like a slave-wife. Oh, my sweet love, what possessed you so to demean yourself – you, the flower and lamp of Carthage, whom everyone had reverenced and adored, you the epitome of gracious dignity?

I know it now, my darling. You were the helpless victim of the gods. It was no friendly goddess who sent me to you. It was I who awoke your slumbering desire, it was I who ensured that it would never leave you. What did they care for you – Astarte and Asherat in whom you trusted? It was Carthage they loved, not you. You were never more than their instrument. As soon as you had served their purpose they were ready to destroy you. They hated you for your beauty; they tricked and deceived you. They robbed you of the joys of love then tormented you with longings. They spoke to you of your solemn vow, then urged you to remarry. They revived your yearning for children, tortured you with reminders of your childlessness. They pointed to the hero whose followers you had welcomed with such humanity. How brave he was, how unfortunate, how noble in his bearing, how tall and strong and handsome, how grateful for your kindness, how ready to be of service. Asherat must have sent him to Carthage to protect you against Iarbas. You and the city were safe for so long as he was there. But when he and his Trojans left in the spring, what would happen then? Iarbas would still be there, a constant danger. You would always be faced with Iarbas.

Oh, how tired she was, how tired and lonely. Iarbas was bent on marrying her, and most of the Senators supported him. They had said it would be for the good of Carthage. They had said she should sacrifice herself, break her vow and marry a barbarous savage. How could she bear it? Soon she would have to accept or reject him. She would never accept him; she would rather die. But she would be alone. The Trojan king would have left Carthage by then. There was no one else with his prestige, his leadership, his loyalty to her, his military experience. There would be no one to whom she could turn, no one to protect her. She was alone. She would always be alone.

She was condemned by her vow to perpetual widowhood and childlessness...

She had begun to fall in love with him, but she would resist it, she must resist it. It was because of his son. He was so like him. Poor child – he had lost his mother. Her heart had gone out to him when she **had** seen him looking at her at the banquet. She had felt that she must take him in her arms; she had felt like a mother towards him. Heavens, how beautiful he was with those large grey eyes and long lashes, and the faint down upon his cheeks. And now he had fallen in love with her. How incredible that he should love her; how touching that he should tell her he desired her. She had never meant to let him be her lover but she could not refuse him. Asherat had sent him to her to console her loneliness. How could it be wrong to give herself to him? It made him so happy. Soon his father would take him to Italy and she would lose him for ever. How lovely he was; how he adored her. If only she could keep him with her. She was teaching him the art of love so that they could enjoy it together, but he was only a boy. It was so long since she had enjoyed it – so long, so long...

Oh why could she not marry his father? He was the only man whom she could ever marry. Were they not meant for each other? And yet he seemed indifferent to her. For all his courtesy he always kept his distance. He was never absent from her thoughts. She could not sleep for love of him. It had become torment to see him. How could she, the Queen of Carthage, she the virtuous widow, admit to her passion for this stranger, tell him that she loved him, ask him to marry her? She would be repudiating her beloved husband whose piteous ghost still haunted her. But if she said nothing the opportunity would be lost for ever. Time was running out. Soon he would set sail for Italy. She must sacrifice to Asherat and implore her to help her. She must go to the temple daily in secret, saying nothing of her purpose to anyone. She would perform the necessary ceremonies herself, and pray un-ceasingly for guidance – for a dream, for a sign...

It came at last. She dreamt they went hunting together with all their followers. Then everyone vanished. She became the quarry and he was pursuing her; and then he caught her and she was his.

No, my darling, you did not tell me everything. How could you explain your sweet compassion for my father's grief when both of you thought you had lost me? You were in the cave alone with him. You put your arms around him because you could not help it, and told him that you loved him; and then you gave yourself to him and became his slave.

Thereafter you could think of nothing but love – love and its consummation. You were devoured by passion. Soon you lost all touch with reality. Sometimes you would spend the whole day together making love, unwilling to be parted from him for a single moment, careless of affairs of state, refusing to leave your bedchamber. And he – yes, for a time he too was caught up in a trance of lust. He had never known that any woman could give him so much pleasure. You knew how to whet his sluggish appetite, to perfect his enjoyment. The variety of your caresses was infinite. You taught him how to prolong each exquisite moment until both of you were almost dying of ecstasy. Afterwards he would fall asleep and lie there, sprawled out, snoring like a drunkard.

I saw him. Do you remember? It was the day before you both went hunting again. This time only a few people had been invited – the few Senators who had not been angered by your marriage; no Trojans except perhaps Achates – to have invited any more would have caused a public outcry, and by then most of them had little respect for either of you.

You had invited me to come with you to show that you trusted me and loved me still; but my father decided against it. He was never happy when he saw us together – surely you must have noticed it? He had been overjoyed that I was safe, but somehow he was still jealous of me. Not only that but I was an encumbrance, my presence made him uneasy, like a twinge of conscience. He knew very well that he was neglecting me, and did not wish to be reminded of it. I made you uneasy too. You could scarcely bear to look at me after that morning. You knew only too well that I was racked with misery, that it was beyond your power to cure me of it. It was brave of you to invite me to the hunt, but my father overruled you. You lacked the courage to tell me, fearing my jealous anger, and appealed to Anna to do so.

I was sharpening my arrows in the armoury when a message came that Anna wanted to see me. I was holding one in my hand, and some malignant spirit made me take it with me, unthinkingly.

I knew at once that something was amiss from the way that Anna looked at me. Her face was tired and pale.

'I am sorry, Ascanius, but you cannot go hunting tomorrow. Dido has asked me to tell you.'

'But she invited me,' I said, my voice trembling.

'There has been a change of plan. Your father and she will be going alone. I know she is sorry. She wanted to take you.'

I drove the arrow savagely into her arm. She gave a cry of pain but did not weep. She stood there staring at me, the blood pouring from her wounded arm. Imilce came rushing in to see what was the matter. Horrified, I fled from the room.

It was Imilce, not Anna, who told my father. She must have thought I was mad – mad and dangerous. My father was furiously angry. By that time he had lost all affection for me. He did not even bother to see me. On his instructions, all my weapons were taken from me and I was confined to my room. That evening when Imilce brought me food, accompanied by a guard, she told me I was to be expelled from the palace.

'When?'

'Tomorrow morning.'

'Where will I be sent?'

'To a house where other Trojans are quartered. Two captains are to take charge of you.'

'Does the Queen know?'

'Yes, she knows. She was very upset. She wanted to see you, but your father would not hear of it. My poor mistress!

What possessed you to do such a thing? You should thank the gods that the wound was not more serious.'

I could not answer. She looked at me, and her face softened.

'I am sorry you are so unhappy, Ascanius. We are none of us happy. Perhaps the gods mean to punish us.'

She went away, leaving me alone.

I sat there thinking. I was quite calm now. No one except you and Anna would ever understand why I had wounded her. I would have liked to ask her forgiveness, but that was not possible now. Soon I was going to kill myself; but not yet. I had no weapons now. I must wait for the gods to give me the opportunity. When they did so, I would grasp it. My father could rely on me; in that I would not disappoint him. But before I died, before I left the palace, I must say farewell to you even if my father was there, even if a guard tried to stop me: because I had loved you once, because I had loved you.

I opened the door and saw that the passage was dark and deserted. Everyone must be having their evening meal: you and my father too perhaps, for even the most besotted lovers have to eat. There had been the remains of a meal in that room in your apartment where the fire had been burning, but you had been there alone. Perhaps you were alone there now. Perhaps you would take my head upon your lap. You would only have to kiss me and I would die of happiness. You would be quit of me then, both of you.

The door of your apartment had been left unbolted. Perhaps you had forgotten about it? I opened it silently and went in. A small lamp was burning in a niche. I picked it up. A fire was burning in the adjoining room, and food and wine were set out upon the table, but the room itself was empty. I passed through it into another smaller room. It was your wardrobe. The whole room was filled with an intoxicating scent. Shimmering robes and dresses hung from walls and pegs in diaphanous folds. And all these delicate feminine things had adorned your lovely body. I knew I would go mad if I lingered there. I opened the further door and burst into your bedchamber.

My father was lying sprawled across the bed fast asleep. His mouth was half-open and he was snoring, satiated, like a hog. You were awake. You were half-sitting up, your white shoulders resting upon the pillow. You were stroking his hair gently as you used to stroke mine. Your face was calm and happy. At the sudden noise, you looked up startled. You saw it was me and gave a little gasp, then put your finger to your lips.

'Don't wake him,' you whispered, looking at me anxiously. 'He would be very angry if he saw you. What is it, Ascanius? Why are you here?'

I stood staring at him.

'Has he been making love to you?'

'Yes, Ascanius. We love each other. I belong to him. He is my husband.'

'But you let him do what he likes. You don't behave like a queen any longer. Oh, what is it, Dido? What is the matter with you?'

Your eyes filled with tears.

'I am in love, Ascanius. I cannot help myself. And I want a child desperately. Soon it may be too late.'

'Too late?' I repeated.

'I have never borne children. Do you think your father wants a barren wife? Suppose he were to leave me?'

'But he loves you, Dido,' I said despite myself, looking at her incredulously.

'Yes, he loves me at the moment. I try to please him, but he is anxious about something . . . So long as I please him . . . I used to try to please you, Ascanius, but your father must never know . . . I know about Anna. The wound is not serious. She forgives you. It was my fault; I was afraid to tell you. I am sorry, my darling, I have not been a good mother to you, but you are not my son and I cannot protect you. Now you must go. He may awake at any moment.'

Oh Dido, how subservient you had become; how you had fallen from your royalty!

'I came to say goodbye to you,' I whispered.

'Goodbye to me? But you will soon come back to the palace. Your father is a good man, but something is troubling him. He won't tell me what it is . . . So long as he stays with me . . . I could not live without him. Goodbye, my darling. I understand why you were so angry. You are truly sorry for what you did? Then come here and let me kiss you.'

Oh, my sweet love, we never saw each other again.

XIV

I stopped, unable to continue.

The whole glade was bathed in silence. The trees stood motionless, mute witnesses to the reawakening of that grief of long ago.

'For all these years you have never ceased to love her,' said Anna softly.

'It is true,' I muttered, looking into her blind eyes. 'I could never forget her. Never.'

I was silent for a moment thinking of Dido in all her beauty. I was an old man now. My hair was sparse, my shoulders were bowed. My sons were grown men. Soon I would die, knowing that I had been the obedient servant of Almighty Zeus, the pious son of a pious father. Yet at this moment nothing mattered to me but Dido who had cursed us all before she died, who had tried to thwart our mission. She had failed. We had left Carthage. We had reached Italy. The oracles, the prophecy of Helenus, all had been fulfilled. My father had founded a second Troy; and now, after thirty years, I had founded a new capital as Zeus had commanded. We had done everything that he had ordained. Yet all this counted for nothing now. Nothing mattered but Dido who had suffered because of us: Anna must tell me of her last days upon earth so that I could be with her till the very end.

'She never meant to be your enemy,' said Anna, 'she never meant to thwart your father's mission. It was Asherat who was your enemy. Dido was no more than her instrument. Yes, I will say it although she is my goddess. What did she care then how much my sister suffered? All that mattered was to keep your father from Italy. In the end she abandoned her just as your father did. Dido had failed to serve her purpose and could be left to die.

'She was never happy for long after she married your father, Ascanius. Even when all seemed well I could see that she was anxious, apprehensive about the future. She always reproached herself because of you. She was more fearful than ever of Iarbas. She had always loathed him from the very outset, sensing that he coveted her, that he was only biding his time and meant one day to possess her. But now the courage with which she had faced him hitherto had quite deserted her. He learnt of her marriage almost immediately – no doubt it was Soubas who told him. He was wild with jealousy and rage. He sent her a contemptuous and insulting message reminding her that he was her overlord. He threatened her with war for having rejected his suit and chosen to unite herself to a miserable adventurer. She never told your father of it until it was too late; but she clung to him more than ever for protection.

'She loved your father desperately, Ascanius. She could scarcely bear to let him out of her sight. Each time I used to see her eyes following him with a kind of anguish. It was as if she always feared that one day he would not come back to her although he was her husband. She belonged to him; but he only seemed truly hers when they made love together. She was haunted by the thought that he might cease to care for her; and Italy was always in the background. To give herself to him whenever he wanted, to surround him with comforts and luxuries, to share her power with him, exalt his prestige, obey his wishes, defer to his decisions, shower gifts on his followers – all this would not suffice to keep him in Carthage for ever. She must conceive quickly, and bear him children. Only then would she feel less uncertain of her hold on him.

'Of course she had always grieved that she was childless – for herself as well as for Carthage. But now it became an obsession. Each time after making love she would pray to Asherat secretly to make her fruitful. As week succeeded week she began to feel desperate. She offered sacrifices daily, consulted wise women, practised secret rites; and all the time her anxiety mounted. Eventually she became almost frantic. She used to feel that the servants were staring at her, whispering together, wondering whether she was pregnant. By then she could hardly endure to show herself outside the palace except to go to the temple. She knew that all her people thought her marriage ill-omened, and guessed that it was rumoured that she was barren.

'They were still devoted to her in their fashion although discontent was mounting. They thought her love for your father abject and shameless. They complained that they saw her so seldom. But she was still their Queen, and she was precious, irreplaceable. They still obeyed her. It was because of her alone they endured the Trojans, much as they disliked them. It was because of her that they obeyed your father's orders. But they felt him to be a usurper whatever she might say.

'It happened soon after you had left the palace. Your father had gone out early to supervise work on the citadel. Dido had remained in her apartment. Before leaving, he had kissed her with great tenderness; and she had asked him gently if you might come back to the palace. You were his son, she said. It was not the first time she had asked him, but before he had rebuffed her. Your father was touched, and promised that he would see you. She was overjoyed, hoping as always that you would be reconciled.

'Not long after he had gone I went to see her. She was playing on her harp and singing to herself, and I knew that for once she was happy. You never heard her sing but her voice was as pure and dulcet as a nightingale's. I remembered how she used to sing Phoenician love songs to her husband long ago in Tyre, and he would listen to her entranced. After his death she had sworn that she would never sing again, but since marrying your father she had begun to do so once more. Poor Dido, little did she know how dearly she would pay for having renounced her vows.

'Beside her, draped across a chair, lay the cloak she had woven for your father. She had finished embroidering it earlier that morning. It was of the most exquisite workmanship, and she had taken endless pains over it. I can see it now, that resplendent purple cloak, bordered with gold thread. I shall never forget it. It symbolized the whole change that had come over her since her marriage.

She smiled at me when she saw me, but her thoughts were far away. I sat there for some time, listening to her singing, and then suddenly it happened. Imilce burst into the room panting for breath, and gasped out that the Trojans were preparing to leave Carthage. She had seen them herself loading their ships, all of them in high spirits.

'Before she had finished, Dido had rushed out of the room. The next moment I saw her run across the forecourt without her cloak, calling out your father's name desperately. Everyone stood gaping at her. I cried to Imilce to follow her, but it was too late.

'She ran all over the city, through the streets, through the crowded market, down to the harbour, looking for him everywhere. She was crying out and weeping, and tearing her lovely hair. People watched her aghast, thinking that she had gone mad. She ran down to where the Trojans' ships were beached, and saw with her own eyes that they were being loaded. Guards had been posted to keep the Carthaginians at a distance. They would not let her come close to the ships, nor would they tell her where your father was. All they would say was that they were acting on his orders.

'By then I had become desperately worried about her. I had sent some guards to find her and escort her back to the palace, fearing that in her frenzy she might have done herself some injury. I stood waiting anxiously outside the forecourt. At last I saw her coming slowly back to the palace, supported by two soldiers and surrounded by a gaping crowd. She was utterly spent and could scarcely stand. Her skirt was bedraggled, her hair was in disorder and her face was streaked with dust. She looked at me as if she did not recognize me. Then all of a sudden she stiffened, told the two soldiers to leave hold of her, and drew herself up. I saw she was staring fixedly towards the street that led to the market place. A man was coming out of a near-by house. It was your father. He did not appear to see her, and began to make his way down towards the harbour. She called out his name and he stopped. Then he turned round reluctantly and came towards her.

'Her eyes blazing with anger, she shouted at him that he was a traitor. Did he think that he and his Trojans could slink away from Carthage without her knowledge, without a single word of excuse or explanation? Then all at once her love for him overcame her anger, and tears began to stream down her face. How could he even think of setting sail now when the weather was so stormy? He would be exposing himself needlessly to terrible dangers. Was he really so anxious to escape from her? Did their vows mean nothing to him? Was this the way to treat a loving wife? Did he not love her any more?

'She had sacrificed everything for him. She had lost the affection of her people and aroused the wrath of Iarbas because of him. Who would protect her now? Iarbas might seize her and lead her away as his captive. Did he not care what happened to her? If he were to leave her now she would be utterly desolate and alone. She would not even have the consolation of bearing his child later. Could he not have pity on her?

'Her voice had died away almost to a whisper. I looked at your father standing there silently listening to her. I do not know how he was able to remain so little moved. It was as if he had already steeled himself against anything she might say. When he did answer, his tone was cold, almost formal.

'He would always be grateful to her for her kindness, he said, and he would always cherish her memory. He had never intended to leave Carthage without her knowledge; but he was under no obligation to stay with her for he had made her no such promise. Nor had they ever been married. They had both been under a spell in the cave but he had been aware of no presence but hers. They had exchanged no pledges. No one had united them in marriage. There had been neither witnesses nor bridal song. It was to Zeus above all, not to Asherat, that he owed allegiance. It was Zeus who had bidden him undertake his mission. And Zeus had given him that very morning a sign, a clear and terrible warning, how neglectful of his duty she had made him. He could not tell her what this warning had been; but because of it he had ordered his followers to prepare to leave Carthage instantly. She and her city had become dear to him, but he must obey Zeus as she obeyed Asherat. She had always known that Italy was his ultimate destination. It was useless to reproach him for leaving her. He had no choice in the matter.

'All the time he was speaking, Dido stood staring at him, scanning him silently from head to foot. No one could have told from her face how much she must have been wounded by his chilly indifference to her pleadings. I know now what she was thinking. She, the Queen of Carthage, had taken this man as her husband and made him her co-ruler. For all these weeks he had let her call him husband; and now, with brazen effrontery, he denied they had ever been married. He had repudiated her publicly and told her he was leaving her. He had made her an object of ridicule, a laughing stock.

'Suddenly the self-control with which she had listened to him snapped. In a frenzy of rage she began to curse him and all his descendants. She told him he was false and treacherous. He had a heart of stone. He was a monster of inhuman piety. He had come to Carthage a shipwrecked beggar and she had befriended him. In her blind folly she had trusted him, loaded him with gifts, shared her kingdom with him. And now he was basely deserting her. Let him go to his precious Italy then! As if any of the gods cared whether he ever reached it. But if there was any justice in Heaven, he would be punished for his treatment of her. He and his followers would be wrecked on some barren rock in mid-ocean, and die there of thirst and starvation. They would call out in agony for her then, but she would leave them to their fate. And when she was dead her spirit would haunt them like an avenging Fury.

'For a moment she stayed there glaring at him. Then she ran across the forecourt and into the palace sobbing bitterly. Your father stood looking after her. For the first time he seemed to feel sorry for her, but he made no attempt to follow her. I left him without a word and hurried after Dido. When I reached the hall I found she had collapsed and fainted. Her maids carried her up to her room and laid her on her bed. I could see they were anxious about her but I sent them all away. I fetched water and sponged her face and hands. Presently she began to revive and sat up slowly, her face still dazed. I pressed her to eat something. She shook her head and put her arms around my neck.

' "You are so good to me, Anna," she said. "No one has ever loved me as you do." Then she began to weep. "Oh, what am I to do? He would not listen to me. Is he still there?"

'I went to the window. "No, Dido," I said gently, "he has gone."

' "He has gone back to his ships," she said bitterly. "His men were hanging garlands on them, they were so joyful to be leaving. And they stopped me from going closer. They would not tell me where he was. I befriended them and this is how they treat me. In my own city. I could have told the people to attack them and burn their ships. And I did nothing. Nothing."

'She was silent for a moment, her face full of misery. Then she burst out: "I cannot order the people to attack them. They hate them so much. They would massacre all of them. But I can't go back to the ships again. The way they treated me – it was too humiliating. He might even refuse to see me. How can I tell him now how much I love him still despite everything? He no longer cares for me. But if I do nothing I will lose him for ever."

'Suddenly she looked at me. "Would you go for me, Anna? He would listen to you more readily than to me. When you looked after Ascanius he was so grateful to you. He said you had saved his life. Could you go to see him quickly and beg him to stay?"

' "Yes, Dido. Of course I will go. You know I would do anything for you."

'She embraced me: "Tell him I am not his enemy, Anna, and

[216]

ask him to forgive my anger. It was the shock of finding out so suddenly that he was leaving me; and then the way he spoke to me – as if our love for each other had counted for nothing. Tell him I will not stop him going to Italy, I swear it. Only beg him to wait a little longer, and to stay with me here until then. Ask him to wait until the sea is calmer. He has left all his belongings here – the sword I gave him, and the cloak . . . he must take them with him when he goes. Tell him that is all I ask of him. I ask it as a favour. I make no claim on him. Now he no longer considers me his wife I do not even ask to see Ascanius." She buried her face in her hands.'

Anna stopped for a moment, controlling her emotion. Presently she went on more calmly.

'I cannot remember all that I said to your father. I suppose I still loved him although not as Dido did. I pleaded with him to change his mind, and told him how much sorrow he had brought upon both of us. I spoke of you and how I had nursed you through your fever, and I could see he was very moved. I almost thought he was going to give way, and then I said something and his whole face changed.' She broke off suddenly.

'What was it, Anna?' I asked quickly.

'I asked to see you, Ascanius, and he refused. And after that he refused everything. He refused even to set foot in the palace. All he would say was that he must leave Carthage immediately. In the end I had to go back to Dido and say that all my appeals had failed.

'At first she was frantic with grief and despair. Then suddenly she became quiet. She got up and went into her bower. She spent a long time praying there. When she came out she was quite calm. She told me she was resolved to free herself for ever from her love for your father and had prayed to her dead husband for forgiveness and for guidance. She knew now exactly what she must do, and all her orders must be unquestioningly obeyed. A funeral pyre must be erected in the large inner courtyard of the palace, and on it were to be placed all your father's belongings. As soon as the Trojan fleet had set sail she would set alight to it, and her love for him would perish in the flames.

'By the late afternoon an enormous pyre of pine and ilex logs towered up into the sky. Propped against them was a ladder, and on the top a massive platform had been erected. As soon as she heard that the pyre was completed Dido began to gather together all your father's belongings and everything that could remind her of him. She was weeping passionately, but refused to let anyone help her. She carried them all down to the courtyard herself – the clothes and weapons he had left behind, the hunting costume he had worn, the sword and sword-belt she had given him, the cloak she had made for him, everything. All these she placed upon the platform at the top of the pyre together with a bronze image of him which had been cast soon after their marriage. By the time she had finished she was utterly distraught, and could hardly speak for tears.

'I begged her to lie down and rest.

' "No," she cried. "There is the bed. We shared it until he disowned me." And she began frantically to tear down the canopy. Only when the bed too had been taken away could I persuade her to come to my room. We lay down together side by side, our arms about each other, and fell asleep, the lamp still burning.

'The gods had cursed her, Ascanius. They meant to drive her mad. All night a lonely owl hooted ominously from the roof-top. She was tormented by dreams and nightmares. First it was her husband calling to her, his voice sepulchral and hollow as if he spoke to her from his tomb. Then she awoke screaming that your father was pursuing her, hounding her down relentlessly, his face distorted with fury. Thereafter she could not sleep. She was haunted continually by memories of him; and suddenly a terrible hunger for him took possession of her. Her whole body seemed to palpitate and quiver until she was writhing with passion. She began to cry out as if he could hear her, imploring him to come back to her for her longing for him was unendurable. She must go to him, she must go to his ship and awaken him so that he could satisfy her there and then upon the deck. She would abandon everything for love of him. She would go with him to Italy just to wait upon him and serve him. It would not matter how contemptuously he and his Trojans treated her.

'Then her frenzy suddenly took a different form. She had betrayed her husband and degraded herself: she was depraved and corrupt, obsessed with carnal pleasures, no better than a strumpet. I tried desperately to soothe her, I tried in vain to calm her; by then she no longer recognized me or knew what she was saying. Soon she broke from me and began to walk wildly about the room. Over and over again she went to the window and looked out on to the city below steeped in darkness. She wrung her hands and tore her hair, crying that she had lost the love of her people; her virtue was smirched, her reputation shattered. I put my arms around her and tried to reassure her. It was not true, I said. They knew she was a great Queen, for she had founded Carthage. They loved her still, their loyalty was unshaken. Gradually she began to grow calmer and to listen to me.

' "It is true," she said, "I was a great Queen until the Trojans came . . . And now that they are going . . ." She broke off. "Look, Anna, the dawn is breaking. I must go to the watchtower."

' "The watchtower?" I repeated.

' "It is my duty. I must watch our enemy leaving."

' "I shall come with you," I said.

' "No, my sweet sister. I must go alone."

'I looked at her doubtfully.

' "You promised you would obey," she said, and kissed me tenderly. For a moment she held me very close to her. Then she went out of the room.

'After she had gone, I stood still for a moment uncertain what to do. I was far too anxious about her not to feel full of misgiving that she should leave me even for an instant. I had promised to obey her, and must let her go to the watchtower: but to wait patiently in my room for her return was quite beyond me. Suddenly a voice spoke within me: I must go to the temple quickly and pray for a lasting cure to all her misery. For a moment I hesitated; but the voice was too insistent to be ignored. I felt it must be Asherat herself who was speaking to me.

'I made my way down to the hall and across the forecourt in the gathering light of dawn, and started to walk towards the temple. Already people were passing on their way to the market. All at once I felt uneasy and stopped. I must not leave Dido alone in the palace. Anything might happen during my absence. I must go back to her at once. And at that moment a terrible cry rang out behind me – the sound of screams and wailing coming from all over the palace. In an instant it seemed to be taken up all around me. The Queen, the Queen, she was dying.

'I ran, Ascanius, cripple though I am. I ran across the forecourt and stumbled into the hall calling to her aloud in an agony of fear. The whole building was echoing with cries and lamentation. Someone guided me to the courtyard, helped me thrust my way through the weeping, grief-stricken crowd, and carried me to where she lay. She had climbed the pyre, unsheathed his sword and fallen upon it. She lay across the bed transfixed, blood pouring from her breast. She was dying before my eyes.

'I bent over her sobbing, trying to staunch her streaming life-blood with my dress, crying out that she had deceived me. Her eyes opened slowly, heavy with approaching death.

' "They have gone, Anna," she murmured, faintly; "I could not go on living . . . I have been punished for betraying my husband as I deserved . . ."

'I put my lips to hers to catch her dying breath. Then her soul fled from her body and she died.'

For a long time neither of us spoke. At first I could think of nothing but Dido's agony and Anna's selfless devotion. Gradually my mind began to clear, and I saw how little I had known. Some of it would always be obscure. Only the gods knew whether Dido and my father had truly been married in the cave, as Dido had always believed, as the huntress herself had told me. Had she indeed been Juno or Asherat, or had she been a mortal endowed with supernatural powers? I would never know. Juno was not our enemy now. But that she had been so then could not be doubted. Yet had she not been Dido's secret enemy also? Each impulse, each emotion, each aspiration of our daily lives was governed by the gods. They were both good and evil, kind and cruel, benevolent and merciless. To us in the end they had been benevolent. But to Dido they had been merciless from the moment she had befriended us. She had not meant to keep us from Italy then. She had befriended us because of her goodness and humanity.

I thought of my father with whom I had long since been reconciled. Yes, I understood why he had left Carthage. It was not for nothing that he was called pious Aeneas. Sooner or later he had been bound to leave her, and she had always known it. Yet the harshness of his treatment of her had been unbelievable. To others he had been by no means lacking in humanity; to her he had been cruel and ruthless. Something had occurred in the space of a single morning that had made him turn suddenly and violently against her. To me he had spoken afterwards of a commandment from Almighty Zeus. But to her he had spoken of a terrible warning. He had been deaf to all her entreaties and he had gone within a day despite stormy seas But I remembered nothing of our departure. I must have been unconscious . . . They must have carried me down to the ship . . .

One morning when I had been alone I had tried to kill myself . . . I had cut my veins with a knife . . . My father had told me later that it had been he who had found me but he had said nothing further . . . he had behaved as if it had been an accident . . . but ever afterwards he had been kind, extraordinarily kind to me . . . Oh God, it was because of me that he had treated her so brutally! it was because of me, and she had never known the reason. And then she had put an end to her life – from grief, despair and humiliation. She had died saying that she had deserved her suffering because she had betrayed her husband. And it was I who had made her betray him. In the sweetness of her heart she had yielded to my pleadings and given herself to me. Was there no justice in Heaven that she should have been punished so, while I had escaped unscathed? Since we had left Carthage, Fortune had smiled upon me. And yet I had never forgotten Dido. Her sweet image had become dimmed by the years, but had still continued to haunt me. Now it would be with me always until I died.

I turned to Anna, sitting before the grotto in the mellow autumn sunlight. Her sightless eyes were closed and her lips were moving.

'I must see her again, Anna, if only for an instant. I must speak to her even if she cannot answer.'

'She will come,' said Anna, 'she is at peace now, for we have told her story. You will tell it to others, Ascanius. It will echo through the ages and live for ever.'

She held out her hand before her, and suddenly a dove alighted upon it. It seemed to have come from nowhere. The next moment Dido was there. She was there before me. She was smiling at me with such sweetness, such tenderness. Oh, my darling, you had come back to me, you had forgiven me. I love you, my darling, I love you!

The vision vanished. I saw that Anna was lying on the ground, a smile upon her face. She was dead. She was with her sister now – the sister whose ghost she had laid. Juno had had pity on both of them at last. I would raise a shrine to her here in this tranquil spot before the grotto. And Anna would lie buried beside it. She would be held in great honour by my people, and one day she too would be worshipped as a goddess, the tutelary genius of this sacred grove.

My sweet love was happy now. Long after I was dead poets would sing of her beauty and goodness. They would commemorate and pity her. They would love her as I did.

$\overline{II}$ = Ans. 2

$\overline{III}, \overline{IV}$ = Ans. 3

$\overline{V}$ = Ans. 3 — ~~Exert~~. 1

$\overline{VI}$ — $\overline{VII}$ = Ans. 1.